Across Barren Plains

OREGON PROMISE SERIES
by Lynnette Bonner

Through Dust and Ashes – BOOK ONE
Beneath Brazen Skies – BOOK TWO
Across Barren Plains – BOOK THREE
Upon the Broken Range – BOOK FOUR – Coming Soon
In the Vale of Dreams – BOOK FIVE – Coming Soon

OTHER HISTORICAL BOOKS
by Lynnette Bonner

THE SHEPHERD'S HEART SERIES

Rocky Mountain Oasis – BOOK ONE
High Desert Haven – BOOK TWO
Fair Valley Refuge – BOOK THREE
Spring Meadow Sanctuary – BOOK FOUR

SONNETS OF THE SPICE ISLE SERIES

On the Wings of a Whisper – BOOK ONE

THE WYLDHAVEN SERIES

Not a Sparrow Falls – BOOK ONE
On Eagles' Wings – BOOK TWO
Beauty from Ashes – BOOK THREE
Consider the Lilies – BOOK FOUR
A Wyldhaven Christmas – BOOK FIVE
Songs in the Night – BOOK SIX
Honey from the Rock – BOOK SEVEN
Beside Still Waters – BOOK EIGHT

Find all other books by Lynnette Bonner at:
www.lynnettebonner.com

ACROSS
Barren Plains

OREGON PROMISE - BOOK 3

Lynnette BONNER
USA Today Bestselling Author

Across Barren Plains
Oregon Promise, Book 3

Published by Pacific Lights Publishing
Copyright © 2025 by Lynnette Bonner. All rights reserved.

Editing by Lesley Ann McDaniel Editing – https://www.lesleyannmcdanielediting.com
Proofreading by Sheri Mast – https://faithfulediting.com
Book interior design by Jon Stewart – http://stewartdesign.studio

Cover design by Lynnette Bonner of Indie Cover Design, images ©
Generated by AI using MidJourney

Scripture taken from the New King James Version®. Copyright © 1982 by Thomas Nelson. Used by permission. All rights reserved.

Paperback ISBN: 978-1-942982-50-0

Across Barren Plains is a work of fiction. References to real people, events, establishments, organizations, or locales are intended only to provide a sense of authenticity and are used fictitiously. All other characters, incidents, and dialogue are drawn from the author's imagination.

Psalm 126:6

He who continually goes forth weeping,
Bearing seed for sowing,
Shall doubtless come again with rejoicing,
Bringing his sheaves with him.

Chapter 1

Eden Houston pressed one hand to the base of her throat as she stumbled to a stop. All around, the rest of the women who had been walking behind the wagon train with her did the same.

The day was perfect. Warm and breezy. But now they studied the large column of smoke blotting the blue of the western sky just over the next rise.

"What do you think it means?" Tamsyn Acheson asked, voice filled with trepidation.

In her arms, she carried a large chunk of wood that she'd found on the trail a few hours earlier. Eden figured she had brought it with her due to firewood being so scarce on this stretch of the trail.

Eden shook her head gingerly. "I'm not sure." She felt the familiar pulse of the pain that had tormented her head ever since she'd been pistol-whipped and knocked unconscious by the man they'd all known as Hoyt Harrington. She was careful to keep any evidence of the pain from her features. The last thing she needed was word of it getting back to Adam. "I don't think it can be anything good."

"Do you think it's from Fort Kearny?" The blond girl was one of the seven Hawthorne children that Eden had a hard time telling apart since there were three sets of twins among them. This one was either

Wren or Whitley. They were the oldest Hawthorne children—about fifteen, she would guess. Their mother was once again round with child.

Eden wanted children, but she hoped the Lord wouldn't bless her with quite so many as eight!

She might have smiled at the thought if their current situation wasn't so dire.

"Do you?" the twin prodded, a bit of wishfulness in her tone.

Eden came back to the present with a start, realizing she'd left the girl waiting for her reply. "Sorry. No. I don't think it's from the fort. We aren't supposed to reach it for a few days." If only the explanation could be something as simple as the fort's cookfires.

Ahead, the wagons of their train stretched in a long line, trundling one after the other up the gentle slope they'd been climbing for the past hour.

Since the first men of their party were about to reach the top of this rise and would likely be able to see what was happening ahead, they should soon have a better understanding of whether the smoke was something of concern or simply a natural event.

Did any folks live this far out from the fort? Could they be burning their fields for planting? Eden hoped that would be the case.

As she and the women continued forward, she kept an eye on the road ahead—paying even closer attention as the first wagon reined to a stop on the crest of the slope with Caesar Cranston riding his big Appaloosa beside.

Outlined against the horizon, Caesar's long white hair billowed around him. He seemed to stiffen as he took in the scenery ahead.

Eden's heart stilled. She held her breath. He didn't move for so long that she'd begun to think she was imagining things.

But then Caesar reined his mount sharply to one side, snatched his bugle from where he kept it hanging down the side of his saddle, and blew the few notes that indicated the wagons should circle!

Eden's heart thrashed painfully in her chest. *Dear Lord. Dear Lord. Dear Lord.*

Where was Adam? Whatever was happening, he'd likely be called right into the thick of it. And injured as his hand was from the burn he'd taken back in town a couple weeks back, she knew he'd be a bit clumsy with a gun, even if he wouldn't thank her for saying so.

She took a breath to tamp down her fear. She might have awoken on this day with frustration pulsing in her chest toward the man she loved, but that didn't mean she wanted to see him put in harm's way. She wished that she could confide in him. However, their lack of trust and confidence in each other could be laid almost squarely at her feet, so she supposed she couldn't complain too much when she had been the one to break their connection.

As though all of them had just found their feet unfrozen from the ground, several women surged toward their wagons at once.

Tamsyn hoisted a handful of her skirts and hurried forward with her wood tucked under one arm. "I have to get to Edi." She spoke over her shoulder as she dashed into the swirling dust that twirled up in dust devils on this side of the slope.

The wind brought with it the sharply disturbing scent of smoke.

Eden gave her friend a distracted wave, unable to remove her gaze from the black mar billowing against the dome of blue sky overhead. Her pulse thundered in her ears, causing the pain in her head to throb with each beat. And her breaths came shallow and rapid even as she hurried to conquer the ascent.

Dread coiled in her belly. Drat this rise that blocked her view of whatever lay ahead. For weeks, they'd crossed open plains where the land stretched endlessly in every direction. But this morning, the terrain had changed. Subtle slopes and dips now rolled beneath their wagon wheels, just steep enough to hide what waited beyond. What could possibly be so urgent that Caesar had ordered them to circle the wagons? In the six weeks they'd been on the trail, he'd never once called for a halt so early in the day.

Willow Riley and Mercy Morran, with her two boys, fell into step on either side of her.

"Lord, have mercy," Willow whispered. "This can't be good."

"My thoughts exactly." Eden pressed her hands to the backs of both women. She ought to pray. It was something expected of the minister's wife, even if she felt dry and deserted by the Almighty. She forced the words out as they continued to walk. "Lord, we ask for Your safety and protection for our wagon train. Give us courage to face what comes next and to do Your will. In the name of Jesus, amen." She swallowed down her guilty conscience. Here she was praying, and yet she had all this anger churning inside. That certainly wasn't the accepting faith a truly righteous woman should display. The person she ought to be angry with was herself, yet all her bottled-up displeasure seemed only directed at Adam recently.

"Amen." Mercy and Willow spoke together, driving another nail into the coffin lid of her guilt.

Mercy clasped the hands of her two boys, her face pale and her eyes wide. "Come on, boys, let's find Pa."

Willow gave Eden a little wave and hurried after them.

Eden glanced back at the three women trailing behind. One was the elderly Mrs. Marigold Hawthorne, grandma to the family of mostly twins. Eden moved toward the woman, taking slow breaths to ease her headache, even as she flapped a hand at Mrs. Goode and Mrs. Hession. "Best hurry to your wagons, ladies. Quick like!" She hoped her voice inspired urgency but not panic.

A panic that she felt to her very core! If this were an attack of some kind, would her health stand up to it?

Several women traded places with their husbands on the wagon bench to take over driving the teams as the men hurried at a run toward Caesar.

But Eden had located their wagon now. It was far up the line—third from the front. Adam must have maneuvered closer to the front of the caravan after they'd all stopped for lunch, because this morning he'd been closer to the middle of the train. She had made cheese sandwiches with leftover biscuits at the nooning, but before she'd had a chance to eat her own, she'd been called away by Tamsyn to help tend to a blistered heel on one of the children. The wagons had been moving out again before she'd been able to return. Her stomach grumbled now at just the thought of food. Had Adam even noticed the sandwich she'd wrapped in a towel and left on the tailgate when Tamsyn had asked for her help?

Giving herself a little shake, Eden forced herself to focus on the present as she swept an arm around Mrs. Hawthorne's shoulders. "Here, ma'am, let me help you up to your wagon. I have to tell you that I love the big red rose painted on the side of your canvas." Eden inhaled purposefully. Now she was just blathering for something to say.

The woman planted her cane into the dusty track they'd been following and gave a nod. "Painted thet myself."

Eden smiled even as she tossed a glance over her shoulder to make sure no one else remained behind. "You did a lovely job. That rose has brought a smile to my face on more than one occasion."

"Well then, it has served its purpose." Marigold gave a pleased hum.

"Mind this rock. We don't need to turn an ankle." Eden helped the older woman navigate the obstruction. "You are quite a talent with a paintbrush, I must say. Did you take instruction?"

Mrs. Hawthorne paused, planted her feet wide, and gave a blank look. She seemed ready to stay awhile.

Eden tamped down her impatience. She wanted to be at Adam's side, no matter that she'd relish the opportunity to wring his neck. She would also love nothing more than to crawl into the wagon and take a nice long nap that might ease her headache. But she was needed here.

"Instruction?" Marigold asked.

"In painting?" Eden pressed one hand to the older woman's back to urge her forward. Thankfully, she tottered onward, if much more slowly than Eden would have liked.

Carefully searching for a sturdy spot to plant her cane, Marigold said, "Oh my, no. A body don't need instruction to copy down what they can plainly see before their very eyes!"

Eden bit back a smile. Mrs. Hawthorne had obviously never witnessed the blobs that fell off the end of her brush when she tried to paint. "Well, I must say you have a singular talent. It's quite impressive. I can almost smell that rose for the perfection of it."

She glanced up to take their bearings and felt the hair prickle on the back of her neck. She and Marigold were quite alone. And the wagon train was still a good quarter mile distant.

Marigold tottered another couple of steps up the incline. "I'm an old woman, dear, so do forgive my meddling ways."

"Meddling?" Eden frowned.

The older woman stopped once more and rested both hands atop her cane. Her rheumy blue eyes settled directly on Eden. "You and the mister don't seem to be on the best of terms?"

Ah! That kind of meddling.

Eden tucked her lower lip between her teeth. She worked her fingers into the tight muscles at the base of her skull. How much ought she to say? She started to take a step, but the older woman's hand shot out, surprisingly quick and strong where it clamped on her arm.

"I can see this ain't something you be ready to speak on, and yet, I've experience with a difficult marriage."

Eden felt her brow tuck into a tight pinch. "I don't want you to think badly of Adam. He's a good man." If only he thought she was a good woman. She would keep trying. One day, he'd see that she was trying to be different now.

Marigold's brows lifted. "A good man who sleeps on a hammock 'neath his wagon nights, 'stead of tucked in warmly by his wife."

Tears sprang to Eden's eyes, and familiar anger, hot and sure, surged. She spun away on the pretense of studying the distant horizon, unable to decide whether it was anger with herself for showing such emotion, anger with Adam for continuing to keep her at a distance, or anger with Mrs. Hawthorne for prying. This constant ache in her head wasn't helping her choose. Yet, if she were to be the wife she wanted to be, she must defend him!

She faced the woman once more as she plucked a blade of prairie grass and shredded the stem. "He does do that, yes. But he has his reasons. He— We— We lost a child . . . a son, you see. And . . . I didn't respond to that loss well. I shut him out for a time and now . . . well, things aren't the best between us." Embarrassment heated her cheeks. Why was she spilling so much to this woman?

Mrs. Hawthorne shifted and tipped a nod to indicate they should keep walking up the track. "My Henry, were he here, Lord bless him, he would tell me I ought to keep my meddling mouth shut." She smiled fondly. "But he ain't here, and your husband, Adam, puts me in mind of my Henry back when we first married—overprotective and trying to do the Lord's tasks 'stead of trusting the Lord to do for Himself."

Eden reached a hand to help the older woman over a rut in the path. Was that what Adam was doing?

"You be wanting children, dear?"

Eden felt her face heat at such an intimate question coming from a practical stranger. She released the woman's arm and strode ahead a couple of paces. They were almost to the wagons now, and she could have left the woman to make it to hers alone, but politeness made her stay and answer, "Yes, I do. More than almost anything."

But would this new pain in her head allow her the concentration to care for a child? Would the knifing shards ever recede? Worrying over that was likely exacerbating the affliction.

Marigold gave an assertive nod. "Thet's why the loss of your first child took you under."

The grief washed over Eden as fresh as it had on the day the grim-faced doctor had told her their son hadn't lived through the birthing. She sobbed, quick and short, before she gathered her strength about her and drew herself together. "Y-yes. I suppose it is."

Breathing hard, Mrs. Hawthorne paused again, settling her hands on the knobby handle of her cane.

Eden was surprised to see tears shimmering in the woman's eyes. One slipped free to sweep down the crepey wrinkles of her cheek.

When it reached Mrs. Hawthorne's chin, she reached gnarled fingers, twisted with age, to swipe at the moisture which she then dried against her skirt.

The woman stared toward the smoke overhead for a long moment as though gathering herself. Finally, she lowered her piercing blue gaze to Eden. "I conceived, carried, and lost seven babes. Two more died when they were no more than walking. Grief takes the legs from under us and sits upon us like a great dragon determined not to let us rise. I been under the weight of that dragon more times than I care to remember. But I'll tell you something the good Lord done for me."

Eden searched the woman's face, willing herself not to put too much hope in her words.

"He give me seeds to sow."

Eden frowned. What nonsense was this? To be polite, she asked, "Seeds?"

A sage nod dipped Marigold's wrinkled chin. "They that sow in tears shall reap in joy. He that goeth forth and weepeth, bearing precious seed, shall doubtless come again with rejoicing, bringing his sheaves with him. From the Psalms. One twenty-six, five and six."

"Don't you think those verses mean the spiritual seed we sow into people's lives? And the sheaves are a picture of people that surrender to God because of our testimony."

Marigold nodded and continued up the slope. "Sure. But spiritual seed isn't just telling others they need the Lord. That's part, but it's also scattered when we show others love, joy, peace, patience, kindness, goodness, gentleness, and self-control. It's honesty. It's respect. It's putting others' needs above our own. And I think the sheaves can also represent other things besides saved souls. Sometimes just the honor of helping another might be the cause of our rejoicing. Maybe God uses our pain to encourage others that they ain't alone. Or thet—" She waved a hand. "—at the very least, someone understands and they don't have to suffer alone."

"I'm not sure I have much to offer others right now, Mrs. Hawthorne. I'm like one of those sheaves, unbound, and facing a roaring windstorm. I'm struggling just to hold myself together, and I don't have any answers."

Marigold's hand fell to rest on her arm once again, but this time it was gentle and soft. "Ah, child. I know just what you mean." After a moment, she released her, and the clunk of her cane beat methodically against the dust of the trail.

Eden fell into step beside her, relieved to at least have someone with a listening ear . . . until the woman continued talking.

"But you listen to me, now, and you listen good. You carry a precious pain inside you. The absence of a life cut down before it even begun. Thet has made you a stronger person than you was on the day before your loss. Sure, it took you some time to escape thet dragon of grief, but the good Lord calls to you now to sow thet seed of pain into ground what needs it. Take your pain, child, and cast it to the soil and see what joy the good Lord will bring from it. You don't have to have all the answers because you know the One thet does!" She gave a definitive nod. "Thet were the gift the Lord done give to me. With every pain, I said, 'Lord, show me how to sow this.' And He'll do the same for you, if'n you'll let Him."

They had reached the woman's wagon now, and Eden had never felt more thankful to see an end to a conversation. "I'm sure He will. Thank you." She offered the placating words as she hurried away, working her fingers once more into the tight muscles at the base of her neck. She shook her head. Sowing the seeds of her pain? No one, least of all her, wanted that crop to grow again.

She put the conversation behind her and hurried off to find Adam and discover the cause of the smoke that still belched into the sky.

Chapter 2

Adam pulled his team of oxen in behind Micah Morran and yanked on the brake handle. Thankfully, his burned hand had healed enough that, though he continued to need a bandage across his palm, he could at least work the reins without too much pain now.

He didn't move for a moment as he assessed the scattered and burned-out wagons in the valley below.

Spring was barely out of the womb, and the drab browns of winter still clung prevalently to the ground and trees. In the muddy expanse, Adam could see where these burning wagons must have entered the lowland through the gap toward the northeast, but nearer to the site of what had obviously been an attack, all the tracks were nothing but a mishmash of chaos.

Whatever had happened here had taken place quite recently because, in stark contrast to the beiges, umbers, and sepias of the landscape, orange and yellow flames still danced and crackled, gnawing greedily at two of the wagons. Two others had been knocked onto their sides. And another had rolled a distance from the others and was missing the canvas top. The stays cut sharp lines against the lighter brown of the dirt track like the bones of a skeleton.

His first thoughts were of Eden, and he searched the direction from which they'd just come and was thankful to see her a ways off, but moving closer with an elderly woman he knew to be the mother of Hiram Hawthorne, the man with all the look-alike offspring. Thankful that she was safe, he turned his attention once again to the decimated wagons below.

Scattered across the valley floor were remnants of the goods that must have once been packed in the five wagons. Here sat a cast-iron stove. There lay a set of copper pots with the consuming flames of the nearby fire reflected in a dance atop them. Papers fluttered in the breeze, and a torn bit of canvas tumbled at the whim of the wind.

Surely this couldn't have been a complete train? Only five wagons?

Adam gave himself a shake, snatched his rifle from beneath the seat with his good hand, and leaped to the ground.

Caesar was snapping orders and his fingers. He pointed one man toward a position on the far side of the now-circled wagons, even as he nudged Gideon Riley toward a gap on the near side. "Look sharp and shoot anything that moves!"

"Where do you want me?" Adam asked.

Caesar scratched his throat, adjusted his hat, and cast a grim look toward the column of smoke towering into the sky. "The scouts and I need to go out there and see what's happened. Figure you better come with us in case you need to give any folk last rites." He narrowed Adam a tight look. "You've seemed the sort to ride the river with, but I have to ask . . . You prepared to defend me and my men if necessary?"

Adam had never felt the weight of the rifle in his hand so heavily as he did in that moment. He ought to be offended that the man felt the need to question him, but he couldn't find it in himself to be so. "I'm no Quaker, Cranston. Protecting life is a key tenet of the Good Book. And anyone who sets himself against those that I care about will find himself between the end of my rifle and the good Lord."

The man nodded. "All right then. And your hand?" He lowered a glance to the bandage around Adam's right palm.

"Trigger finger works just fine." Adam bit back irritation that the injury was casting aspersions on his ability to help. Maybe it was time to lose that bandage, but Eden wouldn't like that.

Caesar led the way, followed by Cody Hawkeye, Jeremiah Jackson, and Striker Moss. Adam brought up the rear. Each of them kept their attention carefully focused on the surrounding countryside as they moved closer to the burning wagons. On the far side of the valley, a few low, tree-covered hills bunched like small wrinkles in the smooth quilt of the prairie.

Nothing moved except a few swaying grasses disturbed by the wind, which whistled eerily through the spout of a lidless teakettle a few feet away.

When they reached the first wagon, they found a woman face down in the dirt.

Adam bent to feel her pulse, then gave the others a shake of his head. Her neck appeared to be broken. Helplessness washed over him as he took up a nearby piece of torn canvas and draped it over her head and shoulders. He weighted the edges with a couple of rocks to hold it in place until they could bury her. Could all of this have been an accident?

Cody grimly strode forward to extract an arrow from the tailgate. The head was blackened as though it had been engulfed in flames but then snuffed out.

Cody sniffed the tip and pulled a face. "Bear grease."

Adam felt his heart sink. Whatever had happened here had been no accident!

"Indians?" Cranston asked.

Cody frowned at the arrow. Shook his head certainly. "Metal arrowhead beneath the grease-soaked rag. And these . . ." He ran his hand across the reddish-brown speckled feathers inset into the other end. "Feathers are too short and look to have come from a chicken." He chucked the arrow, point first, into the dirt at his feet.

Striker muttered something low beneath his breath. "Which means someone wanted this to look like an Indian attack."

"Seems like." Cody nodded.

Adam glanced between the five wagons. "These folks must have left from St. Joseph or another of the towns along the Missouri because no one left Independence ahead of us this year."

Jeremiah indicated a stack of gunny-sacked dry goods on a torn piece of canvas. "Some of the supplies are set out neat-like. As though someone were coming back for them."

Adam felt the hair along the back of his neck prickle. He searched the surrounding hills, and though they weren't very steep or high, he suddenly felt rather exposed and vulnerable down here in the shallow bowl of this valley. "Outlaws?"

"Good a guess as any." Jeremiah shook his head.

Cranston rose from feeling the pulse of a man nearby. He gave a discouraged shake of his head. "Whoever they were, it seems they didn't want no witnesses." He propped his hands on his hips, face contorted into a grim twist. "Scout around. See what you can find. Maybe we can write to their kinfolk."

Brad Baxter cursed his luck as he lay at the top of a knoll and peered through his field glass with his men beside him.

What was another wagon train doing out here this early? And a full-sized one, too. He certainly didn't have the men to take a train that size.

His hands fisted tightly around the shaft of the viewer. They'd barely taken half of the salable goods from that small train!

He was due to arrive at the fort in two days with a load of merchandise for the mercantile. But these newcomers were bound to stop at Fort Kearny also. He moved his study to the larger wagon train. He couldn't see all the wagons due to them being on the other side of the rise across the valley, but he knew from the amount of dust it had raised as it approached that it was a sizable one. A train that size would take at least another week to reach the fort. He could likely sneak down tonight with his men and plunder more of the goods, but now that these newcomers were wandering amongst the wagons, they might recognize anything he took! Or take it for themselves.

He sighed and lowered the field glass. His contract to supply goods for the fort had been hard won. Only won in fact because his brother was now the colonel there. He didn't want to lose it, and sure as the sun hung in the sky, if they found out some of the items he supplied were stolen, they would do more than cancel his contract. And Boone would be one of the first with a rope in his hand, no matter that blood ought to be his strongest loyalty nor that he had plenty of skeletons in his own closet!

Brad's neck itched, and he stroked the prickling skin with his thumb and forefingers. Dangling from some lonely tree was not his idea of a good ending.

Beside him, Mike Malkovich squirmed and glanced his way. "What now, boss?"

Brad pressed his lips tight. Raised the glass to his eyes once again. He was right, wasn't he? The risk was too great?

His stomach rebelled at the thought of leaving all that revenue in the valley for some roving band of Indians to take. He narrowed his gaze on the Indian in the group below, who even now was studying one of the arrows they'd used in their attack. Of course, Brad and his men had snuffed out the fires just as soon as all the pilgrims had surrendered and been dispatched. Couldn't have their merchandise going up in smoke. Problem was, one of those pilgrims had put up a fight and his wagon had been too far gone to save. Another had tried to make a run for it, but of course hadn't gotten far.

Brad moved the monocular a few inches to the right.

The other problem was that they hadn't taken time to brush their trail, and in the soft mud thawing with spring's warmth, it would be

visible to these newcomers if they wandered further afield. Which...
He cursed. They were even now beginning to do.

His vision snagged on a bit of movement near the new arrivals. His brows arched. What was this piece of skirt? His lips nudged up at the corners.

A slender woman with blond hair left the larger group of wagons and headed down toward the few men scattered in the hollow below. She paused at the center of the chaos, one hand covering her mouth as she spun to take in the destruction.

His destruction.

He let his gaze linger. Nice. Very nice, indeed. But he didn't have time to ponder on a woman right now.

Beside him, Mike shifted and blew a whispered whistle. "Ain't seen a lady that shiny in a month of Sundays."

Brad couldn't agree more. But he shifted his focus to more pressing matters.

The Indian scout he'd eyed earlier suddenly raised a hand and motioned for his companions to join him. He'd found their trail.

Brad lowered the monocular with a sigh. Time to get out of here, and they'd better do it silently and quickly. It would take the men in the valley less than thirty minutes to follow their trail up the hill, but that would be all the time they needed to disappear into the forested trails that would dump them out just this side of Fort Kearny.

Thankfully, he'd minded his old man's advice to never load his wagons too close to the site of the attacks. The concealing trees were the only thing that might save them from being caught red-handed.

Brad pointed for his men to retreat down the backside of the rise they were on. "Round 'em up," he whispered.

"But, boss, there's still so much..."

Brad's hand shot out and gripped Mike's throat. His fingers dug in behind his voice box. He leaned in close to glower into the choking man's face. "What was that?"

Mike shook his head, arms flailing as he tried to breathe. Blue veins popped out on his forehead. His eyes widened more and more with each second that passed.

Satisfied that he'd made his point, Brad released him. "That's what I thought. All of you move out, nice and quiet like. Killingbeck, stay back to brush our trail."

This time, his men moved to do as he commanded without question. Satisfying. Yes. Very satisfying.

Eden stood in the midst of the havoc beside Adam with tears blurring her vision. The men had gathered seven bodies from amongst the wagons.

"Eden. You shouldn't be down here." Adam looked at her with that unfathomable compassion of his shining from his eyes.

She searched his expression, hoping to see even a spark of what had once united them, but all she saw was that blasted thoughtfulness. Not a husbandly concern, but a ministerial one. The same that he felt for everyone.

He studied her worriedly.

And had she expected anything different? Ever since she'd returned, he'd been treating her like a patched teacup—like something he was afraid to touch lest it fall to pieces in his hands.

And he had every right to think that, she supposed, after the way their mutual grief had buckled her under. It was also the reason she hadn't confided in him about the pains in her head. He didn't need more evidence of her weakness.

Since her return, she'd tried on several occasions to woo him, to remind him of what they'd once shared. Not just the lovemaking but the bond of friendship and mutual respect. But he'd staunchly resisted her. This distance he'd placed between them sprang from a deeper place. In her grief, she had shut him out. She had hurt him. And now he was doing the same to her, even though he would deny it if she brought it up.

She must do better. Prove to him that she had learned to be strong. Yet even now, she couldn't seem to speak the words she wanted him to hear. However, maybe that was best, because here in the middle of smoke-swirling air with dead bodies nearby was not the time.

She turned to take in the victims. "I-I thought you might need some help tending the wounded."

Adam settled his bandaged hand on her shoulder and gave her a brief squeeze, but quickly snatched his hand back to his side. "None of the victims needed tending."

There was a grimness to his words that tightened her stomach. How could anyone justify doing something like this to another human being?

"Do you think you could percolate a big pot of coffee? The men will likely appreciate a cup after this task is done."

Eden didn't move. She recognized the dismissal. He wanted her to leave. But something rooted her feet firmly in place. "This could have been us, Adam." The words were barely more than a whisper.

She studied the two women lying with the group of bodies. She'd watched the men gather them. One woman appeared to have fallen near her wagon. Another seemed to have been running away when an arrow had taken her in the back. Neither woman looked older than mid-thirties. Eden pictured Mercy and Willow, lying on crushed prairie grass with eyes vacant and staring. She shuttered the horror of the thought behind her eyelids.

Eden had overheard Striker telling Adam that all the men appeared to have been taken off guard by the attack because each one had been cut down on the bench of his wagon. The nearest wagon still had a rifle in the scabbard beneath the bench.

"Someone attacked these poor people, and they didn't even have a chance." Nausea roiled in her stomach, and she covered it with one hand.

"Eden." Adam's voice was soft, gentle—like it used to be before she had ruined everything.

A picture of herself scattering seed flashed into her thoughts, and she irritably pushed it aside.

Her husband drew a step nearer. "I know you like to help. The coffee really would be helping. I'm not just sending you off."

But he was. And stubbornness made her want to stay. "Shouldn't we put things to rights with their wagons? At least gather the things into a pile in one of them? If their relatives come looking... A-at least we can give them that."

The words were foolish, she knew. Within days, this valley would be picked clean, whether by the next wagon train, or by the outlaws who had brought this terrible destruction, or any other number of people who might pass this way. Even now, Hiram Hawthorne was removing one of the wheels from the nearest wagon to replace one of his that had cracked a few days earlier.

Despite that, Eden needed to do something. To act. To right what she could of the wrong that had been done here.

There was something about the death in this valley that filled her with the same feelings that had overwhelmed her after the loss of their newborn son. She could not be overwhelmed again. *Would not* be overwhelmed again.

"Please, Adam. I must face this. I *need* to face it."

His feet shuffled, and she felt the directness of his scrutiny but couldn't bring herself to meet his gaze. From her peripheral vision, she saw him cradle his rifle against one arm and turn to study her more fully.

She held her breath. *Please, God, don't let him fight me on this.*

Finally, he relented and swept a hand toward the scattered remnants that spilled across the valley. "All right." Glum resignation filled his tone.

She wouldn't let herself ponder his disappointment with her right now. She would simply be thankful that he wasn't banishing her back to their encampment.

With a nod she took a resolute step and picked up a teakettle lid. Another step after that, she gathered a fork, and then a small sewing basket filled with threads, buttons, and extra scraps. She took these to the farthest wagon—the one that seemed to have suffered the least damage but was missing the canvas top. As she lowered the tailgate and settled the items into a pile, she tried to ignore the grating sound of shovels displacing dirt where Jeremiah and Striker dug what would become a common grave.

She worked for thirty minutes, and had quite a pile gathered, and the men were nearly done digging the hole, when she approached the wagon with another armful and heard the muffled cries.

Chapter 3

Caesar had appointed Adam to stand guard near the grave while Jeremiah and Striker dug, and Caesar and Cody tried to gather what evidence they could of the crime that had happened here. They would report their findings to the fort when they reached it and bring the arrows and what information they could gather on how many men had likely been part of this attack. Cody and Caesar had followed a trail to the other side of the opposite knoll several minutes earlier.

"Adam!"

Adam glanced up to see Eden frantically motioning him closer.

Striker and Jeremiah both paused digging.

Adam felt his heart thump. What could be so urgent?

After an exchanged look, both Striker and Jeremiah crawled out of the hole and drew their pistols as they followed Adam toward Eden and the far wagon.

As they drew nearer, he heard her speaking softly toward the side of the box. "Don't be afraid. We are your friends. You can come out."

Adam scanned the area, seeing no one. He scrutinized the wagon. "What is it?"

Eden held up a hand for him to be silent, and flapped a motion for Striker and Jeremiah to put away their guns. She also pointed for him to lower his rifle.

"Please come out. You can trust us. I promise we aren't going to hurt you."

Silence.

Adam frowned and looked at Eden. Had she heard something? His eyes shifted to the dead bodies they hadn't buried yet, and he hated the concerns that immediately sprang to mind. Surely, she wasn't... And yet, he'd seen how stress and grief had broken her in the past. Could it be that she was imagining something?

She stood with her hands pressed palm to palm at her lips, her gaze fixed unwaveringly on the box of the wagon in which she'd been piling the supplies she'd fetched from the scattered remains of the raid.

When the silence lingered, she pointed to a compartment built into the lower portion of the wagon's bed. "Adam, please open it. Carefully."

The compartment was similar to ones he'd seen on other wagons. Built for storing extra tools and supplies, the compartments were a blessing until... Well, until they were not. He'd read articles of some who had regretted adding the compartments which lowered the clearance of their wagons—clearance that was needed on stretches of the trail further west, he'd heard. But the compartment wasn't large—a foot deep at best. Surely not large enough for a person to fit into?

Feeling his concerns rising, he nevertheless strode forward and took hold of the wooden handle that would lower the hinged door of the compartment that lay between the wagon's front and back wheels. For a moment, the door stuck fast, and then it gave with a pop.

His heart lurched, and he took half a step back. For there, staring up at him, were three sets of wide and frightened eyes.

"Oh, children." Eden's voice broke. "I'm so sorry for what you endured here today. Please come out. None of us are going to hurt you."

The two younger children, both with fear shimmering in their eyes and tears streaking their cheeks, turned to look beside them at an older boy who, from the look of him, was probably nine or ten.

Adam held still, not wanting to frighten the children. But he couldn't deny the relief coursing through him. Eden wasn't losing her mind. He hated himself for the thought, even as it registered.

The older boy glanced from him to Striker and Jeremiah and then back. After a long pause, he finally nodded to the two younger children. "Go ahead. Just stick close to me."

The children tumbled out of the compartment and stood staring up at them, wide-eyed. The oldest boy, who had just spoken, settled himself between the other two. Were they all siblings?

The youngest one, a girl, seemed like she might be three, but what did Adam know of children's ages? Maybe she was four? The middle boy thrust his chin high, blinking hard to hold his tears at bay. He might be seven.

The older boy's solemn gaze moved past the adults and his lower lip trembled as he noted the bodies they'd yet to put into the ground.

Adam shifted slightly to block his view. There was a brief glint of anger in the boy's gaze before he lowered his focus to the top of the girl's head.

"You three siblings?" Adam asked.

Someone had to get the conversation rolling.

The oldest boy raked his mess of wild, bronzy blond curls out of his eyes and nodded. The sun had baked the boy's skin to a golden brown that proved he spent a good deal of each day in the elements.

"We're very sorry about . . . all this." Eden's voice was soft and full of concern.

Adam swallowed. She would have been such a good mother.

He forked his fingers through his hair and resettled his hat, pushing what-might-have-beens aside. "I'm Adam, this is my wife, Eden." He swung a finger between the two men. "Mr. Striker Moss. And Mr. Jeremiah Jackson. And you three are?"

The little girl's bright blue gaze fastened curiously on Jeremiah. Her blond hair was just as riotously curly as her brother's. "My name's Afton. I like the color of your skin and your eyes." She smiled. "You look nice."

"Afton, hush." The oldest boy said sharply, settling a hand on her shoulder.

"It's all right." Jeremiah squatted so he could meet the child's gaze directly. "Well now, little lady, that's some coincidence because I like the color of your skin and eyes too." His teeth flashed white against his walnut skin.

Afton glanced up at her brother. "I like him."

The boy leaned to see past Adam again. "Our ma and our pa . . . did anyone make it?"

Adam shook his head. "I'm sorry, son."

Tears immediately sprang to the oldest boy's eyes, but it was the middle boy who sobbed and threw his arms around his brother. His wavy hair was the darkest of the three children. But his eyes were just as blue.

The oldest boy patted a hand soothingly across his brother's back. He notched his chin a degree higher as though determined not to give in to the tears that wanted to spill. "You already met Afton. This here is Asher and I'm Wyatt."

Eden stepped forward and held out a hand to the little girl. "Why don't I take you all up to our wagon and get you something to eat?" Her head tilted as she waited for their decision.

Relief shot through Adam. "Yes. Good idea." Finally, Eden would be away from this tragedy. And it would be good for the kids to escape this, too. And then concern swept through him. He shot a look at Eden. If she saw to the needs of these children, she would inevitably fall in love with them. It was simply her nature. Then what would happen when they needed to give the children up? For they *would* have to give them up. There would be family somewhere wanting to care for them, surely. And he'd just gotten Eden back. He had no desire to lose her to grief once again.

Thankfully, the oldest boy shook his head. "If we're digging a gr-grave, I should help."

Guilt for his relief impaled Adam's heart. He had to admire the kid's gumption, even though he ought to insist that they all escape to the safety of his and Eden's wagon. Yet he couldn't bring himself to say a word.

"Ash," Wyatt set his younger brother back from himself. "You and Afton go on up to the wagons. I'll be along shortly."

Asher shook his head vehemently. "If you're stayin', I'm stayin'! I can dig just as good as you!"

"Me too." Afton folded her chubby arms stubbornly.

Eden met Adam's gaze. *Now what?* her eyes asked.

The only thing he knew was that he didn't want his wife growing attached to these children. And that thought made him feel like the lowest of the low.

It was Striker who stepped forward. "You know, that grave is a tight fit for just Jeremiah and me. And we're almost done with the digging anyhow. Of course, we'll want you here for the burying. But what would be a big help right now is if you could sit down with the parson and his wife and help write to any family you or any of these in this train might have back east?"

Relief coursed through Adam. A perfect solution.

Wyatt shook his head. "This was all of us." He motioned to the wagon on the other side of the grave. "That was my uncle Dan Thornton. He was my mother's only brother. And that..." He swung his arm to a closer wagon. "Was owned by my father's only brother, Samuel Slade. Uncle Sam's wife was named Maude. And her two brothers drove those last two wagons. We ain't got no other family."

Eden stepped close to the boy and settled a hand on his shoulder. "And your ma and pa? What were their names?"

Adam couldn't help but feel sorry for the boy when his lips trembled and he blinked rapidly a few times.

After taking a moment to gather himself, Wyatt swallowed. "W-Wyatt and Ella Slade." He cleared his throat. "May I see them?"

Eden's gaze once more flashed to Adam. Even Striker and Jeremiah were looking to him this time.

Adam shifted. What was the right thing to do? Death had come. There was no preventing that. He would like to protect the children from the sight of their deceased loved ones, and yet, would it help the reality settle in better if they were allowed to see them?

He was still trying to decide what was best when Wyatt grabbed Afton's hand and thrust it into Asher's. "Stay here, both of you." With that, Wyatt darted around him and ran to the covered bodies.

Thankfully, Asher and Afton seemed inclined to listen to their brother's sharp command.

"Adam." Eden covered her mouth, soft eyes fixed on the boy who laced his fingers behind his head as he looked down at the shrouded bodies of his family.

"Stay. I'll see to him." Adam could almost palpably feel the boy's grief as he strode toward him. Behind him, he heard Eden murmuring soft words of comfort to the younger two children.

He clenched his teeth. No family, they said. But surely there had to be *someone*.

When Adam reached Wyatt's side, he sank to his haunches, arms resting across his thighs.

In the distance, a hawk screeched, and here the wind swept softly through the prairie grasses, dry and rustling after the barren winter.

For a moment, he and the boy remained silent, but then Adam decided that processing the morning's attack might help Wyatt. It was best to try to learn the details as soon as possible anyway.

"Can you tell me what happened, Wyatt?"

The boy shook his head, but it seemed more a gesture of confusion than denial. His brow furrowed. "Afton is sickly like."

Adam glanced back at the wagon where Eden now squatted before the other two children. She was wiping Afton's tears with her sleeve. The chubby little girl with a head full of shiny blond curls didn't appear sickly, but what did he know of children? Was it something Eden could catch?

"Go on," he urged the boy. "Start at the beginning."

Wyatt released his clasped fingers and crossed his arms instead. "We broke camp and ate breakfast, oats and milk, same as always. Afton, she gets sick near every morning. Stomach aching and sometimes, well . . ." He flapped a hand as though to indicate that the details were not important. "This morning Pa said Ma needed some exercise and that I had to stay in the wagon with Ash and Afton." He paused, brow slumping.

Adam held his silence, not wanting to push the boy to tell more than he was comfortable with. His father's command had likely saved his life.

After a moment, Wyatt continued. "I was reading them a book when I heard the first shot. Just one. But Pa . . ." His voice broke, and he took a moment to gather himself. He gestured at the legs and boots of one of the partially covered bodies. "He screamed at the team. I've never heard him yell like that at any animal." The boy took a moment to gather himself. "Then he yelled at me to get Asher and Afton into the hidden compartment in the floor of the wagon. He put it there on account of wanting to hide stuff from bandits if they came." Wyatt drew in a shuddering breath. "I should have— I should have—" His gaze shifted to one of the covered women, and Adam could only assume she had been the boy's mother.

Adam pivoted to look straight into the boy's face. "You and your siblings were your ma and pa's greatest treasure, Wyatt. I can tell you that were they here, they'd tell you how proud they are of you for staying with Asher and Afton. Doing your duty takes courage."

"I saw one of them." Wyatt's gaze seemed miles away. He stared at a piece of canvas as though seeing an image in his mind's eye.

"One of the attackers?"

Wyatt nodded.

Adam felt his concern rise. If the attackers knew they'd been seen . . .

"How?" Adam glanced back toward the wagon.

"There was a crack between two of the boards. Not big. But enough to see through." Tears were suddenly cascading down the boy's cheeks. "I saw him shoot Ma in the back while she was lying on the ground."

Adam rose to his feet on instinct and pulled Wyatt against himself. He might not want Eden growing close to these children, but he'd be a cad not to see that the boy needed some support in this moment. He settled a hand against the back of the kid's head and, when Wyatt wrapped his skinny arms around his waist and hung on as though for dear life, Adam felt a lump rise to his throat.

"Can you describe this man? The one you saw?"

The boy nodded. "I can draw him."

Adam didn't want to disparage the boy who obviously only wanted to help. But the amateur strokes of a child's drawing probably wouldn't help them give a good description to the authorities at Fort Kearny when they arrived. Still, what could it hurt to let the boy do his best?

"Sure. You can draw him. Eden has some paper in the wagon that she uses for writing letters to her parents. But maybe you could tell me too?"

The boy stepped back, pressed his palms over his damp cheeks, and then looked up at Adam with a frown. "Don't you think a drawing would be better?"

Maybe he'd pushed the boy far enough for this morning. He stepped back. "Sure. We can start there."

"I'll do it as soon as we're done here." Wyatt dropped into the hole that Jeremiah and Striker had been digging and took up one of the shovels that leaned against the side. He thrust the shovel into the dirt and tossed a scoop onto the mound up top. "First, we'd best get on with the burying. I don't suppose your wagon train wants to linger here in this place."

Adam couldn't help but admire the kid's maturity. He must have been raised by good people. Jeremiah and Striker approached, obviously ready to continue the job themselves, but Adam held out a hand for them to hold off. For now, he would let the boy put some of his angst and frustration into the work of digging his family's common grave.

Eden was on her knees before the two younger children when she heard footsteps and turned to see who approached. Adam. She relaxed and sank back against her ankles. She had lowered herself to the two younger children's level to better comfort them, for they'd been clinging to each other. Their horror over this situation was plainly evident in their trembling lips and pale faces.

Asher had been trying to be strong for his sister, and all Eden wanted to do was pull them both into an embrace and shield them from all this atrocity. Yet she didn't want to frighten them by doing the former and had no power to do the latter.

From this angle, looking up at Adam as she was, she could see many of those same emotions in his expression. His gaze was soft and full of concern as it lingered on the two kids.

She swallowed. Swiped away a piece of grass that had fallen into her lap. How long had it been since she'd seen that look of loving concern on his face for her? She couldn't ponder his compassion for these strangers, or her anger would get the better of her. Already, he'd shown more love and concern for these children than he had for her since she'd returned to him.

She resisted a wince. Maybe that wasn't exactly a fair assessment.

Eden held a hand to her eyes and looked to where she could barely see the top of Wyatt's blond hair as he tossed shovelfuls of dirt out of the grave. Striker and Jeremiah stood on guard nearby, both looking like they'd rather be in the hole with Wyatt.

Eden knew that normally people who died along the trail were simply buried in shallow graves and covered over with stones to keep wolves at bay. They'd all been instructed about that in one of the early meetings. However, in this situation, with Caesar and one of the scouts off investigating, Jeremiah and Striker were apparently willing to do the job properly.

And Wyatt. The poor boy shoveled faster and faster as though throwing that dirt over his shoulder could erase some of what had happened to him here today. "Should he be doing that?"

Adam's lips flattened into a grim line as he glanced over his shoulder. "I think he needs something to do right now. He jumped to it without being told. Let's just let him work until he gets tired."

Again, that thoughtfulness for another's needs. If only he had extended his signature kindness toward her when they'd faced their loss. Maybe she would have found the courage to speak of her anguish. Maybe he wouldn't have left her. He hadn't been cruel—that wasn't in his nature. He'd simply been... indifferent.

The pain in her head felt like two giant hands had taken hold of her and were trying to split her skull.

Once more, she yanked her thoughts from frustration with Adam before her familiar despair overtook her. There were more important things to consider right now—like the children's needs.

"Adam, this wagon is mostly unharmed. Just the team is missing. And the canvas, of course. Do you think we should try to take this with us? At least as far as the fort? From there... The children will be able to get an escort back home. That way they'll at least have some of their supplies."

Adam frowned. "You heard Wyatt. He said this was their whole family. No one back home to take them in."

Eden gestured to Asher. "He says they had a neighbor who might take them in." Her voice broke as she said it, for already she knew that leaving these children in someone else's care and continuing to the Territories was going to break her heart. But doing what was right for the children had to come before doing what she might want.

Asher folded his slim hands, blue eyes fastened on Adam. "Can you take us home?"

Adam squatted to the boy's level and gave him his full attention. "I'm afraid I can't do that. But maybe we can find someone who can. For now, my wife and I will take good care of you and your sister and brother. How does that sound?"

Big tears pooled on Asher's lower lids. "But we don't know you."

Adam's eyes closed for the briefest of moments before he gave the boy a gentle jostle. "I know, son. I know. But I'll tell you what, you trust us for a few days until we can figure out the next steps, and then we'll move ahead from there. Okay by you?"

Eden bit down hard, clamping her teeth to keep her anger locked inside. Adam's solution to everything. Just trust me and let me make all the decisions. Had he asked her if she wanted to take care of these kids? No. He'd just assumed she would. Of course, she would have said yes if he'd asked. But she would have liked to have been asked.

Asher sighed. His gaze drifted to where Jeremiah had now joined Wyatt in the hole. "Don't suppose we have any other choice."

My, how Eden knew that feeling.

She'd come back to Adam because she loved the Lord and what other choice did she have but to obey His command to respect her husband? And yet, her heart lagged behind, resisting the release of past hurts. She might be here in body, but her spirit was still so angry at Adam for leaving her behind and moving on with his life instead of waiting for her and giving her the space she needed after the death of their son.

Despite her feelings, she understood that her brokenness had been very real. She had essentially abandoned *him* long before *he* abandoned *her*, so she had no right to be so angry with him. No matter that she knew that to be true, the hot roil of it churned her stomach. It was easy to keep the shield of anger in place, especially since Adam continued to keep an impenetrable wall between them.

Adam gave Asher another squeeze. "No other choice, no. Not at this time."

Afton suddenly rubbed a hand over her belly. "I'ma be sick."

Oh no! Eden shot to her feet and stretched her hand to the little girl. "Come on, let's step over here. I'll stay with you." Had she been hurt somehow in the morning's attack? Nausea was maybe just a result of too much stress on her little body?

She held the girl's hair until she was done and then helped her rinse her mouth with water from a canteen and a scrap of torn cloth that Adam had brought over, then pressed her hand to the girl's forehead. She didn't feel feverish.

Adam watched Eden intently and she gave him a shake of her head.

She had no idea what might be wrong with the girl, but when Afton sagged against her and rested her head against Eden's skirts, it was almost her undoing. She bent and lifted the girl into her arms, where she snuggled the child close and held her tight. Afton settled her head on Eden's shoulder and popped her thumb into her mouth.

Eden met Adam's gaze over the girl's shoulder.

His lips pressed into a grim line. He stepped closer and took one of Afton's hands, giving it a gentle squeeze. "You feeling better?"

She nodded, but didn't speak.

Eden started to soothe one hand over the girl's back.

But as soon as Afton nodded, Adam lifted the child out of her arms and set her on her feet.

Eden clamped her teeth and folded her arms that suddenly felt barren and empty.

Adam bent and pressed one hand to the toddler's back. "Why don't you go stand by Asher, okay? We'll be right over."

Afton nodded and moved across the grass toward her brother.

Eden started to follow, but Adam held out one hand in a motion for her to wait. She frowned, irritated that even when he wanted to speak to her, he didn't touch her.

Adam stepped close and started talking before Afton even reached Asher's side. "I'm not sure we should bring these kids to our wagon if they are sick. We don't know what you might catch."

The anger Eden had been tamping down all morning boiled over. "Oh, yes. Because that's just exactly what the Good Book says. 'Look after orphans and widows, but only if they are healthy,' right? What book is that in again?" She hoped he could read her anger in the lift of her chin.

Adam sighed, and his shoulders slumped. "You're my first concern, Eden."

"Really? Could have fooled me on that count for several weeks now."

Adam's gaze shot to hers. "What have I done to make you think I don't care about you?"

Leaving me behind. Rejecting so much as a touch. Even refusing to eat with me most evenings. Each thought fired, and only realization of their location kept her from leveling each accusation at him. She stepped closer, not surprised when he withdrew a matching step.

Eyes narrowed, she kept her next words to a fierce whisper so the children wouldn't hear. "Whose place would you have me send these children to? Maybe to Mercy and Micah, who already have two boys and might be immune to whatever she has? Or maybe to the elderly Mrs. Hawthorne? Surely, *she* could survive whatever illness you are afraid your precious wife—the one you refuse even to touch—might contract?"

Adam's chin shot up, and though his feet remained unmoving, he leaned back as though she'd launched a physical attack.

Eden took a breath and pinched the bridge of her nose. "I'm sorry. I..." Again, she realized this place was not right for such a conversation. But when might they ever be in such a place, when Adam refused to be alone with her? She sighed. "I'm taking Afton to the wagon. Please call us before the burial. She should be there whether she'll remember it or not."

With that, she brushed past him and strode over to take Afton into her arms again. She could feel Adam's gaze drilling into her back the whole way.

Eden didn't miss the irony over the fact that mere moments ago she'd been upset that he volunteered her for this task without asking her, and now she was upset with him for trying to tell her she oughtn't be the one to care for the children.

The man was a conundrum! But for the moment, she was done cowing to his every whim.

Chapter 4

It didn't feel right, this burying of so many people in one grave, and yet, here they were. Most of their wagon train had gathered around to pay their respects, but several of the men stood along the perimeter of the gathering with rifles cradled at the ready.

Eden settled her hands on the shoulders of the two youngest children, who leaned against her as Adam said a few words over the service. Beside her, Wyatt stood with his arms folded tight as though to keep himself together. She reached to rub his back, but he shifted away from her touch, so she let him be.

The ache in Eden's head made concentrating on Adam's words difficult. She was thankful when the service concluded with Wyatt and Asher throwing handfuls of dirt into the grave. She led Afton over and helped her do the same.

And then everyone disbursed back to their wagons.

Striker and Jeremiah went to work filling in the grave.

Adam paused next to the hole, his gaze on the lone wagon without a covering that the children had been hidden in. Though his gaze was on the wagon, he spoke to the two men shoveling the mound of dirt. "We should bring the children's supplies with us, if we can."

Jeremiah paused and leaned one arm atop his shovel's handle. "I don't mind driving as long as ol' Strike don't mind me leaving him to ride ahead alone."

Wyatt stepped forward. "I can drive the wagon." His chin nudged upward.

Adam exchanged a look with Eden. She knew he was thinking it was much harder work to handle a team all day than the boy realized. Not to mention the strength needed to keep the tension on the reins all day. And the blisters that often formed on the hands of grown men, much less the tender skin of a young boy.

"Well now," Adam nodded. "That's right manly of you to offer. And I'm sure there will be times when we might need you to step up and do just that, but we also will need your help to watch your siblings, if you're of a mind to."

Wyatt turned a look on his brother and sister and seemed torn. "They could ride with me on the wagon bench."

"They could." Adam drew out the word. "Is that what your pa had them do?"

Wyatt frowned. "No, sir. We walked behind."

Adam nodded. "It's hard work sitting still on the seat of a wagon all day. I think that might be more than Asher and Afton can handle, day in and day out, to the fort. So if you could, it would be a big help for you to walk with your siblings to keep an eye on them." Adam was quick to add, "Then on the days when we do need you to drive the wagon, we'll call on you? What do you think?"

Wyatt's frown eased a little. "Yes, sir. I'm happy to help."

Adam nodded. "So you've no objection to Jeremiah driving your wagon?"

"No, sir."

"And Striker?" Adam turned his gaze on the man who was still shoveling. "Be okay with you if Jeremiah drives at least to the fort?"

"Fine by me."

"Good." Adam nodded with satisfaction. "It's settled then. We should see if an extra covering is available that didn't suffer too much damage."

Wyatt pointed to one of the still-smoldering Conestogas. "My uncle kept an extra oilcloth in that box on the side of his wagon there."

The box was scorched, but it didn't appear that the flames had consumed all the way through the wood.

Eden felt relieved to have that settled. The children had lost so much already. She'd hate to see them lose all of their possessions as well.

All day the wagon train remained on the crest of the low mound where they had circled up. Guards remained posted, their rifles resting across wagon tongues and benches alike—all of them facing the surrounding terrain and on the alert.

She had found the cheese sandwiches she'd made at noon wrapped in a towel and set inside the wooden box they used to store biscuits and such. Adam must have assumed she'd already eaten and packed away the leftovers when he was done. But that had worked out fine because she'd been able to offer them to the children. They had eaten rather mechanically, but she'd been thankful to see them getting some sustenance in them before the burying.

Now Eden held Afton's hand as they walked through the gloom of dusk to the golden light of the large campfire that Mr. Cranston had ordered built in the center of their encampment. He and Cody had returned about an hour ago and proclaimed they would remain here for the night, then Cranston had called a meeting.

She hadn't seen Adam since they'd concluded the graveside service for the Slades and their extended family. Saying he wanted to take advantage of the chance to hunt, he had left Afton in her care and taken the boys with him. She had brought the girl to their wagon and they had both slept for hours—Afton likely exhausted from the ordeal she had survived that morning. Eden had no excuse other than that she'd fallen asleep after realizing Afton had drifted off, and then she'd woken feeling much refreshed, scant moments before the little girl.

Now as she walked with the girl, she hoped Adam and the boys would be back in time to join the meeting.

As though conjured by her thoughts, they rode into the circle of wagons.

Eden took a breath to calm the increase in her pulse. Even when she was angry with him, the sight of her husband sitting broad and tall in the saddle could still set every sense on alert. Would that he weren't so stubborn and mule-headed!

Asher sat behind Adam's saddle, which was tethered to a travois loaded down with the carcass of a large deer. Wyatt rode on a horse beside Adam and his brother.

"Bluey!" Afton exclaimed.

Eden paused to take note. They had left with only one horse and Wyatt walking beside. Where had the Paint come from? It was a gorgeous horse with large patches of mahogany brown and a white blaze down its nose.

Afton wriggled loose of her grasp and ran to the blue-eyed horse that Wyatt rode.

At the sight of the tiny girl running full tilt toward the large Paint, fear constricted Eden's chest. She stretched out her hand. "Afton, maybe you should—"

The horse lowered its head to whuffle Afton's hair with a soft whicker.

The little girl threw her arms as far around the horse's big head as they would go. "You came back."

Wyatt swung down and ruffled Afton's hair. "Come on now, Afton. Leave old Blue be. He needs a drink of water."

Afton released her grip. "I tan get it!" She turned with excitement sparkling in her eyes, but then froze as though just then remembering that she was with strangers and didn't know where to find a bucket. Her shoulders dropped, and she clasped her chubby hands before her.

Sorrow swelling in her chest, Eden exchanged a look with Adam, who was helping Asher dismount.

After setting Asher down, Adam swung Afton to a seat on his arm. "Tell you what." He gave her a jostle. "Looks like there's a meeting about to start. The horses drank at a creek just a bit ago and can wait for a few more minutes. How about we hear what our wagon master has to say and then you can come with me and the boys to water and bed down the stock, hmmm?"

Afton hung her head, but she managed a small, "Otay."

Eden gave Adam a nod even as she pushed away thoughts of what a good father he would have been. She swallowed and turned toward the meeting, stretching her hand to Asher.

But it was not Asher who took her right hand. The warm hand that slipped against hers and entwined with her fingers was much too large and calloused.

Eden glanced over with a start.

Adam looked down at her with brows raised and a twinkle sparkling. Heavens. The man looked much too good with a child in his arms. Was it hurting his burned palm to hold the girl? If he could drive the wagon all day without complaint, she supposed that he could hold the little girl for a few minutes.

Eden faced forward. "What are you doing?" She tried to pull away, but he held on. She canted another glance in his direction.

He offered a tilt of his head. "I'm holding my wife's hand."

A glance behind revealed that the two boys were following—and they were exchanging amused glances over Adam's display of affection.

Eden felt pleasure, but also shame and embarrassment, flood her features. She yanked harder for the release of her hand. "Adam, we're going to a meeting. You can't hold my hand in public!"

It felt like a pretense. A show put on for others when naught was right between them.

He grunted and let her go. His jaw hardened. "Thought that would please you."

A little voice niggled at her that she'd been too hard on him. At least he'd been trying. She opened her mouth to apologize, but he handed over Afton, then stepped out in front, leaving her and the children behind.

Eden sighed and dropped back between the two boys, allowing Adam to lead the way. How did she explain that she wanted him to hold her hand because that was what he wanted to do, not because he thought it was what she expected?

She felt those dragon claws pierce her heart. Was everything broken between them? It felt like things would never be right again.

She blinked hard to keep the pressing tears at bay. Eden patted Afton's back and tried not to wish that she was another child—a boy child who would be just a little younger than she was right now had he lived.

Heart heavy, Adam strode into the circle of people gathered by the campfire and paused by Micah Morran's side. He'd thought that holding Eden's hand would make her happy. After all, earlier she'd accused him of refusing to even touch her.

He swallowed, even now willing away the feel of her slender fingers laced between his own. She obviously had no idea what her touch did to him, or she would understand why he'd been keeping his distance. She made him weak with the want of her. And he was determined she not fall with child until they were settled and had a competent doctor close by.

Micah glanced over, did a double take at what Adam could only presume was a glower on his face, and then focused on the children who stopped by his side. "Adam. Good evening. Care to make introductions?"

Adam took himself in hand and forced a response. He pointed to the child in Eden's arms. "This here is Afton. And these . . ." He turned to gesture Asher and Wyatt closer. ". . . are her brothers, Asher and Wyatt Slade."

Micah reached to shake the boys' hands as he might have if they were important men. Adam's heart swelled with appreciation for the man, even as it filled with an equal measure of concern over the situation now facing them.

"Pleased to meet you, sir," Wyatt said politely.

Micah introduced Mercy and their two boys, Avram and Joel, who promptly asked the boys if they would like to play catch while the adults had their meeting.

Wyatt and Asher both looked to Adam, and he gave them a nod. Lord knew that if they could forget this day for even a couple of minutes, they deserved to do that. The boys dashed off to a nearby field with Mattox, Micah's big black dog, trotting on their heels.

"I play too!" Afton squirmed to get down from Eden's arms.

Eden worked to hold onto the little girl, glancing at Adam as though to ask what she ought to do.

He ought to take the child and relieve Eden of the burden, but the moment he'd picked Afton up earlier, he'd known he'd made a mistake. These children claimed they had no family. However, surely there would be someone close to the family who would want them—maybe the people Asher had mentioned. He needed to guard his own heart as much as he wanted Eden to guard hers. And if he was going to do that, carrying that sweet child around probably wasn't the best idea.

He was relieved of making a decision when Willow Riley stepped forward with a small golden and red fruit in her palm. "Would you like an apple?" She smiled and held it out to Afton, who froze and eyed the orb hungrily.

Slowly, the child nodded.

"Well! Isn't that a wonder," Willow exclaimed. "Because I have this one right here just for you!" She nudged the apple closer.

"Tank you," Afton said shyly as she took the apple off Willow's palm.

And for some reason that quiet politeness was almost Adam's undoing. He felt tears sting his eyes. Quickly, he blinked away the moisture.

These were good children. He hated to think of them being separated from their parents. Hated to think about decisions that would need to be made regarding their future. Hated to think about the inevitable parting that would surely crush Eden again.

With Afton seated on her hip, she stood staring into the flames of the large campfire, one hand working at the muscles in the back of her neck. She'd been doing that a lot lately. Perhaps it was the mattress in the wagon? It was naught but ticking stuffed with straw. Once he'd known that she would be joining him, he ought to have purchased goose down. Maybe he could rectify that when they reached the fort in a few days, but it was unlikely the fort would be stocked with down.

Eden glanced over, and her gaze softened when it met his. She shifted her focus to Afton, and her expression melted even more.

She was already smitten with the child, he could tell from the gentle smile on her face, and the fort was still a whole week ahead. Sakes alive, he'd only just gotten her back. Would he lose her to the darkness of grief again so quickly? And this time without her family nearby to aid in her recovery?

Willow said something to Eden, who nodded, and then the red-haired woman moved off to join a few others.

Beside him, Micah shifted. "If you'll recall, Parson, I know something of the grief and worry you two have faced over the loss of your child. Eden is strong."

Adam returned his attention to Micah with a start. His feelings must have been evident in his expression.

He shifted his feet and tried to settle into a relaxed posture. If only he could believe that Eden was strong enough to make it through this again.

"She proved her strength by traveling on her own that whole way to find you." Micah studied the stars above as he spoke, keeping his voice quiet, for which Adam was grateful. It was best that a conversation such as this stayed just between the two of them. "And she also proved it by standing with Willow against Harrington. And by allowing herself to grieve hard in the first place, I'd wager. It's a strength to let oneself feel so deeply and yet come out the other side a different, stronger person. Most people, they stuff all that missing and longing and horror down deep and simply try to continue living. I was one of those. I'm guessing you were, too. But . . ." He hesitated. Shifted. Glanced over at Adam. "I know I'm headed into meddling here, but you'll recall that you've meddled in my life a time or two."

Despite himself, Adam smiled. "I'm apparently better at meddling than grieving." He offered a palm to let Micah know he was free to continue.

"My first wife, Georgia, she felt that grief strong like your Eden did. She was taken from me before she could come out the other side. And, Lord, forgive me, I didn't see it as a strength. But facing that mountain of emotion? That's a strength." Micah slapped him on the back and gave him a jostle. "Eden is strong. You can be, too. You both are going to make it."

Adam couldn't help but feel irritation at Micah proclaiming him weak when it came to facing emotions. He'd *had* to be the strong one. He'd wanted Eden to know that they were going to be okay. But now, he wondered . . .

He pondered as they waited in silence for the meeting to start. It had taken a sheer amount of grit and strength for Eden to come after him like she did. And he would have to admit that keeping his distance from her might be a weakness on his part. Earlier, she'd snapped at him about not touching her for all these weeks, and that had felt like an arrow to the heart. She thought he didn't want her? He didn't want her to think that.

Though, when he'd tried to hold her hand just now, she'd also gotten upset. Why? And did he want to pursue it further? Because doing so would drag him into dangerous territory. Did Eden even know how close she'd come to dying herself in the birthing? He didn't think she did. There had been so much blood! She'd been so pale and limp.

He shook the image away. Maybe he was just as weak as Micah had implied he was, because he never again wanted to face the prospect of losing Eden and having to continue through life without her. One time of facing that wall of impenetrable pain was enough for him. And yet...

He loved that woman to the very depths of his soul.

He couldn't leave her feeling unloved. He would need to find the strength to face these emotions and tell her the whys and wherefores of his actions.

Confound Micah and his meddling. He smiled self-deprecatingly even as he thought it. "Speaking of meddling..." He eyed Micah. "How are things between you and Mercy?"

Micah smiled his understanding of the question. "Mercy is still... coming to terms with our need for a quick marriage, if that's what you're asking."

"You handling that?"

"I might ask you the same, since I see you hanging in the breeze beneath your wagon nights, instead of inside it."

Adam shifted and followed the flight of a moth toward the heavens. "It's complicated."

Micah gave him a side-eyed look. "Good Book says love is patient and kind. I'm doing my best to be that way with Mercy. Lord knows she has plenty of experience with a man who was about as far from a man of the Book as could be."

Adam thumped Micah on his shoulder. A gesture that he hoped conveyed how proud he was of the man for doing his best to follow the Bible, because in that moment, he was finding it hard to vocalize that pride. He gave the man a nod and another thump and then turned his attention to Cranston, who had stepped into the middle of the gathering.

Chapter 5

Tamsyn Acheson and her brother, Edi, strode through the dim dusky evening outside the row of wagons. As they passed between two wagons, she could see the golden glow of the campfire far across the circle, along with the shadowy outlines of those who were gathering. They'd only taken a few more steps when Joel and Avram sprinted by with the two boys from the other wagon train as they babbled about playing catch. Edi grinned and started after the boys, but Tamsyn grabbed her brother's arm before he could take more than a couple of steps.

Edi turned toward her and frowned. "I play ball, too," he gritted.

Tamsyn shook her head, despairing of the confrontation she knew was coming. It would be easier to simply give him his way, but she really wanted to be at this meeting. If she were to let Edi go play with the boys, she would need to keep an eye on them all since she wasn't sure how the two new children would respond to Edi.

She motioned to the campfire in the distance. "Mr. Cranston has called this meeting, and we need to listen to what he has to say in case it's important."

Please, let him come without a fight.

Edi's lips clamped, and his gaze drifted longingly to the boys, who had paused to toss Joel's belt ball back and forth between them.

Though the blue gloam of twilight still lightened the sky, with the sun already dipped below the horizon and the moon rising to take its place, she doubted that the boys would be at the game long.

"They won't be able to see for more than five more minutes, Edi."

Part of Tamsyn felt guilty for insisting that Edi stay with her. He might be a full-grown man, but his mind was still that of a boy. However, in addition to her concerns about how the new children would take to him, she couldn't have him off on his own when she needed her complete attention on this meeting. It was much easier to keep an eye on Edi when he was right by her side. He tended to wander off if left to his own devices.

When he looked back at her, there was a glitter of stubborn rebellion in his eyes.

Tamsyn felt her heart thud in her chest. She and Edi had been allowed to join the wagon train solely because of the kindness of Mr. Striker Moss and his fellow scout, Jeremiah Jackson. Mr. Moss had witnessed one of Edi's fits before they'd left Independence and could have prevented her from traveling with their party. However, on her promise that she would keep Edi in line, he had agreed that they could come.

For several weeks now, Edi had been doing fine, but she could feel the tension building in him. Feel an impending explosion.

Edi shook off her hand. "Edi tired. Tamsyn mean!" He gave her a sudden hard push.

"Edi!" Arms flailing, Tamsyn stumbled to catch her balance and crashed backward into a firm, warm chest.

"Whoa, there. What's going on here?" Striker Moss's hands slipped up her arms to curve around her shoulders and help her regain her balance.

Her eyes fell closed. Of course she'd crashed right into the very man she wouldn't want to witness this type of behavior from Edi. But she couldn't linger, or her brother would make his escape. He was already stalking toward the boys.

"Sorry. Terribly sorry." She could only hope that Mr. Moss would be so intent on getting to the meeting that he would let the incident slide. She lurched to escape the man's grip. "Edi—" She started in her brother's wake.

"Miss Acheson." Mr. Moss's sharp tone stopped her in her tracks. "Miss Acheson." His voice was softer this time, and he took her hand and drew her around to face him.

The warmth of his fingers was an allure that she could not afford to dabble in. She tugged for the release of her hand, and he obliged, though he did step between her and her brother's retreat.

His dark eyes could have passed for black in the dim light of dusk. His hair, normally a bit long and wild, lay wet against his head. He'd obviously just had a dip in the creek, but had forgone the use of a razor, it seemed, by the remaining stubble on his jaw.

He looked down at her, searching her face. He seemed to have lost the words he'd meant to speak.

She pointed toward her brother's retreating back. "I need to get Edi." Why was it that she could barely find her voice? And why was she wishing that she'd not withdrawn from the warmth of his gentle grip that filled her with such reassurance? When he didn't move from her path, she cleared her throat and tried again, a little louder. "I need to get Edi."

"Edison!" Though he kept his scrutiny on her face, Mr. Moss barked her brother's name like a father about to chastise a son.

Beyond his shoulder, she saw that Striker's sharp command stopped her brother in his tracks.

Edi turned and faced them, head hanging.

Never taking his gaze off her, Striker continued speaking to her brother. "What have I told you about treating your sister with respect?"

Lord help her, she couldn't seem to draw her gaze away from Striker's searching scrutiny, but she heard Edi's feet shuffle.

"I sorry," Edi mumbled.

Striker didn't relinquish his hold on her gaze, but he did step back from her and thankfully stepped out of her path.

She rolled her lips into a tight press and lowered her focus to her clasped fingers.

Striker turned and settled his study on Edi instead.

Finally!

"You tired tonight?" he asked her brother.

Edi nodded, looking ashamed.

"You think you can get yourself ready for bed without Tamsyn's help?"

Her brother's brow furrowed. "Yes."

"Good." Striker's gaze once more leveled on her. "Why don't you do that. But no playing ball. If you want to do fun things, you have to be kind to your sister and show her how much you love her."

Edi hesitated, and for one brief moment Tamsyn thought he would give Mr. Moss a fight, but finally he sighed and shuffled back toward their wagon. "Night."

Tamsyn felt her irritation rise. "I wanted to go to the meeting." She fisted her hands in revelation of the irritation tightening her chest, but for some reason she didn't march away from him like she'd planned to.

Softly, he said, "Please enlighten me as to why you were flying through the air and landing in my arms? Not that I'm complaining, mind you."

Heat flooded her, and she spun away from him, massaging her fingers over her forehead. Instead of answering, she gave him a glower over her shoulder. "I wanted to hear what this meeting was about."

He swept a hand for her to lead the way.

She shook her head, thrusting a gesture to Edi's retreat. "I can't go to the meeting and leave Edison on his own." She took a step.

But once again he took her hand. "He'll be fine. I—"

"Mr. Moss!" Her heart stuttered, but it was reality that spun her to face him as she once again yanked her fingers from the temptation of his gentle grip. She drew a step back and folded her arms. Hopefully that would keep him from taking one of her hands. "I'm all Edi has. Do you understand that? He will be with me until the day one of us takes our last breath, and Lord willing, it will be him who draws his final breath first."

His brow puckered as he looked down at her, and she realized how that had sounded.

Tamsyn looked away, following the flight of a firefly as it flitted from one blade of grass to another. "Not that I'm wishing for his demise, mind you. It's only that he needs a caretaker."

She flicked Mr. Moss a glance, hoping to see understanding in his expression. What she found instead was a pair of cinnamon eyes, soft with amused admiration. She jerked her gaze back to the firefly, which had been joined by another now. She must make him understand.

"I'm his caretaker. I will always be his caretaker. There is no future for me other than as his caretaker. Please understand that." She hoped he did because as tempting as the man was, it was vital for her to make it clear right up front that she wasn't now, nor would she ever be, free to court or marry anyone.

How she would take care of Edi once they arrived in the Territories was another matter. A matter that had been increasingly vexing her of late. Up until now, she'd been so focused on getting them into a wagon train and supplying their journey, that she hadn't given the end of the trail more than a fleeting thought. Yet now, the reality of providing for a family as a single woman was beginning to weigh heavily.

She turned to face the man again, being certain to keep her distance. "Do you understand that, Mr. Moss?"

He nodded. "I do." He said the words, but there was a hint of challenge in his expression and also maybe a smidge of anticipation.

Tamsyn swallowed and retreated another step. "Good. G-good. Then, I'll thank you to stay out of our business." Beneath the concealment of her folded arms, she scrubbed her thumb over the pads of her fingers, wishing she could as easily dismiss the feelings the man maddeningly evoked as she could dismiss his help.

This time when she stalked past him, he let her go, but his words trailed her into the darkness. "You're fighting a battle that you don't have to fight on your own, Tams."

She kept walking, willing away the temptation to lean on someone else. She'd tried that. Thought she could rely on Mother and Father, only to be chased into the cold with Edison in the long run. And the pain that had raised had made her realize that it was much better to rely exclusively on herself—that way she wouldn't be eviscerated by others' eventual rejection.

She stomped through the night until she had almost reached her wagon. There, she paused in the darkness just outside the firelight because Declan Boyle was seated on a stone by her fire pit with one of the two oldest Hawthorne twins sitting on an overturned pot beside him. The girl had a book in her lap, and Declan had leaned close, but his gaze wasn't fixed on the pages. He looked over at the pretty blonde and murmured something too quiet for Tamsyn to hear.

Tamsyn pressed one hand to her brow. Wonderful. She couldn't seem to escape romance no matter where she went tonight. She shifted and bumped her elbow against the galvanized bucket dangling from the side of the wagon.

Declan looked up and jumped to his feet in surprise. "Och. What ye doin' here? Mr. Moss asked me tae sit wi' Edi till the meetin' were o'er." He swung a gesture to the girl, who bolted to her feet and closed the book, seemingly unable to meet Tamsyn's gaze. "Miss Whitley here was juist teaching me tae read." He gripped the back of his neck and hung his head.

Even in the firelight, Tamsyn could see the red that filled his features.

Tamsyn lowered her head, drawing in a breath. Edi was crawling into his bedroll beneath the wagon. Striker had planned to give her a night's reprieve, and she'd practically bitten his head off. She glanced toward the glow of the large fire in the distance. She really did want to hear what Mr. Cranston would have to say.

"Thank you, Declan." She motioned for the teens to resume their seats. "Please don't let me stop your . . . lesson." She started to turn away, but then paused and looked back. "But Declan . . . Please remember that my brother is nearby, hmmm?"

Declan hung his head and shifted his feet through the grass with an embarrassed grin.

Whitley pressed her lips together and rubbed at something on the cover of her book.

"Yes'm," Declan said.

For the second time that night she retraced her steps, once again heading back toward the meeting. She wasn't very hungry, but she had a feeling she was about to eat crow.

By the time the meeting wound down, Eden felt ready to cry from the pain in her head, and Afton seemed to be growing heavier by the moment. Caesar had kept the meeting brief, thankfully. He'd cautioned that they would need to hurry to Fort Kearny to report today's crime to the leaders there. He'd encouraged them to plan for short meal stops, early starts, and late encampments.

Wonderful. Just what she needed. A more strenuous schedule. She'd already have the additional task of trying to care for these three children.

The boys had arrived partway through the meeting, since complete darkness had fallen, and now Adam turned to her. He frowned and reached to take Afton.

The little girl plunked her thumb into her mouth and rested her head on Adam's shoulder. One hand gripped her half-eaten apple, and her eyes drooped at half-mast.

You and me both, child.

"Ready?" Adam asked.

She nodded and stretched a hand to Asher. This time Adam let her be and the little boy slipped his tiny hand into hers. "You kids hungry?"

What was she going to feed them besides the venison that Adam had fetched? Children needed milk, and butter, and fresh bread. She had none of that.

Somehow she blustered her way through the evening meal and even managed not to look too inept at cooking. She buried some potatoes in the coals of the fire while she fried the steaks that Adam had shown the boys how to butcher. That, along with a quart jar of canned corn, seemed to satisfy them all, though Afton mostly only picked at her food—not surprising, considering the size of the apple that Willow had given her earlier.

After the cleaning was done, they set Wyatt up with paper, a dip pen, ink, and a lantern because he kept insisting that he wanted to sketch the outlaw he'd seen shoot his mother. Eden's heart grew heavier each time she thought of what these children had experienced.

She took Afton into the brush for evening ablutions and then returned to the wagon.

Though her head had felt better after her earlier nap, it had returned to feeling like two miners, each with a pickax, were hacking at the bones behind her ears. The pain was so intense that she was starting to see black spots dancing in her vision.

But with a breath for gumption, she reminded herself that she merely needed to be strong for a few minutes longer. She would soon be able to collapse onto her bed at the back of the wagon.

Adam had hung his hammock from the underside of the wagon and was showing Asher how to climb inside. Eden hefted Afton into the wagon box and motioned for her to crawl onto the tick and lie down. By the time she checked on Asher a second time, he was already sound asleep.

Now she needed to put a clean bandage on Adam's hand. She retrieved one from the basket, and the small bar of lye soap, filled a bowl with hot water from the kettle near the fire, and set the bowl on the tailgate. "Adam, I'll change your bandage now."

With Wyatt sketching in the light of the campfire, Adam approached. His gaze swept her, for the first time since her return, like a man hungry for his wife.

She tried to set the bandage on the tailgate, didn't realize she was too close to the bowl, and almost knocked it over. She caught it just in time before it spilled everywhere and then plunked the clean bandage down beside it. She swiped at her face then. "What are you looking at?"

Humor touched the corners of Adam's eyes. "I'm looking at my wife."

Eden felt consternation tighten her brow. The pain in her skull stabbed her through with shards of agony. She couldn't ponder on this now. She needed sleep. She held out one palm.

Adam settled his bandaged hand into hers, but instead of laying it face up where she could untie the strips of cloth, he turned his hand to grip her fingers. "Eedie, you are my very breath."

Eden closed her eyes, then purposely turned his hand upright and bent her head over the knot in the dirty bandage covering his palm. If she'd known that speaking to him firmly like she had would elicit such a change, she might have done so sooner. And yet the timing of his proclamation couldn't be worse. She could hardly concentrate for the pulsing shards in her head.

"I know," was all she offered.

"Do you?"

She raised him a quick glance, gave up on the knot, and reached for the scissors. She simply wanted to fall into her pallet and sleep. "I do."

He fell silent then and thankfully let her change the bandage in peace. She was thankful to see that the burn on his palm was dry and healing well. She smoothed on some of the beeswax balm that Tamsyn had given her and then started to cover it once more with the clean rolled bandage, but Adam withdrew.

He pressed the thumb of his good hand into his palm and massaged the balm against the scar of the burn. "I think this is healed enough to leave off the bandage now." Without giving her time to protest, he offered a nod and a "thank you" and then strode to Wyatt's side by the fire. "How are we doing over here?"

Wearily, Eden tossed the water and returned the clean bandage to her basket. She didn't have the strength to fight him on this tonight.

"Eden." Something in Adam's voice spun her to face him.

He wore an expression of awe as he stepped closer to the fire and angled Wyatt's paper toward the light.

Wyatt stood nearby, periodically prodding the dirt with the toe of one boot.

Eden hurried closer. The moment her gaze landed on the drawing, she pulled in a surprised breath. "Wyatt! This is amazing!"

The page held so much more than a simple sketch. The boy was an artist! On the paper, the man's face, stroked and shaded in only black ink, seemed to jump off the page as though he might start speaking at any moment. He had a short-cropped beard, shoulder-length hair interspersed with white streaks, and well-proportioned features. And from the way Wyatt had drawn the eyes, Eden knew they would be a dark brown. Wyatt had even captured the textures of what must be a leather duster and the dark bandana that he wore around his throat.

Wyatt stood by, uncertainly fiddling with the shaft of the pen.

Adam gave her a look that revealed he felt just as amazed with the boy's skill as she did, then lowered his focus to the boy. "Where did you learn to draw like this?"

Wyatt frowned. "Can't everyone?"

Adam released a wry chuckle and shook his head. "No."

Wyatt shrugged. "I just remember what I see and mark it down sometimes." He held up the pen. "I like this pen. It holds lots of ink. I never was allowed to draw with ink before. Pa said it was too expensive." His voice hitched and he hung his head, still fiddling with the wooden shaft of the instrument in his hands.

Adam exchanged another look with Eden. "You've never drawn with ink before?"

Wyatt looked worried and stood on his tiptoes to get another look at the paper Adam held. "I didn't quite get his ear right because of that blob of ink right there, but it's pretty close." He lifted soulful eyes. "Do you think it will help?"

Eden settled a hand on the boy's shoulder and held out her other for the pen. "You did a wonderful job. This is going to be very useful to the lawmen at the fort."

When he handed over the pen, Eden nudged him toward the wagon. "Join your brother in the hammock and try to get some sleep. We'll show this to the men come morning."

It was only after watching long enough to assure herself that Wyatt had listened that she felt Adam's gaze on her. "I cleared a place for Afton to sleep near the tailgate."

"Oh, I didn't notice." Eden was more than ready to fall into the painless oblivion of sleep for a few hours. The last thing she wanted to do was move the girl again. "I don't mind sharing the bed with her for one night."

Adam squinted one eye shut. "The thing is . . . With the boys in my hammock . . ."

"Oh!"

Eden spun to face the wagon, pressing one hand to her forehead. "Yes. I see. Give me just a moment to resettle her."

She took a step, but Adam brushed past her. "I don't mind moving her. I just wanted to make sure you were all right with me joining you."

Eden blinked at his back as he climbed into the wagon and disappeared inside. Early in the trip, she'd tried to get him to join her several times, all of which he had rejected repeatedly. And now he wanted to make sure she wouldn't object. It was as though they were strangers.

Sorrow welled in her heart. She had done this to her marriage. She closed her eyes against the pain pulsing in her skull and tipped her face to the coolness of the sky. *Lord, if You can fix my marriage, I'll do my best to be strong so that I don't break it again.*

A cool breeze swept over her face. In the distance, she heard the plaintive warbling of a screech owl. Closer, the trickling of the nearby creek and the croaking of a bullfrog.

The canvas at the back of their wagon rustled. "Eden?"

She turned to face Adam.

"You coming?"

"Yes." Weariness swept over her as she trudged over and allowed Adam to assist her into the dim interior.

She was too tired to even fret over the awkwardness as they both turned their backs, and she donned her nightwear. Behind her, she could hear Adam tugging off his boots and undoing his suspenders. But she didn't even glance at him before she crawled onto the far side of the pallet and fell into the bliss of sleep.

Chapter 6

Adam frowned when he turned around and saw that Eden was already fast asleep on the bed. She must have been some exhausted after the stress of this day.

And yet, he was a coward of the most extraordinary measure, because he felt relieved that he wouldn't have to speak to her again today about his feelings. He didn't think he'd done a very good job of assuring her of his love earlier. She hadn't seemed like she really believed him, despite her words to the contrary.

He set his boots and his suspenders off to one side, but left his pants and shirt on in case he might need to help the boys in the night. For that same reason, he pulled the canvas at the back of the wagon together, but didn't cinch it. He wanted to be able to reach the boys quickly if he needed to. After checking on Afton, he turned toward the bed.

Was she really already asleep? Or simply avoiding him? He moved slowly between the crates that lined each side of the wagon.

Eden didn't even shift when he lay down beside her. Her breaths were gentle and slow, the sound soothing in the darkness. My, how he had missed that sound. He wanted to look over at her, but he needed to remember that this arrangement had to be temporary—for her health and safety. Even if he talked to her about all that he was feeling, he remained committed to her being near a doctor before . . . anything else.

He turned his back on her and closed his eyes.

The sound of crying woke him and he shot a hand above his head in the darkness to feel for the bottom of the wagon so he wouldn't whack his head when he sat up. When his hand found only air, he remembered that he was sleeping inside the wagon with Eden. He gave himself a little shake and pressed his fingers to his eyes as he paused to listen. Was it just one of the children experiencing troubled sleep?

The sound came again and this time he realized it came from directly beside him.

Eden.

His brow furrowed, and he turned to look at her. The moon glow filtered dimly through the canvas—just enough for him to make out the shadow of Eden's face.

She groaned and squirmed a little, then thrashed her head from side to side. She whimpered, and one of her hands gripped the base of her skull, even though Adam could tell she was still asleep.

He felt his pulse hammer. Seemed like she was in pain. Something to do with when that outlaw had knocked her out a few days back? But she hadn't complained of pain even once since then, so likely not that.

He raised to one elbow and leaned toward her. "Eden?" He shook her shoulder gently. "Wake up, Eden. Are you all right?"

She moaned and twisted her head away from him. Her breathing stuttered.

Had she taken sick? He pressed his fingers to her forehead but didn't find it hot or sweaty.

She jolted upright with a gasp. Her breaths puffed rapidly through the darkness.

He sat up slowly and studied her as best he could.

She worked at the muscles along the back of her neck, and when her elbow brushed his chest, she gasped and pivoted to face him.

He lifted his palms even though she likely wouldn't be able to see that in the dark. "It's just me. Just Adam."

That seemed to ease her, but she didn't relinquish her massaging.

His heart threatened to climb right out of his throat. Something was certainly wrong.

Despite his resolve to keep his distance, he found himself reaching for her. "What is it? Are you in pain?" He brushed her hand aside and gently began to massage the muscles that seemed to plague her. "Is it here?"

She shook her head and suddenly seemed more at ease. She brushed his hand away. "I'm sorry to have disturbed you. I'm sure it's nothing."

His brow furrowed. "Eden . . . This is not nothing. What is it?" Slowly, he reached for her again. Her braid slipped like silk across his knuckles as he worked the pads of his fingers into the muscles at the base of her skull. "Is it a cramp?"

"No." She seemed reluctant to offer more.

"What then?"

She sighed. "I didn't want you to know."

A tightness threatened to clamp off his breathing.

Stay calm.

"Didn't want me to know what?"

Again, his mind flashed to the incident with the outlaw, and his heart began to hammer. Surely she would have said something sooner if she'd been in pain all this time?

"I'll be fine. Let's just go back to sleep. Morning will come early."

The fact that she didn't want to tell him raised his concerns even further. "Eden, I know things have been a bit difficult lately. But you can trust me. You know that, right?"

She loosed a breath on a little huff and lay back down. "Go to sleep, Adam."

He twisted to see her in the dim light. It had to stem from her getting hit in the head! And he was a fool of the worst kind. Of course, she didn't know that she could trust him. After all, he'd left her and headed west on his own when he hadn't known how to help her overcome their grief. That must have hurt her.

And yet, he was more than just a husband. He was a minister of the gospel. Didn't his call from the Lord rise above his duties as a husband? After all, the Word said that anyone who put his family above the Lord was not worthy of the Lord, and that those who did not take up their cross were also not worthy.

So hadn't leaving been the right decision, when she had refused to even speak to him, much less join him in their call? He still didn't know what else he could have done. Though, if he had faced the emotions like Micah said he should, perhaps...

He massaged at the pain in his chest.

The decision to leave without her had felt like tearing his own heart out. And maybe it had been just exactly that. The Word also said that a man and his wife became one flesh. But now, it felt as though he and Eden were torn asunder. Two parts of the same flesh that could never heal enough to be whole again. But if there was one thing he believed in, it was miracles. It might take one to repair his and Eden's relationship, but he was committed to waiting for it.

To participating in it.

He eased onto his side, facing Eden. He could see in the faint light that she was staring up at the canvas overhead. He reached out and took her hand. Felt her stiffen. He soothed his thumb over the softness of her skin. "Eden... If we don't learn to trust each other again, we will never be able to repair what we broke."

She did not pull away from him as he had half expected her to, since that was what she had done out by the fire. But neither did she turn to him and rest her hand atop his cheek as she would have done in the early years of their marriage. She simply lay staring into the darkness. And then she closed her eyes.

Finally, when he was beginning to wonder if she had fallen back asleep, she spoke quietly. "If we are ever to repair what we broke, Adam, then you must not think of me as weak."

He frowned." I don't think of you as weak. In fact, Micah just reminded me tonight how much strength it took for you to come find me. And I realized how true that was."

She angled her head sharply toward him, and then gave a gasp and closed her eyes.

He rose onto his elbow and frowned down at her. "You are in pain. Please, Eden, you must tell me what is wrong. We are meant to help each other, to be a strength for each other."

"Like you were a strength for me when I was drowning in grief?" Bitterness touched the edges of her words.

Despair swept through him. He leaned back from her and turned his face to the shadows of the canvas overhead. "You know that I tried to be there for you. But *you* left *me*. You moved to your parents' and refused to speak to me when I came by." His conscience cried out for him to admit that he hadn't wanted to face all the emotions, but he clamped the words tightly behind his teeth.

"I was mad at God, Adam!" She froze for a long moment as though the words had surprised her as much as they'd surprised him.

He searched her face in the darkness, wishing he could read her expression through the shadows.

"Yes. I was." She squirmed and released a quiet breath, lowering her voice. "I'm sorry to say it. But it's true. And you were just . . ." She flapped a hand in the darkness. ". . . willing to go on as though nothing had happened."

Adam ground his teeth. He certainly hadn't been going on as if nothing had happened. Maybe he hadn't shown as many emotions as she'd wanted him to, nor recognized the strength it had taken for her to face them, but he'd felt the loss of their son to his very core.

His conversation with Micah prodded him again. Of course, she hadn't been able to know the depths of his grief when he hadn't shared it with her.

Eden continued even more softly than before. "I had been willing to give up everything for God—family, home, security . . . And He couldn't even be bothered to save my—our—son. Why, Adam? Explain it to me."

He rubbed a wrinkle in the coverlet between his fingers. Shook his head. Pressed his lips together. Fought for control. *Lord, I'm so bad at this. How do I explain something that I don't even understand myself?*

Scripture came to him as though whispered directly to his soul, and he spoke through his brokenness. "In this . . . world, you will have . . . tribulation. But take heart . . . I have . . . overcome the world." He barely managed to squeeze the verse through the fist clamping his throat. "This world is not our home, Eedie." He fumbled for her hand again in the darkness. "We are just passing through. Our son is there in our real home, healthy and whole. That's the promise I have to cling to."

When she didn't respond, he glanced over. "Are you still? Mad at God?" He held his breath.

Please, Lord, show me how to help her. Increase her faith. Increase my compassion.

"I read the book of Job. Clean through." Her voice rang soft but steady.

"And?" He let his thumb stroke the length of her little finger.

She turned on her side and tucked her hands beneath her cheek, looking up at him.

He lamented the loss of the warmth of her hand. He gripped a fistful of the coverlet instead. "And?" he prodded.

"I realized I didn't want to be Job's wife."

A furrow tightened his brow.

Eden's shoulder moved in a quick shrug. "God took everything good from Job. But he left his wife. She told him he ought to curse God and die. Maybe she was part of his test. I don't want to be part of your test, Adam. I want to have the faith of Job. No. I *do* have the faith of Job. And like Job, I say, 'Though He slay me, yet will I trust Him.'"

Adam inhaled so sharply that it sounded like a gasp, and then he hung his head. Here he'd been praying for Eden's faith when maybe it was his own that needed shoring up. At least she had gone to battle for her faith. He'd simply accepted the lot handed to him and moved on with his life. And yet, his faith in the Lord had never wavered.

He eased down beside Eden again. This time they lay face-to-face. "'Work out your salvation with fear and trembling.' I think that's what we've both been doing, Eedie. Just in our own separate ways." He paused, but knew he must go on. He beat back the coward in him. "You accused me today of not touching you. And you're right. But not because I don't love you."

She rolled away from him, settling to her back with her hands once again beside her. "Adam, you don't have to—"

"No. Please let me finish." He raised her hand and kissed the back of it. "What we went through, Eden. It almost broke me. I'm not sure you know how close you came to . . . I came to losing you, too."

"I know, I was weak."

Shock washed through him. Did she blame herself for the death of their son? "No, Eden. You're so small. And your body, well, you couldn't help what happened in the birthing. It wasn't your fault."

She didn't move or respond, but she didn't tug her hand back either. Progress.

He forced himself to speak before he lost his courage again. "Then later, you were strong and faced the emotions when I only wanted to run from them. But now . . . the thought of losing you . . ." He stroked her cheek with the back of one finger, immediately wishing that he hadn't given in to that inclination. He withdrew and rested that hand against the coverlet before him. "I don't know if I'm strong enough to go through that. I love you so much, Eden, and I'm merely a man. You understand?" Even now he longed for the freedom to draw her close, kiss her, love her. Now it was his turn to flop to his back and turn his gaze toward the canvas overhead. "I've been keeping my distance for your protection. And maybe a little selfish weakness on my own part. I fear losing you. Do you understand?"

This time she did reach out. She touched his face and turned his head toward her, then she rested her hand against his cheek. "Yes." Her eyes fell closed.

Relieved to finally have the subject out in the open, he closed his eyes, too. And it was only when he woke in the morning to find that she'd somehow eased out of the wagon without waking him, that he remembered that she hadn't explained what had pained her in the night.

Chapter 7

The morning bugle had sounded earlier than normal, and it was still dark as Tamsyn put the coffee to perk and added Edi's oats to the pot of boiling water.

Relishing the warmth of the fire, she wrapped her shawl snugly about herself, folded her arms tight, and turned her face to the blush of dawn that faintly tinged the horizon to the east. Wisps of sparse clouds stroked peach and lemon against a dome of cornflower blue. Cold as it was today, at least the heavens promised a day without rain. Remnants of stars still pierced the canopy of the sky above her. And a crescent moon floated like a canoe above the vast sea of prairie grasses that stretched in every direction.

Footsteps drew her focus back to the dim light of dawn on the prairie. Surprise lifted her brow. "Parson. Good morning."

He nodded and returned her greeting, feet shuffling. He twisted his hat through his fingers. "I hear you are some hand with medicine?"

She leaned forward and lifted the lid on the oats to check them. Who had he heard that from? She'd helped a few in the wagon train, true enough, but she didn't feel confident about people seeking her out for medical help, did she? Still . . . he was the minister. She couldn't very well turn down a man of the cloth.

Decision made, she looked at him. "I've learned a fair bit over the years. Something ails you?"

"Not me." He glanced back toward his own wagon. "It's Eden. Something isn't right. She's in pain, but doesn't seem to want to talk about it. I wondered... Well, I wondered if you'd be willing to speak with her? I'm concerned that it might be from when she got hit by that fellow."

Tamsyn frowned. If Eden had been in pain from that all this time and hadn't said anything, she could have made things worse for herself. "I'll talk to her as soon as I get Edison settled with his breakfast."

His shoulders seemed to ease. "Thank you. I appreciate it. While you're there, could you check on the little girl, Afton? The boys say she's sickly like. And..." He dug in an inner pocket of his duster and withdrew a money pouch. He worked at the drawstrings as he offered, "I'm happy to pay you."

"Nonsense. Put that away."

He lifted his brows and met her gaze.

She shook her head. "We're all in this together. I'm happy to do what I can to help your family."

"Afton is not my family."

He said the words abruptly and with enough force that she wondered at the emotion behind the statement. Of course, it wasn't her place to go prying.

He withdrew something from the pouch and held it out to her. "And the worker is worthy of his hire—or her hire, as the case may be." He smiled and nudged the money closer. "Go on. Take it."

Reluctantly, Tamsyn held out one hand.

He nodded. "Thank you. I'd best get my team hitched."

As he stalked off, she glanced down and heard herself gasp. A silver dollar lay in her palm. She had never considered that people might be willing to pay for her knowledge of herbs and such. Could this be a way that she could supplement her and Edi's income when they reached the Oregon Territory?

And yet, what if she made it known that she had medical knowledge and then was called in to help someone she didn't know how to help? What if someone died because of her lack of knowledge? It was a risk. Yet, wouldn't having *someone* to help in a time of need be better than having no one at all?

She tucked the silver dollar into the pocket of her skirt and pulled Edi's oats off the fire.

She didn't have to make a decision today. It was something she could ponder. Doctoring might pay a little better than trying to sell items made with the wool from the sheep Edi loved so much.

Something inside her eased. Perhaps this was guidance from the Lord that she hadn't even asked for!

By the time she settled Edi with his breakfast and stepped over to Eden's wagon, it was to find her making light conversation with the three new children by her fire as she ladled oats from a pot for each of them.

Tamsyn tucked the warmth of her shawl around herself as she cast a critical eye over Eden. Her hand was steady on the handle of the pot. And though she was bent to ladle the oats, her form seemed strong and sturdy. From the way she was smiling at the children, she didn't seem to be in too much pain. Could the parson be mistaken?

"Morning."

Eden glanced over and paused, seeming surprised to see her. "Morning. Is there something you need?"

Tamsyn tilted her head. "The parson seemed to think you might have need of some herbal remedy for pain?"

Eden thrust her tongue into one cheek and moved to set the pot on the tailgate of their wagon. "Ah."

"He's concerned that it might stem from the incident when that outlaw knocked you out?"

Eden propped a hand into the small of her back and turned to face her. Her gaze flitted from one place to another in the encampment.

For a long moment, Tamsyn thought she wouldn't speak.

Finally, Eden offered. "I've been having a little pain in my head since the incident with Mr. Harrington—or *Donahue*, yes."

Tamsyn didn't want to dwell on thoughts of the villain who had traveled with them for some of the way from Independence. "A little pain?"

Eden waved a hand and scooped a bowl of oats. She offered it. "Can you join us for breakfast?"

Tamsyn shook her head, irritation with her friend's evasiveness climbing. "Eden... A little pain?"

Eden plunked the bowl onto the tailgate and took up a mug of coffee instead. She leaned one hip against the wood. "It's been getting worse."

Tamsyn felt her chest tighten with concern. "Eden, why haven't you said anything?"

"It's difficult to explain." She stared into the depths of her cup.

Tamsyn tilted her head and narrowed her eyes.

Eden squirmed. Twisted her coffee cup. "I don't want Adam to think me weak. It's just an ache in my head. I can handle it."

Tamsyn fought to think through her limited knowledge of medicine. Back home, she remembered Dr. Johnson telling Mother that Edi needed rest after he'd fallen and hit his head against a stone. He'd taken Edi onto the porch and made him step into the sun while he studied his eyes, and then he'd proclaimed that Edi had to stay abed for three days. What had the man been looking for in Edi's eyes?

The sun was still too low on the horizon for her to try something similar, but maybe... "Don't move." She motioned for Eden to stay still and quickly stepped over to the fire. She grabbed the outer end of the longest branch of burning wood and lifted it like a torch. Back before Eden, she looked deep into her friend's eyes. "I need you to stand still and look into the light for me."

"Tamsyn, really, I'm sure this is all a fuss over nothing."

"Just humor me. Now, chin up."

Eden blew out a breath of frustration but did comply.

The burning firebrand wasn't nearly as bright as stepping from shadows into sunlight, but nonetheless, when Tamsyn lifted it before Eden's face, she gave a slight wince and held up one hand.

Tamsyn frowned at her.

"Sorry. The light hurts my eyes."

Tamsyn remembered now that Edi, too, had wailed as a boy when the doctor made him turn his face toward the light. She had dismissed it as a natural inclination to avoid looking into the sun, but now she wondered if Edi had experienced more pain than usual at that time.

"Let's try again. I'll hold it farther away this time. Just try to bear it for a moment so I can study your eyes, okay?" If only she knew what she was looking for.

Eden tilted her chin in compliance, but not without protesting, "I really should be getting the children's dishes cleaned up and instructing them about today."

Tamsyn concentrated on Eden's eyes, glancing back and forth between them. She frowned. "Wyatt, come here for a moment, would you?" she asked.

"Yes'm." The boy came immediately to stand before her.

Tamsyn held the torch before him and studied his eyes. Both pupils immediately contracted when she moved the light before them, but Eden's . . . She held the light before her again and willed herself to be calm over what she saw.

One of Eden's eyes responded normally to the light, but the other responded much more slowly.

"Eden, you're not going to like what I have to say."

Something in her tone must have set Eden on alert, because she studied her intently. "What is it?"

"From here to the fort, you must do absolutely nothing but lie in your bed in the back of that wagon."

Eden released a soft laugh of disbelief. "Tam, do be serious." She swept a gesture to the three children near the fire. "I can't lie around and do nothing."

Tamsyn took her elbow and nudged her toward the wagon. "You can and you will." Truth was, she wasn't even certain what Eden had or what the proper treatment was. So uncertain, in fact, that her heart hammered with the fear of it. What if something terrible happened to Eden because she didn't know exactly how to help her?

Eden thinned her lips into a tight line and dragged her feet.

"Go on." She pushed a little harder. "I mean it—nothing but rest. Between Mercy, Willow, and me, we'll take care of the children. I want your eyes closed and your body prone."

Eden used the portable steps to crawl into the wagon, then turned to look at her. "All the way to the fort?"

Tamsyn nodded. "All the way." Tamsyn started toward the children.

"Am . . . am I going to die?"

Tamsyn froze and turned back. "Of course not. But resting is what your body needs right now to recover from the blow you took to the head." Would that she knew for certain her assurances were true. She nipped the inside of her lower lip lightly between her teeth. Then realized that might not project much confidence, so she forced a smile instead.

With a sigh, Eden turned for her pallet.

One battle down. Tamsyn turned to the wide-eyed children, who were all staring at her with bowls of porridge untouched.

Wyatt tucked his lower lip between his teeth. "Is Mrs. Houston going to be okay?"

Tamsyn squatted before the children. "Yes. I think so. A few days before we came upon you, we discovered that a bad man had been traveling with us. He hit Mrs. Houston on the head with his pistol."

Afton's brow slumped, and her lips pursed into a frown. "That's not nice!"

Tamsyn resisted a smile at the little one's cuteness. "You're right. It's not. A sheriff came and took that man away." Tamsyn left out the part where her brother had needed to knock the man unconscious when he'd taken Willow and Eden captive.

Now onto her next task. She studied the little girl. "I hear that sometimes you don't feel good?"

Afton nodded. "Sometimes."

"Can you tell me more about it?"

Wyatt stepped forward and opened his mouth but Tamsyn shot up one hand for his silence and kept her focus on Afton.

The little girl's lips twisted as she pondered, and then she lifted one shoulder. "Sometimes my tummy feels wike all the baby chicks is pecking inside."

Tamsyn lifted her gaze to Wyatt.

He shrugged. "Pa used to . . . raise chickens. Before we left home." When his voice broke partway through the explanation, Tamsyn felt compassion fill her for the boy. He was doing remarkably well at handling the grief he'd experienced yesterday and keeping an eye on his siblings at the same time.

She turned her gaze back to Afton.

The little girl spread her tiny hands. "First, it hurts a wittle. But then more."

"When does the hurting usually start?"

One tiny shoulder lifted. "After breakfast."

"I see." Tamsyn looked to the half-empty bowl of oats in the girl's hand. "And how about today. Are you feeling okay?"

"Yep."

"Okay, well that's good. Mrs. Houston is going to rest for a few days, so if you start to feel sick, I need you to let me know, okay? And I'll help you." She pointed. "My wagon is that one right there, and that big man is my brother."

"Otay."

Tamsyn glanced at Wyatt, and he gave her a nod to indicate that he understood as well.

"Good." Tamsyn rose, realizing she needed to get back to check on Edi's job of hitching the horses. Sometimes he forgot a step. She was going to have to recruit some help if she had any hope of handling both her own morning chores and Eden's.

"I need to get back to my wagon, but will you three be okay?"

Wyatt nodded confidently. "I'll be sure to put the fire out and wash the oat pan."

Tamsyn rose and settled one hand on the boy's shoulder. "You're a good lad." She ruffled Asher's hair. "And you are too."

"Wha' 'bout me?" Afton spoke around the fresh mouthful of oats she'd just spooned into her mouth.

Tamsyn smiled, thankful to see that the little one seemed to be doing fine this morning. Maybe it was simply a passing illness that she'd picked up, and she would be well from here on. She bent and tapped Afton on her nose. "And you are a very good girl."

Afton offered a sticky grin as Tamsyn stood and turned toward her wagon.

Her gaze collided with that of Striker Moss, who had stepped between her and Edi at some point in the last few moments.

The softness in his eyes sent her heart into a romp. She clasped her hands. "Mr. Moss."

She gave him a sedate nod. She had tracked him down the evening before and offered an apology for her reaction, which he had graciously accepted. But she had hurried away before the moment could grow too intimate. The man could never know the way he affected her, because she knew he would never give up his attentions after that and he would wear her down. But it wouldn't be fair to ask anyone to be responsible for Edi all his life. That was her burden to bear, and hers alone now.

He stepped closer and took in Wyatt, who had already started to put out the fire. "Everything okay here?"

"Yes. Fine. I was just returning to my wagon after seeing to Afton."

The man's gaze softened even more when it lowered to the little girl. And drat if that didn't make her romping heart frolic even more.

He bent low, propped those broad hands against his knees, and peered right into Afton's face. "You feeling better this morning?"

"Mmm hmm." She nodded, blond mop bouncing, even as she worked the rather large spoon into her mouth again.

Her appetite certainly didn't seem to be stunted by whatever sickness she'd been battling.

Striker grinned when a blob of oatmeal landed on the front of the girl's dress. "I'm right glad to hear that."

Tamsyn would have stepped close to help clean Afton up, but that would put her much too near to the scout. "Wyatt, I'll return in a little while to help you pack away the cast-iron tripod and the pan. You sure you can manage washing it?"

"Yes'm."

Tamsyn gave him a nod and hurried toward her own fire, feeling the scout's gaze drilling into her back the whole way. As if she didn't have enough worries over Eden, now she would be worried all day that he thought she'd snubbed him—when, in fact, that was the very thing he ought to think because it would keep him at a distance.

Eden lay in the back of the wagon, staring at the canvas overhead. Outside, she could hear that conversations were happening, but they blurred into the background if she didn't concentrate on trying to hear what was spoken. Weariness swept over her. She ought to be out there fighting Tamsyn to take care of the kids. But the pain in her head was constant and sharp today. A few minutes of rest would feel so lovely and Tamsyn was very kind to have offered to see to everything.

And Adam—the one who had set all this in motion with a visit to Tamsyn—he would certainly do his part.

She closed her eyes. Perhaps just for a little while, she would sleep. It only took a few moments for the darkness to claim her. The sleep was tormented with disturbances, however.

First, labor pains took her nearly to her knees. But no, not labor, the pain was too high, contained behind her eyes.

Then a man's face swam before her. The doctor who had delivered her son. His frown brought back a rush of painful memories. She moaned and tried to twist away from the pain, but everywhere she moved, the sharp agony moved with her.

A cool hand settled against her head. A soothing voice, familiar, deep, and soft, accompanied by another more feminine and tight with concern. Drops of moisture touched her tongue, something bitter and sharp. That was followed by hot tea, sweet and tangy. She swallowed, grimacing, then swallowed again, hoping that her smile conveyed her thanks for the sweet tea.

Her eyes were too heavy to lift, and oblivion overtook her once more. She fell, headlong, floating as though through an expanse of blackness, deeper, deeper, deeper.

Chapter 8

Adam stepped down from the wagon and turned to offer Tamsyn his hand as she descended. It had been a long day filled with concerns. At noon, he'd checked on Eden, but she'd been deep in sleep and unresponsive to his attempts to get her to eat some bread and venison.

"Is she going to live?" He hadn't meant to voice his concerns, but the words blurted out before he could stop them. His heart seemed to forget to beat as he waited for her reply.

Grooves etched the skin around Tamsyn's tightly pressed lips as she rinsed the small bowl in which she had crushed the herbs for the tonic they'd just dripped into Eden's mouth. Thankfully, Eden had drunk the whole thing. But Tamsyn's silence made him want to crawl outside of himself.

He ought to pray, but his soul felt dry and cracked, and when he turned his gaze to the heavens, nothing seemed to be the right thing to say. What did a man say to the Almighty when he ought to have recognized that the woman entrusted to his care was suffering, but hadn't?

"What was in that tea you gave her anyhow?" he snapped.

Tamsyn lifted her head.

He gripped the back of his neck. "Sorry. I don't mean to bark."

Using her apron to dry the little mortar, Tamsyn then tucked it and the rest of her supplies back into her bag. "I wish I could make you promises, Adam. It concerns me that she's slept the whole day away and still seems rung with exhaustion. I think this came about because she's pushed herself too hard after an injury that was more serious than *we all* realized." She settled one hand on his arm as though to emphasize that point, but released him just as quickly. "I'm hopeful that a few more days of rest will restore her to her normal healthy self."

Adam paced, hands propped against his gun belt.

He suddenly realized that three small pairs of eyes were staring at him and froze. All day long the children had been well behaved and helpful. At noon, Wyatt had seen to feeding his brother and sister the hardtack and dried apples that Adam had dug from their supplies. This evening, he'd thanked Mercy Morran most politely when she'd brought a large portion of venison and Willow Riley when she'd arrived with biscuits. Adam had felt ashamed to have the women cooking for those in his care, but he'd been too consumed with worry over Eden and busy with taking care of his oxen to resist their kindness.

Right now, there wasn't anything he could do for Eden other than to let her rest, but there was something he could do for these children. He may need to guard his heart against growing too fond of them, but that didn't mean he had to ignore them altogether.

He thanked Tamsyn, and as she moved toward her own wagon, squatted to his haunches and motioned the children toward him.

"You three get enough to eat?"

"Yes, sir." Wyatt spoke for the three of them, but Adam waited until the other two had also nodded.

"Good. What do you say that I wash our dishes quickly and then we find Joel and Avram and play a round of ball?"

Wyatt and Asher exchanged a quiet look, then nodded, but it was more like they were agreeing to please him than because they wanted to play. And little Afton looked like she could barely keep her eyes open even as big tears spilled down her cheeks.

Wyatt stepped forward and tugged Afton against his side. "I already washed the dishes, Mr. Houston, whilst you fed the team." He pointed to a pail that contained a stack of wet plates and cups. "But if you'll forgive us . . ." His voice pinched off, and Adam's heart nearly broke as the boy worked to compose himself. "We're not much feeling like playing this evening."

Of course they weren't. Yesterday they'd all been in a great deal of shock. Playing ball had likely simply been something to occupy their hands while their minds tried to process their day.

Adam rose to his feet. "Of course." He still felt as though he were towering over them, so he strode to the rock they'd rolled near their fire and sank down, once again motioning them close.

Afton stuck fast to her brother's side, with her little arms wrapped firmly around one of his legs and her little shoulders heaving with silent sobs. Asher stood off to one side, arms folded and a frown on his face. His dark curls fell across his eyes, and he shook his head to brush them back. The boy's lips were pressed tight, as though he were barely holding all the sorrow in.

Adam felt helpless to ease their agony. "Asher, come here."

He tugged the little boy against his side and wrapped an arm around him. But he was apparently no good at this comforting, because though he tried to nudge the boy closer, he held his little body aloof and stiff. Adam was just about to give up on the endeavor when the child suddenly turned into him and sobbed into his shoulder.

Relieved, Adam settled one hand against his back.

Wyatt hung his head and kicked at the ground with the leg that Afton wasn't clinging to.

"I'm sorry. I'm so sorry." Adam settled his other hand against the back of the boy's head, realizing how small he truly was. These children had been stalwart all day long when they were suffering with sorrow. Afton had sat beside him on the wagon bench silently for most of the day. He'd tried to engage her in conversation a couple of times, but what did he know about drawing out a girl barely out of nappies? But now that he thought about it, of course her silence made sense.

Seeing that her brother was enveloped in his arms, she released Wyatt and threw herself against Adam's other side, and he pulled her in tight.

Wyatt's feet shuffled uncomfortably. He folded his arms, unfolded them, then folded them again.

Adam wished he had a third arm. He leaned his cheek atop Afton's mop of curls and felt moisture seeping from his own eyes. "It's okay to cry. The Lord understands our sorrow and is near to the brokenhearted." His eyes fell closed. If only he'd been able to say that to Eden when she'd needed to hear it.

"I want Sally," Afton sniffled.

Adam lifted his gaze to Wyatt.

The boy's lips twisted in defeat as he glanced toward the wagon that had been their parents'. "Ma made Afton a cloth doll. She named her Sally."

"I see. Well . . ." Adam rose, lifting the little girl with him. "Shall we go and see if we can find her?"

With a loud sniff, Afton nodded.

Adam settled his free hand against Asher's back. "And how about you? Is there something you would like from the wagon?"

Asher exchanged a look with his brother, and when Wyatt gave him a nod, he looked up into Adam's face. "Mama reads to us."

The present tense of the boy's words sent a shaft straight through Adam's heart. He didn't try to correct him, however. "What was she reading to you?"

"*The Count of Monte Cristo*," Wyatt offered.

"Well, then. Let's go find a doll and that book. Would you boys like for me to read to you a little bit?"

Wyatt frowned, but then nodded. "I think Ma would like for us to finish it."

"Okay then. We'll do just that."

The Slade wagon seemed to be relatively untouched by the marauding of the outlaws. Adam thanked the Lord that Mr. Slade had been able to withdraw his wagon far enough to protect his children. The tarp they'd found in Wyatt's uncle's wagon had been singed on one corner, but was otherwise in reasonably good shape—good enough to keep the wagon dry, and that had been a relief. One day, the children would be blessed by these few possessions that would remind them of home. Adam hoped Mr. Slade and his wife were in heaven and able to look down and see that someone was caring for their children.

Jeremiah wasn't nearby, so Adam helped the youngest children into the back of the wagon, knowing the man would understand if he arrived and found them here.

Afton wanted not only her doll, but a specific small blanket that her mother had apparently made just for her. Wyatt climbed in on his own and pointed out the crate that the books were stored in and sure enough, *The Count of Monte Cristo* lay right on top next to a well-worn Bible. Adam flipped through the pages of the Bible and found many passages underlined and words written in the margins. That was a treasure that he hoped Wyatt would one day be blessed by. He took it up but then glanced around the interior of the wagon. There was no reason that the children couldn't sleep here in their own wagon. It would likely be a sight more comfortable than his hammock beneath his.

He knew that Jeremiah wasn't sleeping in here, but rather on the ground beneath when he took his few hours of sleep each night.

He looked at Wyatt, who stood in the entrance at the back of the wagon, helping Afton down to the ground. "You kids could sleep in here tonight. Mr. Jackson has his own pallet and won't need this one." He gestured to the stuffed tick laid out at the front of the wagon.

Wyatt's lips twisted to one side. "We're grateful to Mr. Jackson for driving our wagon so's we can keep our supplies. But . . . That was Ma and Pa's bed, and it wouldn't feel right sleeping there. If it's all the same to you, we're fine in the hammock."

Adam nodded in understanding. "Of course. You're more than welcome to it."

Relief swept over the boy's features, and he rushed out of the wagon so fast that Adam figured it had taken a great deal of courage for him to merely enter.

When they returned to Adam's wagon, Mercy Morran approached and offered to take Afton into the bush.

Adam gratefully abdicated the task to his thoughtful neighbor. "Thank you."

While she helped the little girl, Adam and the boys walked off to take care of their own evening needs, and after washing up, they settled once more around Adam's fire, and Adam pulled out the book. He was already reading to the boys when Mercy returned with Afton, so she helped the little girl into the wagon and onto the little bed they'd made up for her, then lifted a wave as she returned to her own wagon.

The boys' eyes were soon drooping, and even Adam was thankful to put this day to rest. He closed the book, mid-chapter, and neither of the boys protested when he directed them to the hammock.

By the time he put out the fire, both boys were sound asleep, and when he climbed inside the wagon, Afton was already deep in slumber under her little blanket with her doll clutched tightly in one arm. The sight of her soft pink cheeks in the lantern light and the innocence of her countenance swelled a protective warrior in Adam's chest. He must do everything in his power to ensure justice was served for these children. But how did he go about finding the perpetrators? And all while protecting Eden from growing too attached?

If nothing had been done to track the outlaws down by the time they reached the fort, he would have to decide how to handle that. But it was a concern for another day.

Today, the concern that occupied his mind was that when he blew out the lantern and fell into bed beside Eden, she didn't even stir. She lay so still and quiet that his heart set to pounding in concern, and he reached out to press his fingers to the pulse in her throat.

Relief swept through him when he felt the soft but steady beat of her heart beneath his fingers. His tears took him by surprise, as did the gulping, silent sobs.

In the darkness of his wagon, he drew his wife close to his side and turned his face to the canvas overhead. He wanted to pray, but he felt hollow, empty, and worn down.

All he could think to offer was, *Lord, You know what we need.*

And that was enough to ease the tension in his chest.

With moisture still pooled in his eyes, he drifted off to sleep.

Adam couldn't have been more relieved when he woke the following day to find that Eden was awake, though still sleepy.

Before he even thought about what he was doing, he leaned across the bed and pressed a kiss to her forehead. Her skin was soft and warm beneath his lips, and that tantalizing scent of her favorite toilette water that always reminded Adam of peaches and cream swept over him.

He ought to have pulled away immediately, but he could only seem to withdraw enough to look into her face flushed with sleep.

She smiled sleepily as she stretched. "Morning."

He brushed a strand of hair off her forehead. "How are you feeling?"

She seemed to ponder. "Much better. There is only a small touch of a headache left."

"Good. But I still want you to rest the day away."

"Adam, do be serious."

He tapped her nose. "I've never been more serious. But perhaps you could allow Afton to join you for a little while? I think she is very much missing her mother. I was up with her twice in the night and had to soothe her back to sleep."

Eden's face softened. "You did that?"

His brow tightened. "Yes. Was that wrong?"

"No! I just think it's . . . sweet"—she poked his chest—"to think of you being so fatherly to her."

Adam captured her hand, even as his intuition shouted a warning. He leaned back onto one elbow. "Just doing my duty. You know we can't keep them, right? They're bound to have someone somewhere who wants them."

He could almost see the pout on her face, even though her expression didn't change. "You don't think Wyatt is old enough to know if they have any other relatives that might want to take them in? And you don't think that God is good enough to have sent us on our way early from Independence so that we would be there, approaching that valley of destruction, at just the moment those children needed us?"

Adam let go of her and scrubbed one hand over his face. Then scooped it back through the tangle of his hair. She was right, of course. God could have done those things.

Eden had a small frown on her brow now. "Adam, I believe that God sent us there, but it raises a question in me."

When she hesitated, Adam urged, "Go on."

"The God who orchestrated that we arrive in such a timely fashion could have also protected the family from the attack in the first place. Why didn't He do that?"

Adam pondered for a long moment, working through his thoughts. "I think that one of God's most cherished gifts to humanity is our free will. God values it because it makes relationship real. If we didn't have free will, any submission to God would simply be a slavery of sorts. Somewhere out there is a man—maybe more than one in this case— who God loves and wants a relationship with. He allowed that man to make a poor choice to attack those wagons. God loved the Slades, too, of course. But that gift of free will sometimes creates a clash between two people God loves. It's like I said about our son, earlier . . . We see this limited time we have on earth, and that tends to be our focus. But God sees all of eternity. If the Slades had a relationship with God— and from what I've seen, I believe they did—they are with him in a much better place and in the blink of an eye, in light of eternity, their children will join them there. But in His infinite mercy, God sent us at just the right time to meet a need."

Eden glanced over at him.

He rushed to conclude. "That doesn't mean that we are the ones meant to provide for these children for the rest of their lives, you understand."

That was true enough. They also owed it to these children to do everything in their power to reunite them with people who already cared for them, even if that wasn't with family.

Eden pierced him with a look. "It also doesn't mean that we are *not* the ones to care for them."

Adam sighed. If he were honest, he'd have to admit that she was right on that score. "I concede you could be right, but we at least owe it to them, and to ourselves, to do due diligence to try to ferret out a few more details. Please, Eden, I know you love so easily. Please don't get too attached."

She reached up and touched his cheek with such a seriousness shining in her eyes. "Don't worry, Adam. My heart has plenty of experience with pain. And I'm the stronger for it."

Her words were like a knife straight to his chest. Was she referring to him abandoning her? Or to the loss of their son?

She continued. "And I learned that even through the deepest loss, the Lord can and will be my strength, if only I'll let Him. We must love these children, Adam. That's why the Lord put us there, and they need that love in their lives so much right now. If any people on the earth know that truth, it's you and me. And if the time comes when we have to let them go, God will give us the strength to do so." Eden's voice grew stronger then. "Do not ask me not to love. That may be the very reason we went through the trial we did—so that our God-given gift of love would come out forged like steel and ready to be lavished on those who need it. The Lord has shown us what we can survive,

Adam. Don't hold back for fear of losing what you refuse to take hold of in the first place!"

Unaccountable tears blurred Adam's vision. She was right. He'd been holding back—wanting Eden to hold back—out of fear of pain. And yet... There was wisdom in that, wasn't there?

A thought almost bowled him over then.

Just like he'd been holding himself back from Eden out of fear and pain and what the future might hold. Here he'd been thinking of himself as the strong one who needed to hold them together. But maybe it was Eden who'd been the strong one all along!

He rolled away from her sharply and swung his feet to the floor. Stood. Scooped both hands back through his hair as he stared at the wagon floor beneath his feet for a long moment. Then he gave himself a little shake. "Rest. Go back to sleep if you want to. Tamsyn, Willow, Mercy..." He flapped his hand toward the opening. "They've all been a big help, and I'm sure we'll get the kids fed. I'll bring you some oats in a few minutes."

With that, he swept past the still sleeping Afton and out the opening of the wagon.

Chapter 9

Wyatt lay in the hammock beneath the wagon with his hands interlocked behind his head. Asher's foot poked into his ribs, but he was content to allow his little brother to sleep as he contemplated the conversation he had just overheard between the parson and his wife. He doubted they realized he could hear their exchanges through the boards of the wagon bed.

The first night, he'd fallen fast asleep and hadn't heard if they had talked at all. But this discussion . . . He'd heard this one plain as if they were speaking directly to him.

The parson didn't want them.

And the minister's wife only wanted to love them out of some obligation she felt called to live up to.

Understandable, he supposed, since they were all strangers. If the truth were told he didn't want them either.

But he also knew no one back home would want to be burdened with their care. Asher's friend's parents, their neighbors, had too many kids already, at least according to what Ma had said. He knew his parents had often taken food to the family to help them through hard times. It had been one of Ma's greatest regrets when they had left for the west. On the night before they rode away in their wagon, Ma had asked Pa who would help their neighbors when they left.

The parson had been kind to them the night before. Yet now he said he didn't want them.

Wyatt felt all akimbo inside, like nothing would ever be right again.

Was what the minister said about Ma and Pa being immediately in heaven true? His hands fisted behind his head. He didn't want Ma and Pa in heaven. He wanted them here. But if Pa were here, he would cuff him upside the head for throwing a tantrum over a situation that couldn't be changed.

Wyatt shifted to get Asher's foot into a more comfortable position. He would do anything to feel Pa cuffing him upside the head one more time. But of course, he knew that would never happen.

It would be up to him then. He would take care of his brother and sister.

They didn't need the Houstons.

Though . . .

What kind of a job could a twelve-year-old do to provide for his younger siblings? Would anyone hire him? He'd heard of boys traveling west to work on the cattle ranches. He could do that, except . . . he wasn't sure how to be a rancher. He'd work at learning everything he needed to before the time came. Maybe he would stick with the Houstons until he found a ranch to hire on with. He'd heard that jobs like that sometimes even offered room and board. Maybe he could give up part of his salary in exchange for food and a roof for his siblings, also.

He might be small for his age, but he was tough. Pa had always said so. He would just have to prove himself to the rancher.

Above him, he heard the minister's feet tramping the length of the wagon bed, and then thumping into the grass beneath the tailgate.

Wyatt closed his eyes and tried to look like he was still asleep. He didn't want the Houstons to know that he had overheard them until it was time for him and his siblings to strike out on their own.

Good thing he did, too, because he heard the parson's footsteps shuffle his way, and sensed the man bending to peer beneath the wagon to check on them.

Wyatt lay still and forced himself to breathe normally until the man walked away. Then he opened his eyes to stare at the bottom of the wagon.

"Why didn't you want him to know you was awake?"

Wyatt jumped so hard that he almost tipped Asher out onto the ground. When he looked over, he saw one of the blond boys from that family of twins. He peered at Wyatt from above a tuft of bunch grass, his blue eyes twinkling.

Wyatt rolled out of the hammock and then steadied it so Asher wouldn't tip out. "Why are you skulking around like a snake in the grass?" He frowned and nipped the inside of his lip as he tugged his suspenders up over his shoulders. He hadn't meant to sound so put out.

The boy leapt to his feet and threw back his shoulders. "Weren't skulking. Just watching is all. Pa says a body can learn a lot by watching."

Wyatt wanted to snap that he should go watch someone else, but that wouldn't be polite, so instead, he offered. "Name's Wyatt."

The boy grinned. "I'm Silas." He leaned close to mock whisper. "The handsomest of the male Hawthorne twins." His grin grew as he hooked his thumbs into his suspenders. "Can pitch a ball the best, too. You want to join us? That's my brother Soren." He motioned toward his look-alike, who Wyatt only now noticed stood near the head of the wagon.

Soren folded his arms and glowered at his brother. "He's lying about the pitching. And about his good looks too."

Wyatt couldn't withhold a grin. He liked these boys. Playing ball usually sounded like fun, but today he didn't feel like having fun. Besides, if he were going to provide for his siblings, he needed to set playing aside and learn a man's work.

He shook his head. "Can't. Sorry. Gotta take care of my brother and sister."

Silas and Soren exchanged a look.

Then Silas shrugged. "All right. Maybe tonight then?"

The twins were already backing away. In the distance, he could see the two boys they had played ball with on the first night, waiting for the twins.

Wyatt sighed. "Yeah. Maybe." He raised a hand to the boys and then leaned down to shake Asher awake.

Being a grown-up sure wasn't going to be easy.

He would need to make a plan. But Ma had always said he was good at planning.

And he refused to be a burden to anybody.

Eden wasn't sure what had come over her this morning, talking to Adam like that. She'd seen the pain in his eyes the moment she'd mentioned their shared grief. And she suddenly realized something.

Adam had not only been running from her when he'd left for the west. He'd also been running from the terrible gut-wrenching emotions that had clawed and torn at them every day like a beast of prey.

And her return had brought it all back to him!

She flopped onto her back and closed her eyes. *Oh Lord, how we need You. We need Your strength and courage to love these children who need us so much in this time of their loss. We need Your strength to love each other and the courage to step forward into the life that You have called us to. A life where there* will *be pain again. A life where there will be loss again. Show me what Mrs. Hawthorne meant when she spoke about scattering seeds, Lord. I feel at a loss to understand that. And please strengthen me and heal me of these headaches.*

The tick dipped beside her. She opened her eyes to see Afton's little tear-stained face peering down at her.

"Hi, sweetums." Eden reached over to smooth a wayward curl behind the girl's ear.

Afton's face crumpled. "I want my ma."

"Oh, darling, I know you do. Come here." Eden sat up and tugged the little girl onto her lap, wrapping her in her arms and rocking her. "Do you know that I lost a little boy?"

Afton looked up into her face. "Did you find him 'gain?"

A sob slipped out before Eden could stop it. "No. He's in heaven with the Lord. And your ma is there now too. Maybe she can help watch over my son until you and I both join her there someday . . . a long time from now."

Afton pondered. "Can we go now?"

Eden tucked her head close and rested her chin atop her curls. She gave a little shake of her head. "No, sweetie. We have to stay here for now because the Lord is not done with us yet."

"But I want my ma!" Afton shoved her thumb into her mouth, her distress clearly evident, though she did settle her head against Eden's chest.

Eden soothed a hand over her back and continued to rock. "I know just how you feel because I wanted my son so badly, too, after he went to Jesus." She struggled to think how she might ease the little girl's distress. What would have helped her after losing her son? Certainly, it would have helped if she hadn't shut Adam out. But Afton was here in her arms, and clearly not shutting her out. But maybe . . . "Would you like to tell me about your ma? What was your favorite thing about her?"

The little one worked at her thumb for several moments, and at first, Eden thought she might have fallen back to sleep, but then she popped her thumb out of her mouth. "Ma sings."

"Oh, that sounds lovely. And you liked to hear her sing?" Eden relished the feel of Afton's warm curls beneath her fingers. Would their son have had curls? Blond surely, since both she and Adam were fair. But would he have been broad and brawny like Adam? Or would he have taken after her side of the family and been slender and strong like dear Papa?

Eden yanked herself back to the present in time to see Afton nodding.

"And what was your favorite song that she used to sing?" Eden took her thoughts captive. She must not continue down that path of wondering about her son, or she may never rise from this bed for the grief that would hold her here.

Afton looked up at her. "Tan you sing like my ma?"

"Well, I probably won't sound just like her, but I used to love to sing. I haven't done a lot of that recently. But for you, I can try. What would you like me to sing?"

Movement drew her gaze to the back of the wagon. Wyatt's head was just visible above the tailgate.

"Forgive me for interrupting, ma'am. I wanted to see if Afton needed a trip into the brush."

"That's very thoughtful of you, Wyatt. I'm sure she does. But she's rather missing your ma this morning. Do you know what your ma's favorite song to sing was?"

He shifted and looked down at the ground for a moment. When he lifted his head again, moisture glimmered in his eyes. "'Nearer My God to Thee.'"

Eden felt his grief in her very core. "Wyatt, you have been so strong. I know your parents would be busting their buttons were they here to see how you have watched over your brother and sister through this trial."

The boy's face scrunched tight in a way that revealed his struggle against tears. He turned his face to look at something off in the distance as he gritted out. "I don't feel so strong, ma'am."

"I understand. But remember that the Word tells us that when we are weak, Christ is strong in us. You are revealing that strength by loving your siblings through this time."

If possible, his frown tightened even more. "You've got Afton then?"

Eden realized she'd brought him to the point of wanting to flee. "Yes. I'll help her in a moment."

"Thank you, ma'am." With that, he turned and disappeared from sight.

Eden looked down at Afton. "Would you like to hear me sing?"

The girl nodded without a moment's hesitation.

Eden cleared her throat, tucked Afton close, and cried out to God for the strength to sing.

"*Nearer, my God, to Thee, nearer to Thee!*"

Her voice started out broken, but gained strength as the prayer of the words filled her.

> "*E'en though it be a cross that raiseth me,*
> *Still all my song shall be, nearer, my God, to Thee.*
> *Nearer, my God, to Thee, nearer to Thee!*
> *Though like the wanderer, the sun gone down,*
> *Darkness be over me, my rest a stone;*
> *Yet in my dreams I'd be nearer, my God, to Thee.*
> *Nearer, my God, to Thee, nearer to Thee!*"

Oh, how that is true, Lord. Darkness has been over me, but I want to be nearer to you despite this bitter grief! She searched her memory for another verse.

> "*Then, with my waking thoughts bright with Thy praise,*
> *Out of my stony griefs Bethel I'll raise;*
> *So by my woes to be nearer, my God, to Thee.*
> *Nearer, my God, to Thee, nearer to Thee!*"

The truth of that verse stole the rest of Eden's voice. *So by my woes to be nearer, my God, to Thee. Yes. Lord, please, yes.*

When she looked down, Afton was staring up at her, thumb still in her mouth. "There's mo'." She spoke around the barrier.

Eden smoothed her hair and somehow managed to choke out. "Another time, love. I hear Adam hitching the team, and if we are to be ready to leave, we'd better make our way to the privy, yes?"

Afton consented.

"Here." Eden handed her the hairbrush from the crate next to the bed. "You work on your tangles, while I dress."

Tongue caught between her little teeth, Afton went to work, and Eden was pleased to see that she seemed to have been soothed by the song. And maybe by the sentiments in the words.

Adam was caught unaware by Eden's clear contralto as he returned with the oxen. The walls of canvas that hid her and Afton from the camp did nothing to stop her soothing song from drifting across the wagons. He hesitated a moment, simply listening to the words that seemed to penetrate to his very soul. After a moment, he realized he would cause a delay if he didn't get the team hitched, so he went to work as quietly as he could so that he wouldn't disturb the reverence of the moment.

All around, the camp had never been this silent. Men nodded quietly as they hitched their teams to the wagons. Women stood with their gazes transfixed on the blush of dawn, clearly relishing the sweetness of this moment.

Adam knew Eden didn't realize how far her voice was carrying across the plains, but he wouldn't have disturbed her for anything.

After hitching one side of the yoke to the first pair of oxen, he strode to the other side, eyes toward the dome of the sky. *Thank You, Father. Your grace is sufficient for me.*

If these children had come into their lives solely to draw him and Eden out of their grief, he would forever be thankful to the Lord for orchestrating the intersection of their paths.

And yet, even as the thought crossed his mind, he knew, deep in his spirit, that this meeting was so much more than that. And for the first time, he glanced toward the two boys he'd put in charge of holding the reins while he hitched the team and wondered what it would be like to call them sons.

He gave himself a shake. Those kinds of thoughts would eventually bring more pain. It was best he shove them back into the abyss from which they had emerged.

Eden stopped singing, and it was as though the camp had come awake. Women started moving again, men called to one another, and even birds began to chirp.

Life would continue. He and Eden would travel on to the west and serve the Lord as He had called them to, and these children would return to the east and settle with some family.

He frowned at the thought as he prodded the next pair of oxen into place and began the task of hooking the traces and the yokes. Would a family who wasn't expecting a passel of children to raise even treat them with kindness? Offer them love? Make them feel wanted? Take care of Afton, who Wyatt claimed was sickly, though they'd only seen glimpses of it on that first day?

Because these children deserved that. That and so much more.

He realized that was another concern weighing on him. If Afton were sickly and Eden grew to love her and then the child's sickness took her, would Eden have the strength to bear that? Would *he*?

He slapped one of the oxen on its shoulder and gave it a rub. The animal's muscle quivered beneath his touch, and a long tail flicked up to swat him in return. He smiled and stepped back from the cranky steer, returning his thoughts to the children.

No. It was best not to fall too deeply in love with them and that was the truth of it, no matter what Eden said.

"Move 'em out!" Cranston called.

Adam brushed the concerns aside. Figuring out where the children would end up was a problem for another day. And not his problem, in the end. It would likely come down to a decision made at the fort.

Between here and there, he couldn't allow himself or Eden to grow too fond of these children. At least not until it was decided what would happen with them. He and Eden certainly weren't equipped to take care of three children across the plains. They didn't have any provisions for children!

Even as the thoughts crossed his mind, and he took the reins from the boys, his gaze drifted to the wagon falling into line right behind his.

Jeremiah Jackson tugged on the brim of his hat. "Mornin', Adam."

Adam nodded and returned the greeting. The things the children would need would be right there in their wagon, surely?

Again, he nudged the thoughts aside. "Up onto the bench, boys. You can ride a ways this morning and then get down to walk when you want to. Did your sister and Mrs. Houston return?"

"We're here." Eden's voice drifted from inside.

"Can I drive the team?" There was a determination in Wyatt's question that made Adam proud.

"I don't see why not. Better don a pair of gloves first, though." He motioned to the pair on the bench beside where Wyatt and Asher had sat down.

Wyatt snatched them up and shoved his hands inside. Adam's gloves dwarfed his fingers, but the kid didn't seem put off by that. He looked to Adam to see what was next.

"Scoot on over to the left of the seat there." Adam climbed up and plunked himself down between the two boys, then helped Wyatt take the reins in his hands. "Your hands are small, so you'll need to wrap the reins around once. Good. Just like that." He gave the boy a nod. "Now you'll have to show the team who's boss. Keep the lines tight. We don't want our team running over the Riley wagon in front of us." He gave the boy a wink.

However, Wyatt didn't seem to find any humor in Adam's words. He seemed to be all seriousness this morning.

"Yes, sir," was all he said.

Adam felt his smile fade. Deep sorrow filled the gaze the boy bounced off his before he returned his scrutiny to the bony backs of the steers. The kid was likely missing his family like all get out.

"All right, then. We're off." Adam eased back against the bench between the boys and hoped that his thoughts would be able to find some peace on this long and arduous day.

Chapter 10

Wyatt held tightly to the reins until his hands felt like they were on fire. The sun had climbed from the eastern horizon and now hovered directly overhead. He had wanted to turn the reins over hours ago, but for some reason, when the parson had asked him the first time if he was ready to relinquish the task, it had made him angry. He said no. He was fine.

The parson had asked again a couple of times, but each time he had declined, and now he was kicking himself for his stubbornness. The cramps in his hands had moved past merely aching to the point where he didn't think he would be able to open his fingers when they pulled to a stop for the nooning.

The past couple of hours had been better, though. He had almost forgotten about the ache in his hands because the parson had passed the time by reading a few more chapters from *The Count of Monte Cristo*.

Asher had fallen asleep again, not much into the first chapter of today's reading.

Wyatt appreciated how the story helped pass the time.

In many ways, driving the team was easy. Mostly, the steers just fell into line behind the wagon in front and plodded along at a steady clip. It was only occasionally when he needed to rein the team around an obstacle or slow them down slightly that he tugged on the reins.

So he'd been able to listen to the story without too much discomfort from the cramping of his fingers.

The parson's voice droned on as Wyatt took in the scenery around them and tried not to breathe in too much dust from the wagons ahead.

For the past several days, the terrain that they drove through had gradually grown flatter and flatter, till now they drove through an endless sea of grass with not even a tree on the horizon. Wyatt found the vast open space unsettling. Back home, living in the shantytown on the edge of New York, there had been house after house after house. Out here, there wouldn't even be a neighbor for miles around.

Mr. Houston closed the book and stretched his arm back behind the bench to place it through the front opening of the cinched canvas onto the bed in the wagon. "Asher is sound asleep, and Cranston should call us to stop here any minute, anyhow. You've done a real good job this morning, son."

Wyatt felt his jaw thrust to one side. "I'm not your son."

The parson twisted to look at him. After a long moment of silence had stretched, Wyatt saw in his peripheral vision that the man gave a nod. "You're right. I'm sorry about that." The parson scrubbed his fingers into the stubble of his jaw. Gave another nod. Hung his head.

Wyatt's eyes stung. He angled his face away from the man, but there was nothing to see other than the vast stretch of prairie.

They drove in silence for a few minutes, and then Wyatt noticed a low rumble that seemed out of place in the distance. He cocked his head to listen. That sound sent a prickle of unease along the back of his neck. He sat up straight and turned this way and that to check all the horizons, but could see nothing. However, the rumble grew louder and louder.

The parson searched too.

"What is it?" Wyatt asked.

The man shook his head. "I'm not sure."

Off to the south, Wyatt noticed a low cloud of dust that seemed to be roiling on the horizon. He pointed. "Look."

Ahead of them, the wagons began to pull to a stop. Wyatt tried to pull back on the reins, but his hands spasmed and the leather slipped through his grip.

"Whoa." Mr. Houston grabbed the reins from his hands and hauled back hard. The steers pumped their heads up and down, seemingly agitated by more than just their sudden stop.

Calls of surprise came from up and down the line of wagons.

Cody, the scout, thrust one fist into the air and gave a series of yips from the back of his horse, then he put his heels to his mount's side and galloped toward the boiling dust on the horizon. Mr. Moss, the only other mounted scout, rode out fast on his heels, shucking his rifle from the scabbard as he galloped away.

Mr. Cranston trotted into sight on his big Appaloosa, waving his arm in the air like he did when it was time for them to circle up in the evenings.

Wyatt glanced over at the parson. It was odd for Mr. Cranston to be signaling that they should make camp this early in the day.

Mr. Houston leaned over the edge of the wagon bench and waved his arm as Mr. Cranston came near. When the man paused, he asked, "What is it, Caesar?"

A glitter of excitement filled the wagon master's eyes. "Buffalo! If Cody and Striker have anything to say about it, we'll be eating grand tonight."

"Won't this delay us getting to the fort?"

Mr. Cranston glanced at Wyatt and dipped his chin slowly. "By half a day, but we need the meat."

Mr. Houston only nodded. He stood and motioned for Wyatt to trade places with him on the wagon bench. "How about you let me pull us into our position?"

Wyatt gladly abdicated his position without protest.

The roil of dust on the horizon grew larger and larger until it formed a vast, swirling wall, advancing like an oncoming horde. The thunderous pounding of hooves sounded like too many percussionists had been set loose on the prairie.

Wyatt watched in fascination as the first buffalo came into view on the horizon. The herd ran from the south toward the north—miles upon miles of massive beasts that made Wyatt's jaw hang open in awe at the wild beauty of the stampede. He reached over and gave Asher a shake. "Asher, wake up."

Asher sat up slowly, sleepily, but then his eyes widened, and he shot to his feet. His jaw fell open, and Wyatt smiled at the wonder in his expression.

Mr. Moss felled one of the creatures with a single shot. Wyatt looked away. Two more shots followed, and he was thankful to be looking at the wagon bench between his knees. He tried to cordon off the image of the first buffalo falling, however, as ever, once he had seen something he couldn't unsee it. He wanted a paper and pencil, or better yet, the ink pot and dip pen that Mr. Houston had let him use a few days back. He wouldn't draw the death that had his heart aching as he wished that he had not seen the creature fall. Creatures such as that ought to be free, and yet trouble had found them just as trouble had found him and his siblings, he supposed. No. Not death. His drawing would focus on a large bull and a tiny calf barreling toward the viewer with billowing clouds of dust behind them.

No more shots rang out, so he risked lifting his gaze to the bison once more.

It took another fifteen minutes for the herd to trundle past, and thankfully, the scouts let the rest of the creatures live.

He watched the herd as Mr. Houston urged the team into the proper place in the circle, set the brake, and then leapt to the ground. He reached up and helped Asher down, but Wyatt jumped before he could help him. He wasn't some little kid who needed assistance.

He tugged off the gloves, wishing that his hands weren't spasming so drastically. He held the gloves out to the man, hoping that the pain wasn't showing on his face. He must learn to do these tasks so that he could take care of his siblings. "Thanks for letting me drive."

Was that a glitter of humor in the parson's eyes when he accepted the gloves from him? "Sure thing, s . . . kid."

Wyatt started to walk away but then hesitated. "Would you . . . That is, do you think I could draw again tonight?"

The minister smiled. "Sure. I'll fetch the paper and ink for you as soon as I get the team unhitched. Meanwhile, you boys stay in the center of the wagons, okay? I would hate for that herd to circle back and catch you unaware."

"Yes, sir." Wyatt frowned, took Asher's hand, and stalked off to see if Afton needed any help.

He didn't need the minister telling him how to stay safe. And what did the man care anyhow?

At least he'd agreed to let him draw.

Eden sat by the fire on a crate that Adam had pulled from the wagon for her since there was no wood here. Afton snuggled against her chest with her thumb thrust firmly into her mouth. Eden's lower back ached from holding the girl on the seat with nothing to lean against, but twice she had tried to put Afton in her little bed, and both times the child had woken and fussed to be held again.

Wyatt apologized and grew gruff with his sister, telling her that she needed to go to sleep, but Eden had assured him that she didn't mind comforting the little one who was obviously distressed over the loss of everything familiar and those she loved.

Wyatt had spent some time drawing, but a few minutes earlier he had thrust the paper beneath his thigh, set the pen beside the ink pot on the small rock at his side, and frowned as he planted his elbows onto his knees. Now Adam sat in the grass by the fire, whittling a stick, and Wyatt sat on a rock across from Eden, massaging his thumb into the palm of his opposite hand. Asher had fallen asleep already in the hammock beneath the wagon.

"What did you draw, Wyatt? May I see it?" Eden asked.

His brow slumped further. "It's not finished yet." A glint of warning in his eye told her not to push.

Eden drew a breath and reminded herself to tread carefully. She didn't want him to feel forced into anything. "It's okay. But I'd love to see it when you are done."

She hoped he would believe her. A talent such as his should be encouraged.

"Would you like more meat?" Maybe changing the subject would ease his seeming distress.

But he only shook his head, continuing to rub his hand and frown.

The three buffalo had been divided between each of the wagons, and everyone had meat left over. Adam had roasted theirs on a spit over the fire and then hung the leftovers in a canvas bag from one of the stays on the side of the wagon. If they portioned it, they would be able to eat off it for at least a week, which would save some of the canned goods. That was good since Adam had only packed the wagon for himself, and now he had four extra mouths to feed. The day would come when they would need to break into the supplies in the Slades' wagon to keep these children fed, but that was a problem for another day.

After all her resting, the severe pain at the back of her head was barely a twinge. And tonight, she was simply enjoying sitting here with her family around her.

She caught herself at that thought. She might love these children and take care of them, but it was best that she not think of them as family. And yet . . . It was already too late for that.

She closed her eyes and breathed through the realization. Adam wasn't going to like that. Her heart wasn't going to like it if the time came for goodbyes. Despite that . . . She thought of Mrs. Hawthorne's words about scattering seed. If she'd learned anything from the loss of her son, and almost losing Adam, it was that she ought to love lavishly while she had the chance. She would never want to give up the wonder of the love that had filled her each time she'd felt her son kicking in her belly. That wonder outshone all the grief and pain that had come after.

And loving these children would never be a feeling that she would regret, even if it did bring her pain later down the road.

"Wyatt?" Adam's voice broke the silence. "Is something amiss with your hand?"

The boy straightened and rested his palms against his knees, seemingly trying to look casual. He shook his head. "No, sir."

Adam glanced from the boy to his hands and back and then rose and stalked into the darkness on the other side of the wagon. Eden heard water trickling into a pot from the barrel strapped there. Adam returned only a moment later and settled the pot of water onto the hook above the fire. Then he stepped over to the wagon and rummaged through a box in the back.

When he returned to the fire, he stopped in front of Wyatt. "Roll up your sleeves, please."

Looking perplexed, Wyatt did as he was told.

Adam uncorked a bottle he held. "Hold out your hands."

Again, Wyatt complied.

Adam splashed a generous portion of the liniment onto the boy's hands, corked the bottle, and set it aside. Then he took Wyatt's small hands in his own larger ones and began to massage the liniment into the boy's palms and the heels of his hands. He even worked the oil almost all the way to Wyatt's elbows, sliding his strong thumbs over the muscles of his forearm.

As he worked, Adam talked. "I let you drive too long today. I'm sorry about that. From now on, I'll know that you have a stubborn streak a mile wide and we'll make sure this doesn't happen again." He grinned down at the boy.

Eden thought Wyatt would smile back at him, but the boy remained serious. A tight little furrow settled between his brows.

"A man has got to work hard if he is going to take care of his family. I don't want you all to worry about needing to take care of us for long."

So much anger with her husband surged to life that Eden closed her eyes as though that might be able to hold it inside. But her heart panged at all the pain packed into Wyatt's statement. Afton was so soundly asleep now that she was limp in Eden's arms. And she needed to move or she was going to explode. She rose and settled Afton onto her pallet and this time the child didn't even stir. Eden's boots clomped rather loudly as she descended the crate stairs Adam had set up earlier.

Adam met her gaze as he turned toward the fire to retrieve the pot of now-warm water.

Eden hoped he could feel the full measure of her animosity as she leveled a glower on him while returning to her seat.

That boy had obviously overheard their conversation this morning! And now, in a time when he should be thinking of nothing but grieving the loss of his family, he was worried about how he was going to take care of his siblings.

There was a slump in Adam's shoulders when he turned back to the boy and set the pot of water on the ground at his feet. "Set your hands in there and let them soak for a while."

Again, Wyatt complied, head hanging as he refused to meet either of their gazes.

Adam sank wearily back onto the grass. "Wyatt, we don't want you to feel like you are a burden to us. This whole situation has been . . ." Adam waved a hand. " . . . difficult, I'm sure." Adam stretched his legs out before him and tucked his hands between his knees. He focused on his boots as he said the next words. "I'm not sure if you know, but my wife and I, we lost a son a couple of years back. So we do understand the grief you are feeling right now."

Wyatt huffed a breath through his nose, but made no other response.

Eden sighed. Yes. They understood that cynicism too. The cynicism that declared that no one else could understand the depth of grief they were feeling.

The fire glowed orange in the darkness, and Eden watched sparks drift into the star-studded canopy above until they were snuffed out in the atmosphere.

Oh, Lord, snuff out this child's pain, just like that. May his journey with grief be short-lived and over just as suddenly as the life of those sparks.

Adam shifted. "We don't want you to feel like you are a burden to us. You are not. We are more than happy to . . . care for you children until the time comes when that is not needed anymore."

This time it was Eden's turn to huff. "Wyatt, it seems that you are not the only one around this campfire with a stubborn streak a mile wide."

She leveled one last look on Adam, but he seemed intent on a blade of grass he picked apart.

"Hey Wyatt!" Joel Morran dashed up to the fire. "The fellas and I are gonna play some catch. Want to come?"

"Sure." Wyatt scrambled to his feet and dashed off to join the boys.

Eden's gaze landed on the sketch that he'd left behind on the rock. She rose and went to pick it up. "Oh!" The sketch elicited such horror that she almost dropped it.

"What is it?" Adam surged to his feet and hurried to her side.

She held the paper for him to see. Contrary to Wyatt's claim that the drawing was incomplete, it was just as perfect as the one of the outlaw that he'd drawn. In the foreground, a buffalo lay bleeding, its sightless eyes staring. In the background, a wagon burned, a woman ran from an outlaw who held an outstretched gun, and Wyatt, Asher, and Afton watched from a compartment beneath the wagon. Wyatt's eyes had been blotted out with great blobs of ink.

Eden pressed the sketch against Adam's chest and looked up at him. "These children need us, Adam." When he reached to take the paper, she stepped back. "I am going to speak to Marigold. No need to wait up for me."

When she reached the edge of the firelight, she glanced back. Adam stood looking down at the sketch with soulful sadness in his expression.

Good. Eden hoped that the boy's agony might get through to Adam's heart. She hefted her skirts above the grass and made her way across the center of the circle toward the Hawthorne wagon parked on the other side.

Chapter 11

Eden was thankful to find that Mrs. Hawthorne had not retired yet. Honestly, she wasn't sure exactly what had sent her looking for the woman other than the fact that she seemed to share a similar talent with Wyatt when it came to art.

The elderly woman looked up as Eden approached their fire. She rose, searching Eden's expression with curiosity. "Good evening, dear. Be there something I can help you with?"

Eden felt a little foolish. She still wasn't even sure what she wanted to ask the woman. "I wondered . . . Would you have time to walk with me for a moment?"

"Of course, dear. Let me fetch my cane."

"I'll get it for you, Granny!" One of the oldest twins jumped up from her seat on a log by the fire and dashed over to the covered wagon. Whitley, Eden thought, because she had more red in her hair than Wren.

"Bless you, Whitley girl." As soon as Marigold had her cane in hand, she turned and gestured for Eden to lead the way.

Tonight they had circled the twenty-five wagons into one large oval on grass that must have been trampled by the great herd of bison not too many days past. Eden remained inside the perimeter of wagons but walked far enough from each camp that they would be able to have a conversation without being overheard. They strode for a full minute before Eden decided where to begin. "The other day, when we were walking up to the wagon train, you mentioned that once you see something, you are easily able to mark it down with paint and whatnot." Eden fiddled with the lace at the throat of her collar. "I believe that Wyatt, the oldest Slade boy, has the same gift."

"I see?" Though the woman seemed to be saying she understood, her words emerged as a question.

Eden explained about Wyatt's most recent sketch. "I just wondered . . . Is he going to be stuck with those memories so vividly for the rest of his life?"

"Ah." Marigold tottered a few more steps before she paused and glanced toward the first stars that were beginning to shine through the dusky blue dome overhead. "The gift has its drawbacks, of a certainty. I saw the boy's sketch of the attacker, and it were a wonder, indeed."

They strode past the boys who were still playing catch inside the circle of wagons at one end of the encampment. Eden was glad to see Wyatt at least participating in the game.

"As for being stuck with the memories . . ." The woman continued. "Do I regret some of the pictures thet get trapped in my mind?" She fiddled with the head of her cane. "Perhaps, some of them. But others . . . Oh, how can I regret such vivid pictures in my mind of the babes I lost—each one so unique and dear? Or how can I regret the memory of my dear Henry's impish smile, or the way his eyes lit like candles when I offered fresh-baked apple pie?" She shook her head. "No. I cannot feel sorrow for any of those memories, even though each one is followed by an eventual heartache. Memories of wonder, beauty, and oft overlooked moments of perfection, sustain us through darkest valleys." The elderly woman turned then to level her gaze directly on Eden. "It will be the same with the boy. Right now, he is simply taking his first steps into that deep darkness. It terrifies him for the unknown that lies ahead. And yet when we are in that valley, the Lord is with us, He comforts us and He brings us out the other side."

The woman reached a gnarled hand to grip Eden's forearm. "Bless you, child, for loving him when it must feel like such a risk. He may want to blot out his sight right now, but in a few months, he will be ever so thankful for the vivid memories. Give him time. Give yourself time. Give Adam time. Keep planting those seeds."

Eden couldn't withhold a huff. "I confess, Mrs. Hawthorne, that I've pondered on your words and I simply don't know how to do as you suggest. This planting of seeds—the meaning of it eludes me."

Mrs. Hawthorne smiled and turned to start them back in the direction of her family's wagon. With her free hand, she reached to clutch one of Eden's. "Loving and caring for children you might not get to keep, thet's a seed. Love is not selfish. Holding a child filled with sorrow and singing a favorite song, thet's a seed. Love is kind. Trying to rebuild a relationship torn asunder by grief, thet's a seed, child. Love keeps no record of wrongs." She squeezed Eden's hand and gave it a gentle shake. "You're doing just fine! Planting so many seeds you can't even keep track of them all. Planting seeds is simply risking a little. Risking doing the right things when you know the pain it might cause later—those are the seeds. Dying to self. Loving others. Not hiding from potential pain. Thet's it."

Eden felt unaccountable relief. The woman made it sound so easy. And yet, Eden knew from experience the difficulty of it.

"Thank you, Mrs. Hawthorne. Thank you so much. These are things that I know how to do." She smiled. "I might not be very good at them, but I'm practicing."

Mrs. Hawthorne chuckled. "We all be practicing, child. All the way to eternity." She wrapped one arm around Eden's shoulders and hugged her tight. "Now, if you'll excuse me, these old bones need as much rest as possible before another long day of walking tomorrow."

"Oh, I'm sorry if I've kept you—"

"Hush, child." Marigold smiled sweetly.

Eden grinned. "Yes'm. Good night. And thank you, ever so much."

The woman nodded and waved as she turned toward her encampment.

Eden felt a great deal of relief as she turned back toward where she could still see Adam sitting by the fire across the way. She smiled. Not hiding from potential pain. That was something she could wrap her mind around.

She took a step, and then froze.

A low ominous rumble coming from somewhere out on the plains suddenly registered. It grew steadily louder, and the sound was familiar since the herd had just thundered by only a few hours ago.

Adam lurched to his feet, searching the encampment. When his gaze landed on her, his shoulders sagged with momentary relief, but then he was running toward her, hand outstretched. "Hurry, Eden! Where are Wyatt and the other children?"

Eden felt her heart pounding in her throat. The herd had passed in front of them earlier, but now, in the darkness, would the entire encampment be pounded to dust beneath their hooves?

Her eyes shot wide. All around, the scouts hustled to mount their horses. Cranston yelled at some of the men to encircle the roped-in oxen that were lowing and snorting and pawing the ground, ready to bolt into their own mini stampede.

And all the while the thundering clamor of the oncoming herd grew more ominous!

Wyatt! They had to find Wyatt. She turned to look in the direction where she'd last seen the boys tossing the ball. None of them were there!

Micah Morran sprinted toward them. He stopped, panting. "Have either of you seen Av and Joel?"

Adam swallowed. "Not with us. Maybe at the Hawthorne wagon?"

"No." Eden shook her head. "I was just there. The boys were just—" She pointed to the empty space, feeling a tremor sweep through her.

Eden's gaze crashed into Adam's. Where had the boys gone?! Surely not . . . She covered her mouth with one hand and turned her gaze to the darkness beyond the wagons. "Adam."

He was already sprinting. "Saddle our horses!" he yelled to Micah over his shoulder. "I'll fetch Hawthorne."

Wyatt was tired to his very core, but he did not want to return to the wagon yet. However, he also didn't feel like playing catch anymore. It was so dark that one of them was bound to get beaned in the head at any moment anyhow.

Mrs. Houston and Silas and Soren's grandma walked by a little way off. He frowned as he tossed the ball back to Soren. The women looked like they were having a deep conversation. But he didn't want to think about Mrs. Houston right now. He didn't want to think about any of this sorry mess, in fact.

At the center of the encampment, the steers lowed plaintively as they began to settle down for the night. Several campfires around the perimeter had already been extinguished as people prepared to sleep.

Wyatt could see Mr. Jackson standing as one of the guards, and in the distance, Mr. Cranston struck up a tune on his fiddle.

Wyatt glanced from the boys toward the outer prairie. Mr. Houston had said not to go outside of the wagons, but what could it hurt? Especially if he had all of the boys with him? He sure would like to see that herd of buffalo one more time. Maybe if they walked out a ways, they would come upon them.

"You fellas wanna see if we can go out and find those bison again?" He wasn't sure what had made the words pop out of his mouth. He hadn't really intended to follow through on the thought. But now that he'd spoken, he couldn't seem like he hadn't meant to.

Joel and Avram shared a look, as did Silas and Soren.

Joel shook his head. "Can't. My pa don't let us go outside of the circle of wagons at night."

Avram folded his arms. "If I go, Joel will tell."

Joel frowned and punched his stepbrother gently in the shoulder. "I ain't no snitch."

Silas cast a lingering assessment toward his family's wagon before he turned back and said, "I'll go with you."

Soren shifted. "Silas."

"What? Go on back to the wagon if you're too scared to come with us. Just be sure you don't squeal."

Soren's chin shot into the air. "I ain't scared. Just smart. Pa will whoop you but good if he catches you. Besides, what if there's a wolf out there? Or maybe a cougar like the one Granny read about to us the other day."

Wyatt swallowed. He was suddenly thankful that Asher and Afton were already back at the wagon with the Houstons. He sort of wished he was too.

Silas shuffled his feet. Folded his arms. "Those are just stories."

True. How many times had he read things in stories that he'd never seen in real life? Wyatt spoke again before he could change his mind. "Besides, what harm can a bunch of overgrown cows do?" He pushed away the picture of his father's frown and turned on his heel. "If you're coming, let's go."

The five boys dashed through the night and slipped between the two Riley wagons, both of which were already dark and silent. There they paused and stared out toward the endless black plains.

The prairie stretched before them, vast and still. And dark. So very dark.

Wyatt pulled in a deep breath. Just a little way. They would only go a little way and then they'd come right back. He would make sure to keep everyone safe. It wasn't like him to disobey, and he wasn't sure what had set this insistence in him, even now—except that minister made him feel rebellious and irritable.

He took the first step.

The hair on the back of his neck stood on end, and he winced as he walked forward, halfway expecting a wolf or a cougar to leap from the shadows. Nothing came but a slight breeze rustling through the grasses. Easing out a breath, Wyatt kept going.

Above them, the dome of the sky was so full of stars! Had he ever noticed how many there were before? He felt certain that back home he hadn't been able to see this many. It made him feel small, so very small, to see the splay of speckles stretching from one horizon to another without so much as a tree to block it.

They'd only gone a little way out into the swaying grasses when Avram stepped up beside him and slipped his small hand into Wyatt's. Maybe because he was the biggest fellow there and Avram wanted his protection in the darkness. Whatever the reason, the feel of the boy's hand, even smaller than Asher's, made Wyatt's heart pitch. If someone led his little brother into potential danger, he would be mad. More than mad.

His feet dragged to a stop.

He might want to escape these awful circumstances that had dumped him into the Houstons' lives, but deep down he knew this wasn't right. He didn't want to get anyone hurt. And if they went much farther, they wouldn't even be able to see the lights from the wagons' fires to lead them home.

"Doesn't look like the herd is anywhere near. We'd best get back and get some rest." He hoped none of the fellas could hear the tremor in his words.

"G-good idea."

Wyatt couldn't tell if that had been Silas or Soren's voice.

They had all turned back toward the wagons when, in the distance, they heard that terrifying rumble!

Wyatt no longer cared if the boys thought him a yellow belly. He snatched Avram into his arms and lit out for the wagons. "Run!"

Chapter 12

Adam felt terror pulsing through him as he ran with Hawthorne on his heels toward where Micah held their saddled horses in the distance.

Where should they even start looking? The prairie was so vast, and in the cloak of darkness, it would take a miracle to find them! The two wagons nearest to where they'd been playing catch were Gideon Riley's. That was as good a starting place as any.

He swung into the saddle and trotted his horse between the two wagons. He couldn't move faster than that for fear of running the boys over if he came upon them in the dark.

In the distance, Cody Hawkeye, Striker Moss, and Jeremiah Jackson galloped toward the sound of thunder, firing their pistols into the air.

Dear Lord! Would the boys have made it out that far? What if one of the scouts accidentally shot one of the boys while trying to turn the herd of bison? *God, please!*

"Wyatt!" Adam called into the darkness, but it was no use. His voice was immediately swallowed up in the thundering noise of the approaching herd.

Beside him, Micah and Hiram Hawthorne also called for their boys, but just like with Adam, their calls seemed to fall flat to the prairie.

Adam's mouth was dry. If the scouts failed in turning the herd… He didn't want to think about tiny trampled bodies, crushed into the grass of the prairie.

God, please!

Suddenly, a shadow loomed before him. And five boys screamed.

Micah leapt from his saddle. "Joel! Av! Thank God!" He swept the boys into a fierce hug and then tossed them into the saddle and turned to run for the minimal protection of the wagons.

Hawthorne bellowed at his sons. "You boys! I oughta crack your heads together!" He thrust a finger toward the wagons and screamed, "Run!"

Silas and Soren lit out in Micah's wake, surprisingly fast for boys so young. Hiram angled his horse after them.

Adam reached a hand down to Wyatt and swung him up on the horse behind him. He could feel Wyatt's arms trembling where they wrapped around his chest.

"I'm sorry! I'm so sorry! I didn't mean to get anybody hurt!"

Fury built inside Adam, layer upon layer, until they skidded their horses to a halt in the center of the wagons.

He didn't wait for Wyatt to dismount. Instead, he swung one leg over his horse's neck and leapt down, then turned to yank Wyatt out of the saddle by his shirt front. He set the boy on the ground and leaned over him. "You could've been killed!" He jabbed a finger toward the younger boys. "Those boys could've been killed! Men could've been killed coming to look for you! I told you to stay in the center of the wagons!"

Wyatt sniffled, seemingly unable to meet his gaze. "Yes, sir. I'm sorry."

"You look at me when I'm talking to you!" Horror, terror, and anger made Adam's head feel as though it were about to burst. He thrust a finger toward the occasional pistol shots still coming from the prairie. "I should be out there helping to turn that herd. Instead, I had to come looking for you!"

Wyatt hung his head. "I'm sorry, sir."

Adam paced a few steps away from him and took a breath. Blew it out slowly between pursed lips. He turned back to look at the boy. Assessed him from head to toe. "Are you hurt?" Before Wyatt could even answer, he turned to look at the other boys. "Are any of them hurt?"

"My boys are fine for now until I find a good sturdy switch." Hiram Hawthorn's voice rang roughly through the darkness. Despite his angry words, he stood with one arm around each of his twin boys, clutching them closely to his sides.

Micah held Avram in his arms and had one hand settled on Joel's head. "My boys seem to be fine, also."

"Thank God!" Adam turned back to Wyatt, noticing for the first time the tears in the boy's eyes. He thrust a finger toward the horse the kids called Bluey, but gentled his tone when he said, "Get that horse saddled, and then go stand over there by the wagon, and be ready to move if I say we need to move." He thrust his lasso rope into Wyatt's hands. "No telling what this herd is gonna do." He hesitated then and assessed the boy. "Are you kids the ones who scared that herd into running?"

Wyatt was already shaking his head. "No, sir! We were walking through the grass when we heard the bison coming in the distance. We weren't anywhere near them. I promise it's true."

Adam took another breath, willing down the trepidation still shooting like wildfire through his veins. "I'm glad you're okay, son." The word *son* slipped out before he could rethink it, and Adam was glad to see that Wyatt didn't protest it this time.

He swung back into the saddle, but just as he was reining to ride into the night, Striker trotted his horse through a gap between two of the wagons. He held up a hand. "Everything's going to be all right, folks. Cody and Jeremiah are staying out to make sure the herd doesn't turn back this way, but we managed to get them turned west, and it seems they are intent on heading away from us for the time being. Everyone get some rest." He swung down from his mount and set to stripping off his saddle. All around the encampment, calls of relief filled the air.

Adam breathed out a sigh. He looked down at Wyatt, whose gaze was fixed on him, waiting for instructions. He tipped a nod toward their wagon. "Leave the horse and go get in the hammock. We can talk about this more later." He held out his hand for the lasso.

Looking like a liberated prisoner, Wyatt handed over the rope. "Yes, sir. Night, sir."

Hawthorne and Micah said their farewells and then returned to their wagons with their boys, and Adam was left alone with his mount.

He fell to his knees, clinging to his horse's reins as he sobbed in the darkness.

"Thank You, Lord. Thank You!"

The next morning, Wyatt woke and wondered what his punishment would be.

Mrs. Houston had pulled him into a fierce hug when he'd returned to the wagon. But she hadn't said anything other than to urge him to hurry to bed.

He had lain in his hammock long into the night, trying to fall asleep, but so many emotions had been pumping through him that he'd had a hard time relaxing.

It had been a long time before the parson had returned the evening before, and Wyatt had wondered what had taken him so long. His footsteps had scuffled wearily when he finally arrived back at the wagon and climbed the crate steps into the bed.

This morning, Wyatt had made sure to be particularly helpful. Whatever punishment was coming, he wanted to ease his circumstances as much as possible. At least that had always worked on Ma. But the Houstons hadn't said a word—at least not about the evening before—as they worked to get breakfast and hitch the team. They had greeted him politely, and Mrs. Houston had measured an extra serving of bacon onto his plate, but otherwise, their camp had been silent this morning.

The whole camp had been rather quiet, come to think about it.

Now, the call for nooning had gone out—he'd made sure to walk along behind the wagons with Asher all morning—and the punishment looming over his head felt like a guillotine about to fall. He approached the Houstons' wagon and slunk onto the grass near the blanket Mrs. Houston had laid out for them to sit on.

He couldn't seem to meet Mr. Houston's gaze when the man walked up.

Wyatt plucked a blade of grass and worked at shredding the fluffy grains of the head.

Mr. Houston washed his hands in the bucket that Mrs. Houston had set nearby and then sloshed some of the water over his face before reaching for the towel. "Ah. That feels good. Thank you, Eden." The man turned, drying his face and hands, and settled his gaze on Wyatt.

Quickly, Wyatt returned his focus to the grass in his hands.

"Wyatt?" Mr. Houston's voice cut through the warmth of the spring day.

Here it came. "Yes, sir?" His voice emerged barely above a whisper.

"You were the oldest of those boys last night."

He swallowed. "Yes, sir."

"Next time, I expect you'll know that you ought to speak up and be a leader for what is right?"

Wyatt swallowed. He ought to confess that it had been his idea in the first place, but maybe it would be better to simply keep his mouth shut. All he said was, "Yes, sir."

The minister nodded. "Good. Then, let's eat."

Wyatt exchanged a look with Asher. That was it? Pa would have tanned his hide into the next season. So why was it that he almost felt worse with just a few words spoken by this man?

He suddenly wanted to make the man proud of him. And that thought returned a measure of the irritation he'd been feeling the night before and yet a rush of relief, too. The ordeal was over, and he never wanted to be in a situation like this again. From now on, he would be a good leader instead of a bad one.

All afternoon, he intended to put his new intentions into practice with the fellas right away, yet that night, when the boys had stopped by to see if he wanted to play ball, Wyatt found that he was too weary. He fell into the hammock at the same time as Asher and fell asleep almost immediately.

Eden smiled at Adam as she dried the last of the dishes. With the three children already fast asleep, and no danger threatening from the horizon, the evening felt downright peaceful.

"That was a sweet thing you did for Wyatt, Adam."

He looked up from the pages of the book that he'd continued reading after the children went to bed. Glanced at the hammock, then lifted one shoulder. "If you could have seen the terror on his face . . . I figured he learned his lesson without needing any more punishment from me."

"He seems to be a good young man."

Adam nodded and turned back to his book. "He does."

Eden quirked a brow at him. "Are you reading ahead in the story?"

Adam smiled. "Edmond was just thrown into the sea in a sack. I have to see if he makes it, or not."

Eden laughed. "Well, I am off for some sleep, dear husband. I'll have to wait to listen as you read the story around the fire tomorrow evening to find out what happens."

Adam glanced up, swept her with a look, then snapped the book closed. "I suppose we should retire. The nights are short enough these days as it is."

Eden's heart hammered. She'd seen that hungry look in her husband's eyes before. But when they were settled in bed, he only pressed a kiss to her temple and said, "Good night, Eden."

She sighed, disappointed. And yet, as she lay there listening to Adam's deep, even breaths, she realized that this evening, with all the children around the fire and Adam reading, and all of them holding on to every word of the story, had been the best night she'd had in a very long time.

Each little step forward was a step in the right direction.

The other night, Mrs. Hawthorne had mentioned "oft overlooked moments of perfection." Tonight had been one of those moments, and she didn't want to overlook it.

As she lay there in the darkness, she thanked the Lord for this one perfect night and prayed for many more to come.

Chapter 13

Mercy Morran had never been happier to see a cluster of clapboard buildings than she was to see those of Fort Kearny. Her heart hadn't been easy since they'd come upon the burned-out wagon train five days back.

Her first husband, Herst, had been a man like the ones who must have perpetrated those atrocities on that wagon train, and she feared another attack at any moment. Micah had tried to reassure her to rest in the only One who could protect them and also in the fact that the men of the wagon train were guarding with extra vigilance, but she had failed miserably at that task.

Now, as they pulled into a field on the outskirts of the fort, Cranston ordered them to circle the wagons, and for the first time in days, a feeling of hope seemed to permeate the air. Mercy felt the excitement, too. A town filled with people and a mercantile!

She knew that Willow would be relieved to be able to buy herself some clothing and other necessities in the mercantile since she had nothing due to that Donahue man burning down her father's store before they'd left Independence. At least Mercy had some of Georgia's clothes, even though she'd kept herself busy nights near the fire, hemming up the skirts that were too long for her and tucking in the waists. What she did want was to buy a book or two to read to the boys in the evenings along the trail. And she also wouldn't mind a bit of dried fruit. That was something she hadn't packed enough of. And there were a couple of other things, she realized. She was unable to withhold a smile, even as she felt heat warming her cheeks.

Micah glanced over at her from where he was seated next to her on the bench. "Uh-oh. I'm in trouble. I can see your excitement blooming at just the sight of that mercantile."

Mercy smiled. "Never fear. Your wallet is safe." She gestured to the wagon behind them. "Where would I put anything? Except . . ." She dragged the word out and turned a smile on her husband.

"Uh-huh. Here it comes." He grinned at her. "What is it?"

"A milk cow?" She winced a little. "With so many children in the wagon train, I just thought that maybe . . ." Her words trailed away as Micah was already shaking his head with a serious bunch to his lips.

He thumbed a gesture over his shoulder. "I don't think we want to share our space with a milk cow."

Mercy's mouth fell open, and he released a bark of laughter. Once he pulled their wagon to a stop at their place in the circle, he planted his elbows against his knees and grinned over at her.

She smacked his shoulder with a laugh. "You're incorrigible."

He set the wagon's brake and looped the reins around the handle, then he leaned across her to plant one hand on the arm of the wagon bench and the other on the bench itself, effectively trapping her between his arms. He was still smiling when he said, "I think I could be tamed, but it would take the right woman to do the job."

Mercy quirked a brow, barely withholding another laugh. "Oh? And do you know such a woman?"

Her husband's gaze dipped to her lips. "Indeed. I believe I do."

Mercy's heart hammered as it always did when she found herself in Micah's purview. He'd been more than patient with her, and she knew that she wanted intimacies with him. But so far, kisses were as far as things had progressed. In the crowded wagon that they shared with their boys, Micah and Joel had been sleeping in the aisle, and

Avram had been sharing half the tick with her. She loved this man all the more for the fact that he hadn't pressured her.

But she'd been trying to work up her courage to make a change to those arrangements for some time now. Her gaze landed on the mercantile again.

Micah was leaning in for a kiss, so she hurried to speak. "You know..."

He stilled and raised his gaze to hers.

Mercy felt the heat that rushed into her cheeks again as she squirmed beneath his scrutiny.

Micah eased back a fraction. "This is interesting, wife. I do confess that I like to see you blush, but I can't for the life of me figure out what I've done to deserve such a pleasure."

Mercy rolled her lips inward and sealed them tight. She fiddled with one of the buttons in the middle of his shirt. "It's just that I had a thought."

"I am most intrigued to hear what this thought is." He grinned, but there was a light of seriousness in his gaze, too.

Mercy felt all a flutter inside. She knew the man was smart enough to have guessed at least the trajectory of this conversation. Was he ready for another step in their relationship? Just because she was ready to move on from Herst didn't mean he was ready as well. He'd loved Georgia with all his heart, after all.

She shored up her courage and pressed ahead. "It's just that I noticed that the parson gave up his hammock beneath his wagon for the new boys. And that got me to thinking that, at least in good weather, Avram and Joel might, well..." She lifted her gaze to his, her heart beating anticipation from the region of her throat. "Do you think that the mercantile might have a hammock?"

Micah's gaze twinkled, and the stiffness that had crept into his shoulders relaxed. "I'll hold the owner at gunpoint until they hand one over!"

Mercy laughed in relief and smacked his chest. "You'll do no such thing."

He leaned in until his lips hovered only a fraction above hers. His voice was barely audible when he said, "Just see if I don't."

Mercy giggled and pressed her lips to his. Then, because others from the wagon train were starting to mill about as they unhitched their teams and began to set up camp, she nudged him to his side of the bench. "And don't forget a milk cow."

Micah shook his head. He hopped down and hurried around to her side of the wagon to lift her down. "A milk cow . . . and a hammock." He leaned forward to whisper those last words into her ear.

Heavens! Was her face as red as it felt? She pushed him back. "Just make sure no guns are involved."

Though Micah laughed, he was gentleman enough to let the matter drop. He stroked the knuckle of one finger along the underside of her jaw, then tilted his head toward the store. "Buy what you need and tell them I'll be in to pay the bill in a few minutes. The boys can stay here and toss the ball around." With that, he sauntered forward to unhitch the team.

Relieved that he'd been open to her suggestion, she turned her gaze toward the town and was surprised to notice that the fort had no fortifications. No log wall with pointed tops, like she'd imagined. Not even any Cheval de Frise. The fort was naught more than a rectangle of buildings built side-by-side around a parade ground surrounded by cottonwoods. The parade ground was large, and it felt surprisingly civilized to walk on the graveled paths that separated the field into rectangular quadrants.

The excited chatter among the women did her heart good. Seeing a civilization again felt a bit like Christmas morning. There was anticipation. The thrill of uncertainty. The joy of the unknown touched with the hope of expectancy.

Even Eden was here today, walking with them toward the mercantile with the hand of little Afton clasped firmly in her own. The boys must still be with Adam. Mercy fleetingly hoped that none of the boys would run off like they had a few nights back. But the men would keep an eye on them and all the boys had seemed to be on their best behavior since the incident. She drew a breath. They would be fine. She needed to quit worrying so much.

Concerned for her friend, Mercy studied the blond woman who walked by her side. "How are you feeling now that you've had some rest?"

Eden smiled. "I feel much improved. Thank you for asking." She touched the back of her head. "Just a touch of pain here, but much more manageable than it was previously. You, Willow, and Tamsyn have been a godsend, helping with so many things."

Mercy waved away her thanks. They'd told her time and again that they were happy to help. But she knew that if their roles were reversed, she would feel the same.

As they approached the mercantile, Eden bent to listen more closely to something Afton was saying, and Mercy glanced up to the second story of the building and found a man watching them. A glare of light on the glass obscured most of his features. But what she could see was that his gaze was not fixed on her but on Eden beside her.

Mercy glanced from the man to Eden and back again. He was definitely watching her. Something inside tightened up at the look in his eyes, but then they were at the steps, and the porch roof blocked the sight of him.

She gave herself a mental shake. The man had probably only been assessing the newcomers. Her history with Herst likely had her seeing shadows where none existed.

Besides, with such a group of them all descending on the mercantile at once, there would be too many of them together for anyone to try anything untoward.

Brad turned from the sight of that beautiful blond woman to face his brother, who sat behind the wooden desk across the room. Boone's office, here above the mercantile, was warm and well-lit with windows on each side. This second-story vantage point also gave Colonel Boone Baxter a clear view of his men and the activities of his fort.

Brad and his men had arrived only two days earlier with the supplies they'd been contracted to fetch. "That wagon train I told you we saw is here."

Boone continued perusing the military report on his desk. "Saw them coming earlier."

Of course he did. Boone never missed anything.

Brad felt an itch slink along beneath his skin. Boone was about to learn of an attack that had wiped out a wagon train. How would he take the news? He'd undoubtedly take some men and ride out to check the scene.

Had Brad's men left any traces of themselves?

For the hundredth time, Brad considered how they had left things. Normally, he would have made a final clean sweep of the wagons and area to make sure no traces that could lead back to his men were left. This time, the surprise arrival of the other wagon train had made that impossible.

He was a fool! If he'd been paying attention, he surely would have seen the dust of that wagon train approaching on the horizon! He'd been too focused on stripping those wagons of their supplies.

That itch again. He scratched his neck, unable to shake the feeling that Boone was going to discover the part he'd played in that attack. And Boone had made it clear on more than one occasion that blood or not, Brad was on his own if he ever broke the law again. Boone might have his own skeletons, but he kept them carefully hidden, and woe to Brad if he ever turned a spotlight of scrutiny on their family name. Brad smirked at that, then drew his thoughts back to his predicament.

He'd only gotten this contract because Boone had given him another chance. Boone, the good son. Always the good son. Especially since their brother had passed.

Boone, the soldier. Boone, the son who had made something of himself. Boone, the one who never made mistakes. Boone, the one Ma and Pa had always been so proud of. Boone. Boone. Boone.

Brad's stomach churned.

It made him sick.

For now, he'd mosey on down into the mercantile and maybe see if he could strike up a conversation with that pretty woman down there. She had a child, though. That was disappointing. When he'd seen her back at the site of the attack, he hadn't pictured her already settled with children. She must be married?

No matter. A woman's marital status had never stopped him before.

He turned for the door, lifting a hand to Boone as he went out.

Boone didn't even look up or acknowledge his departure.

When Gid pulled the wagon to a stop at their place in the circle, Willow couldn't bring herself to move. She simply stared down at the fort, feeling empty and hollow. She needed to shore up her gumption and get to town because all these weeks she'd been wearing her only dress—the one she'd been wearing on the day of the fire—and one borrowed from Mercy that had once been Micah's first wife's dress.

She needed undergarments, and her sturdy boots had also burned in the fire. The ones she wore hurt her feet. She needed shampoo, a hairbrush, toothpowder, and a brush for her teeth, if they even had such an extravagant item way out here in the wilderness. So far, Gid had been sharing his with her.

She needed all these things and needed to hold herself together while purchasing them, but she couldn't seem to move from the wagon bench.

Beside her, Gid set the brake and wrapped the reins around the brake handle, then shifted toward her. One of his big hands settled against the base of her neck, and his thumb and fingers worked into the muscles of her shoulders. "You going to be okay, Willow girl?" His voice rumbled with concern.

Blinking back the sting of the tears, she scooted closer to him and rested her head on his tall shoulder, still staring down at the fort. "I can't believe it's been over a month since I lost him." One tear slipped free and slid down her cheek. She swiped at it.

Gid's arm slid around her, and he tucked her close, turning her into his chest. "He would have loved to see this, wouldn't he? I can't count the number of times he talked of what it must be like to live out here in the wilderness. He worried about bringing you out here, but he was always so excited about the prospect of the future."

Willow felt her sadness mount at that. Yet another thing that had been taken from her. Papa hadn't even told her he planned to go west until the morning of the day he'd passed away from the smoke of the fire.

"I wish he had talked to me about it."

Gid rested his hand against her shoulder and stroked her jaw with his thumb. "I know. Would it help if we talked about our hopes for Oregon?"

Hopes for Oregon? Did she even have hopes for this far-off land that she hadn't wanted to travel to in the first place? Her eyes fell closed, and she breathed in the scent of Gid's soap mixed with the dust and hard work of the trail. It was a scent that she was coming to associate with home, safety, and love.

Love? She pondered on that. Yes. She was growing in her love for this man who had given up so much for her. And love was certainly different than the attraction that she'd felt for him from the first moment that she'd laid eyes on him all those months ago.

Talking of Oregon wouldn't ease the pain of having lost Papa, but it would help her get to know her new husband better, and she truly wanted that.

She eased back from him and spread her hands against his chest as she looked into the blue of his eyes. "I'd love to speak of your hopes for Oregon. But for now, I see Mercy and Eden already headed to the store. I should join them, and we can talk this evening?"

Gid bent and gave her a quick, gentle kiss. "Yes. This evening. Tomorrow. Whenever you are ready. *Our* hopes. Not just my hopes." He lifted one brow, and she knew he wanted her to focus on the future, not the past.

She may not have wanted to make this journey, but she could choose to find joy in it, nonetheless. She nodded to let him know she understood. She would put her mind to thinking about that. What did she want? She couldn't go back to the past. So what did she want from this unplanned, unexpected future that lay before her?

Seeming to accept her nod for now, he reached inside his jacket and withdrew a pouch that jangled with coin. He pressed it into her hands. "Buy what you need."

Willow frowned down at the leather poke, sweeping her thumb over the softness of the hide. "Thank you, Gid. I don't want to be a burden."

"Hey." He touched her chin and lifted her gaze to his. "You are not a burden. You're my wife, and I want to care for you. Get what you need. I'm headed to the livery to see if they have a sidesaddle for you."

That love again, swelling through her with such strength. "I love you, husband."

He smiled. "And I love you, wife." He searched her expression. "You sure you're going to be okay?"

She patted his chest and eased back from him. "I'll be fine. See you this evening?"

He nodded, leapt from his side of the wagon bench, and lifted his hands to help her down. When she had leaned into the strength of him and sunk into his arms, he pulled her close and lingered over a kiss this time. He smiled down at her, touched her chin, then stepped back. "See you this evening, my Willow girl."

With that, he turned to unhitch the team, and Willow was left to strengthen her knees, which practically turned to jelly every time he called her his Willow girl.

Giving herself a shake, she hurried through the prairie grasses to catch up to Mercy and Eden.

Chapter 14

Jeremiah Jackson drew in a bracing breath, pushed his hat off, and let it dangle down his back from the strings as he stepped up on the mercantile porch. He wished he'd had time to wash before stepping through those doors, but Cranston had insisted that he immediately needed ink, a pen, and a sheet of paper so the men of the wagon train could write down their complaint for the fort's colonel.

Unlucky for Jeremiah, he had been the closest scout to hand when the idea had struck the wagon master, and now he found himself entering this store full of white folk with the dust of the trail still itching his skin.

Carefully, he kept his eyes just below those of any person he met. High enough to show them his respect, low enough to offer no challenge. Normally Jeremiah sent Striker on errands such as this one, but his friend hadn't been anywhere in sight when Cranston had issued the order. Probably off helping that Acheson woman. He was careful to keep the humor of that thought from reflecting in his features.

No need to get any white folk riled up over why the lone black man in the store was smiling.

Keeping his hands carefully in sight, he meandered through the aisles looking for paper and ink.

Ahead of him, two sets of the Hawthorne twins wandered also. The two boys, Silas and Soren, were about nine. Their eyes lit up over practically everything in the store, but Jeremiah was glad to see that they kept their hands to themselves. Perhaps because their older sisters, Wren and Whitley, kept glowering and snapping their fingers for the boys to keep up. The youngest set of twins and the baby—Jeremiah had once heard Mrs. Hawthorne loudly thanking the Almighty over the fact that he was a single birth—must still be back at the wagons with their mother. As round as the children's mother was, he couldn't help but wonder if another set of twins might soon be forthcoming.

Jeremiah took up a small pot of ink, a dip pen, and one sheet of paper and fell into line behind the twins. With a frown, Jeremiah noted that the children had nothing in their hands, but as soon as they reached the counter and the jars of penny candy came into view, understanding dawned.

He did smile then, and was happy to see that the proprietress, an older woman with almost completely white hair but youth in the pep of her step, met his gaze with a smile of her own.

Jeremiah lifted a finger and swung it to encompass the four children. "Whatever they want, ma'am, it's on me."

The twins all spun to look at him with surprise in their expressions.

Jeremiah gave them a nod. "Go on. Pick out what you want."

"All right!" One of the boys—Jeremiah still hadn't figured out how to tell the towheaded duplicates apart—surged toward the jars of candy.

But Whitley—she was the one with the redder streaks in her blond hair and more freckles on her nose—snagged her brother's arm before he could touch anything. "Only one piece, Silas, and I'll be the one to fetch it for you. Just point to the kind you want, *without touching*!"

Ah, so Silas was the one with so much spice and spirit. Maybe that would help Jeremiah tell them apart in the future.

Soren turned to face Jeremiah while his brother pointed out the piece of candy he wanted. "Mr. Jackson, sir, is it okay if I take one of those bigger pieces that cost two cents so's I can share with Liberty, Serenity, and Cumberland?"

"Well now, that's right thoughtful of you, and yes, that'd be fine. You go on and pick what you want." It warmed Jeremiah's heart to have the boy thinking of his siblings. He bit back a grin when Silas, who had turned with his precious candy and must have overheard their conversation, hung his head and looked at the stick of red sugar in his hand.

"I can share some of mine, too, Soren."

"We'll all share." Wren gave Jeremiah a smile that all at once conveyed her thanks and her humor over her brothers' personalities.

Jeremiah gave her a nod of understanding.

Lord, You ever gonna bless me with a family and a passel of children of my own?

Longing washed through him, and yet there was hopelessness, too. Heading to the west as he was, he wasn't likely to find a woman that folk would approve of him marrying. He released a breath. It made no never mind.

You are enough for me, Lord. You surely are. I hope You know that this longing for a family isn't no disregard of Your blessings. Help me to be content in all circumstances and learn to lean on You to be my satisfaction.

After the children each retrieved a piece of candy, they thanked him, then darted away, chattering their excitement to each other.

He couldn't withhold a smile. It did his heart good to hear those young ones so happy.

Jeremiah stepped up to the counter and carefully laid Cranston's purchases down.

The proprietress offered him a smile. "That was a mighty kind thing you did."

Jeremiah shook his head. "Weren't nothing, ma'am. Weren't nothing."

He was thankful when she seemed content to let the matter drop. It also eased some of his tension to note that she wasn't upset at having a dusty black man in her store.

She finished tallying his purchases in her receipt book. "It will be ten cents for the ink, pen, and sheet of paper, and five cents for the children's candy, so fifteen cents total."

Jeremiah glanced from the jars of candy to the two bits in his palm. "Tell you what. Why don't you throw in another ten cents of that candy there?" He laid the quarter on the counter.

The woman smiled. "I'm guessing you're about to become very popular with the children of the wagon train."

He grinned. "Who says that candy isn't for me, ma'am?"

She laughed and motioned to the jars. "Any flavor in particular?"

Jeremiah studied the colorful jars, but couldn't decide. "Just a few of each is fine." It made him smile even bigger when she tossed in a few extra pieces and claimed they were "on the house."

He gave her a nod as he took up his purchases. "Right kind of you, ma'am. Right kind. Bless you."

With that, he made his escape from the store and breathed a sigh of relief to be back in the open air where men were less likely to accuse him of stepping out of his place.

He hurried back to the wagon train and deposited the sack of candy in the back of the children's wagon before hurrying toward Cranston's with his paper and ink.

Movement on the store's porch drew his gaze in time to see the proprietress just returning inside.

He frowned. That was odd. Had she followed him outside to see where he went with his purchases?

He gave himself a shake. It made no never mind to him what the lady had done or why she'd done it. He'd given her no cause to suspect him of any wrongdoing. And she hadn't seemed the type to throw accusations where none were deserved. He always did his best to live in the light. As long as he was doing right, he wouldn't give fodder to anyone who might want to accuse him of anything.

For now, he had to find Cranston.

Eden stood with Afton's hand in hers, taking in the vast array of supplies on the shelves. There was nothing out of the ordinary, really. Simply a well-stocked mercantile, however just the sight of civilization gave her a boost of energy.

They weren't out here in the wilds of the unknown all alone. There were others who lived here. Made a life. Received goods from back east. It was all beginning to sink in, this choice that she and Adam had made to travel into the unknown to share the gospel with people who were, as of yet, unknown to them.

Beside her, Afton squirmed. She pointed to a set of dishes. "Those were Aunty Maude's."

Eden blinked and felt a jolt of tension. But then she realized that the dishes must be a pattern similar to those the child's aunt had owned.

She squatted by the girl and picked up one of the blue-and-white pieces of china. The pattern was beautiful. Eden had always been partial to blues. "Your aunt had this pattern, did she?" She traced a finger over the tree on the left side of the plate.

Afton nodded. "I like the birds." She pointed to the two fluttering fowl at the top of the pattern.

"Me too." Eden smiled and returned the plate to the shelf. Pretty as it was, they had no room for such frivolities in the wagon. She tugged the little girl closer. "This pattern is made by a company called Spode. They make lots of plates at one time. So your aunt could have some, and another person could have some, and this store could also have some to sell."

Afton frowned. She pointed to a plate three down in the stack. "Aunt Maude gots mad when Asher chipped that one."

Eden felt a chill slip down her spine, and she tugged Afton closer to her side. She remembered the chaos that had surrounded the wagons they had come upon, and yet the neat stacks of items set here and there, as though someone had planned to come back for them.

Could someone have been robbing those poor folks to bring their supplies here to sell?

She rose and took Afton's hand, feeling a sudden need to escape the store. Could it be the proprietor? She glanced toward the front counter. A harried woman with a cap of silver hair on her head helped Mrs. Hawthorne with a bolt of cloth, while also trying to assist Willow, who seemed to want an ounce measured from a jar of herbs, and another woman wanting a packet of tea leaves. Despite being torn in several directions, the woman served with a smile and a kind light in her eyes. Could such a woman be a thief and a murderer? It didn't seem likely.

Perhaps she wasn't the owner, however? Maybe the woman only worked here and had no idea of the nature of the goods sold.

Eden frowned down at the stack of blue-and-white plates once more. They were ceramic. A popular pattern. Surely chipped edges couldn't be uncommon in such, especially out here on the edge of the world?

She was probably making more of this than it warranted. Afton was three, after all. And one chipped plate looked much the same as another. Still, it wouldn't hurt to mention this to Adam and the men and ask a few more questions. Adam had told her that as soon as he and the men got the oxen corralled, he and Caesar would come into the fort to speak to the commander about what had happened to the Slade family.

But a whisper of worry tickled the back of her mind. What if the colonel was in on the marauding?

She withdrew the chipped plate from the stack, then bent until her face was next to Afton's. She rubbed one finger over the chip. "Nicks like this could happen on any plate if it got bumped." Were the words more to assure herself than the child?

Afton frowned. "Otay." She thrust her thumb into her mouth, then promptly withdrew it. "Nicks always look like a moon smile?"

Eden lowered her gaze to the chip once more. Sure enough, a near-perfect crescent moon marred the edge of the plate. Her heart dropped. She returned the plate to the stack and took up Afton's hand once more. "Come on, sweetie, we're going to head back to the wagons to find Adam and the boys."

When she turned, a man stood at the end of the aisle watching them with his thumbs hooked on the thick leather belt about his waist.

Eden gasped and snatched Afton into her arms.

She was looking directly into the face from the sketch Wyatt had drawn!

Chapter 15

The outlaw wore leather breeches and a linen shirt open at the collar. A faded black bandana draped around his neck. There was something assessing in his gray gaze.

Eden swallowed. Now here was a man she would have no trouble envisioning as a marauding murderer. She settled Afton more comfortably on her hip, wishing he wasn't blocking her way out of this aisle. But with the wall at her back, shelves on either side, and him between her and escape, she knew she must act as though nothing were amiss.

Eden thought again of their arrival at the scene of destruction. This man had no idea who she was, nor that Wyatt had seen him—and an intrinsic instinct told Eden it was best to keep it that way. Yet, when they'd arrived at the scene, surely he hadn't been too far off. The piles of goods meant he'd been coming back to steal more things when the arrival of their own wagon train had derailed his plans. Had he seen them? Was he upset with their interruption of his plans?

Whether he had seen them or not, he must know, based on the timing of their arrival here at the fort, that theirs was the wagon train that had interrupted his marauding. Perhaps he was here in the mercantile simply trying to assess if any of them were talking about the incident?

Whatever his presence meant, it was improper for him to block a woman into a tight position. And he may be willing to kill women out in the middle of the wilderness, but she doubted he would try anything here in a busy mercantile on a military fort.

Eden tilted up her chin. "If you'll pardon us, sir?" She raised her voice to hopefully draw the attention of some of the other women from the caravan.

"Name's Brad Baxter, and you are?"

"A woman who is happily married." He didn't need to know that wasn't entirely true just now. "To a minister." She cocked a brow at him, not even ashamed to be using Adam's profession as a shield.

Mr. Baxter didn't seem put off by what she'd hoped would set him back. With one elbow propped casually atop a shelf, his gaze lowered to Afton. "Your daughter sure is a pretty little thing." His lips curved up at the edges, but no kindness lit his eyes when they lifted back to her.

How long had he been standing there? Had he heard the things that Afton had said about the plates? No. She'd looked toward the proprietress only moments ago, and he hadn't been standing there. Even so... something in Eden clanged a warning that she should not reveal that Afton wasn't her daughter.

"Thank you. We were admiring the beautiful blue pattern on these plates." She searched his face. Would he buy her story?

He lifted a hand and scratched the back of one thumbnail along his jaw. "My sister-in-law there—" He nodded toward the bustling woman at the front of the store. "—said they were quite the most beautiful plates she'd ever seen. She just bought them the other day. You interested in buying them?" There was a glitter of assessment in his gaze.

The nerve of the man! Speaking so casually about the plates he had killed to acquire!

Stay calm. He doesn't know what you know.

Eden waved her free hand and then tucked it back into the folds of her skirt, hoping he hadn't noticed her trembling. "Oh no. We were only looking. We don't have room in the wagon for anything so nice."

His searching gaze seemed to intensify.

And Eden knew it was time to put an end to this conversation. She took a bold step forward. "If you'll pardon us? We were going to buy some tea at the front counter."

For one heart-stopping moment, she thought he might not step out of her way, but then he withdrew with a touch of two fingers to his forehead. "Can't have a pretty lady such as yourself without your tea."

So relieved that her knees felt like melting wax, Eden made a beeline for Mercy, who stood waiting for Willow at the front. She could feel the man's scrutiny the whole way across the store. "Mercy, please, will you come with me to find Adam?" She kept her voice down and did her best to look calm.

Mercy snapped her head up. "What is it?"

Eden tossed a glance over her shoulder toward the outlaw who was apparently related to the woman who ran this store. The man remained at the end of the aisle where she'd left him, and his gaze was still fastened on her. Eden felt a shiver work down her spine. She willed herself to exude tranquility.

Was the owner of the mercantile included in his scheme? Sister-in-law, he'd said. So who was his brother? Did that man know about this one's nefarious activities?

She looked back at Mercy. "I just need to find Adam and speak to him, but I don't want to walk there alone."

Mercy narrowed a look on the man across the store. She leaned forward and lowered her voice. "Did that man do something to make you uncomfortable?"

Eden nodded.

Mercy stepped closer. She lowered her volume several degrees. "Did he touch you?"

"No." Eden shook her head. "Please. I'll explain. But not here. Will you come with me?"

"Of course."

Willow finished with her purchases and stepped up beside them with her basket on one arm. "What are you two discussing in such secretive terms?" she whispered.

"Outside." Eden turned and strode purposefully to the door, willing her arms the strength to hold onto Afton, and her legs the strength to keep her upright.

Brad felt uneasy as the women left the store. He moseyed onto the porch, stepped into the shadows of the alley, and propped his shoulder against one of the porch's log columns.

The blonde had acted like she'd seen a ghost from the moment she'd first laid eyes on him. Not the usual reaction he got from women, though he maybe shouldn't have hemmed her in like he did. Her beauty fascinated him, and he'd been too eager to speak to her.

Foolish. He'd scared her. She'd even left without her tea.

He frowned. Thought back to the attack.

No one from the wagon train had seen him that day, he felt certain. No one who had lived, that was.

However, when he'd seen that beautiful woman wandering in the midst of his destruction, she hadn't had a little girl with her. Wasn't that unusual? The child was too young to be left alone. Perhaps she'd left her child in the care of others while she went to see how she could help? That would make sense. If she were anything like his sister-in-law, Betsy, she wouldn't want her child anywhere near danger. At least that was what he figured, even though Betsy and his late brother had never had any children.

And yet . . . something in him wouldn't sit easy today.

Sure, he'd blocked her into the aisle, but he'd remained standing at a respectable distance. Nothing that should have frightened her. And still she'd fled as though he'd accosted her. Could she know something that was impossible for her to know? There was no way she could know that he had perpetrated that attack, was there?

He frowned. What could he be missing? The unease wouldn't leave him.

He'd brought the goods and sold them to Betsy without her or Boone suspecting anything. But if there was one thing that years of bucking the law had taught him, it was to listen to his gut. No one suspected him of being an outlaw, and he wanted to keep it that way. It was time to move on west again.

His men wouldn't like it. They'd only just arrived a couple of days back. But they would have to live with it.

He watched the woman all the way to the wagon train, where she paused near a man and spoke with urgent slashes of her hand back in the direction of the store.

Blazes!

He spun on one heel and headed toward the livery. Boone was his brother, and the only family he had left, so he'd be back to say his farewells. But first he would alert his men and buy some supplies. Within the hour, he and his men would be on their way.

Adam pounded the last post into the temporary corral, then reached to shake Micah's hand. "Hopefully that will hold them." He withheld a wince when Micah firmly squeezed his palm. His hand was much improved, but still bothered him with its tenderness from time to time. He was only thankful that it had healed over without getting infected. Likely thanks to Eden's constant ministrations.

Because they would be staying here for a couple of days, the men had worked to pen the oxen and cattle into a fence about half a mile outside the fort. Unless one of the animals took it into their head to force their way out, the fence should hold until it was time to move on.

Micah nodded. "That cow of Hawthorne's is the one that will escape, if any of them do."

Adam chuckled. "It's always the females."

Micah grinned, glancing past Adam's shoulder. He lowered his voice. "Better not say that too loudly. Your wife is coming this way."

Adam turned with a smile that quickly faded as he took in the tight expression on Eden's face. She rushed toward him with Afton on one hip. "Adam, where are the boys?" Tension filled her tone.

Concern had him stepping toward her and searching the land behind her for some threat. "They are playing catch with Joel and Av." He pointed them out beyond a wagon where she wouldn't have been able to see them from her angle as she approached.

She almost sagged in relief and no one seemed to be chasing her. What could this be about? He returned his attention to her and gripped her shoulders. "What is it? How's your head?"

Eden waved a hand. "I'm fine. This isn't about me." She looked up at him, pale and trembling. "He's here, Adam." She lowered her voice. "The man from the sketch." She swung a gesture back toward the buildings of the fort. "He said his name was Brad Baxter. And Afton saw some plates that she says were her aunt's, right down to describing a chip in one of them."

Horror whipped through him, and he drew her closer, feeling the need to make sure she was whole. "You're sure it was him?"

She nodded. "It was him. Wyatt even had the white streaks in his hair correct. I just spoke to him in the mercantile. He's apparently the brother-in-law of the proprietress."

That set Adam back. He shared a look with Micah. Days ago, he'd shown all of the men of the caravan Wyatt's sketch so they could all be aware of the danger the man might pose. "Do you think that means people at the fort could be in on it? Family of such a man? Surely they would know?"

Micah wagged his head in uncertainty. "Not necessarily. If they were in on it together, why attack the wagons so many days into the wilderness, and why go to the trouble of transferring the goods to other wagons? They could have simply let the wagons come to them, or even if they attacked out there somewhere—" He waved a hand toward the vast prairie to the east. "—they could have brought the goods here, all contained in the wagons they were already packed in."

"That's true except the likelihood that everyone at the fort is in on it is slim. They could be trying to prevent others from learning what they are up to."

Micah consented with a tilt of a nod. "True."

Adam looked back at his wife. Her blue eyes were large and scared. He drew her closer and settled his arm around her shoulders, dropping a kiss on her temple. "It's going to be okay. We're all going to be okay." He reached to soothe a hand over Afton's riot of curls, then looked down at Eden. "What do you think? Did he make it sound like the woman was in on it?"

She clamped her lower lip between her teeth. Frowned. "He said she bought them a few days ago—the plates. If she were in on it, I don't think he would have worded it like that."

Adam exchanged another look with Micah, still uncertain. But a decision had to be made, and the quicker they did something, the quicker they would know what they were up against. The man was here. That meant he needed to be brought to justice before he was able to attack any other wagon trains. Whether they would need to bring the man to justice themselves or leave that to the fort authorities, remained to be seen. "Okay. We go together. Several of us. Right now to the colonel of the fort. And we go armed."

He heard Eden draw in a little breath.

He looked down at her, taking in her features. Memorizing the pattern of the small spattering of freckles across her nose, the arch of her brows, the curve of her lips. He tugged her close and rested his chin atop her head. If he and the men were killed, what would happen to the women? He cast his gaze toward the sky. *Lord, I'm pleading with You to watch over Eden . . .* The thought was so painful that he had to fight for a breath. *And these kids. And all the other women and children of this caravan.*

Could they even trust the commander of this fort? Would Adam be leading the men into danger?

Go before us. Please help us bring this outlaw to justice.

After giving Eden one more squeeze, he set her back from him and motioned toward the boys. "Get the kids, please. Stay in the wagon. If there's trouble, you'll hear it long before it gets here. Have Wyatt catch up the horses, take the kids, and you flee back east, hear me?"

Her chin shot up. "We're not leaving without you."

He touched her jaw to make sure he had her full attention. "You will, Eden. You must." He ran his hand once again over Afton's head. "It's not just you and me now. I mean, you know, *for* now."

Though she frowned at him, still worrying her lip, she nodded.

With that, though it practically tore his heart in two to leave her there, he gave a nod to Micah, who was saying his own piece to Mercy. Micah kissed the back of his wife's hand, and then they started toward the other men of the caravan. He should have kissed Eden, but she wouldn't have liked it since they were out in the open. And he didn't have time to go back and mend his oversight now. He and Micah would need to gather a force before heading into the fort.

Eden rushed with Mercy toward the boys, calling for them to come. She gave Mercy a hug and wished her safety, then hustled the children toward their wagon. When Eden, the last to enter, finally joined the children inside, Wyatt stared at her wide-eyed with concern.

Eden touched the side of his head. "The men are going into town to take care of some business and the parson asked that we wait here together in the wagon is all. Don't you worry. We're going to be fine."

She drew a breath. Would that she could believe her own reassurance.

"It's him, isn't it?" Wyatt's voice was sharp with apprehension.

For a moment, Eden rolled her lips in and pressed them together, trying to decide how much to reveal. She wanted to protect him from the fear of knowing that the man who had killed his family was merely a short walk away, and yet she also needed him to be prepared to act quickly if they needed to flee, as Adam had said. *Lord, please don't let it come to that. Keep the men safe! Bring them back to us whole and healthy.*

Finally, Eden drew Wyatt close enough that she could rest both hands on his shoulders. "I saw him, yes. The men of the caravan have gone into the fort to speak to the colonel about it."

Wyatt made to brush past her. "I should go with them! I'm the one who saw him!"

Eden tugged him back. "There will be time enough for identifying him once he is caught."

The thought jarred her to her very bones. Would Wyatt have to identify the man? Could the boy live with himself if he did? Because that identification would be the certain end of the outlaw. At least if there were any justice served at this fort.

Realizing the children were all still looking at her, Eden shooed them toward the pallet. Each night she had been reading to the boys by the fire. Today, the count's troubles might help them escape pondering about their own.

"For now, we will continue reading our story, hmmm?" She thought about preparing Wyatt that he might have to wrangle the horses, but decided to leave that instruction until it might be needed.

With the kids settled onto the bed, Eden took up the book and sank onto a crate. She angled the book toward the light streaming in from the open canvas and found the chapter where they'd left off.

And as her mouth spoke the words from the story of the count, her mind continued to pray—for the safety of the men, that the outlaw would be captured, and that the children would also be safe.

Chapter 16

The sharp knock on his door lifted Boone's head from his paperwork. "Come," he called.

The door pushed inward, and when not one, but seven men crowded into his office, Boone settled against the back of his chair in surprise. They spread out in a semicircle before his desk, all of them with serious expressions like men with business on their minds. A black man with light skin and blue eyes, an Indian decked out in buckskins, and five white men, though one of those was almost as dark as the Indian, despite his piercing blue eyes.

Boone rose from his chair and skirted the desk to offer his hand to the first man. "Gentlemen, I'm Boone Baxter, but since you all are here in my office, I presume you know that."

One of them, a tall blond man with broad shoulders and a paper gripped in one hand, shuffled uneasily. "Baxter, did you say?"

A cold premonition swept through Boone as the group of men before him shifted and exchanged glances. Had his cuss of a brother brought trouble on the family yet again? Boone's gaze fixed on that paper, somehow knowing it was what had brought the men here to his office.

"Yes. Baxter. Boone Baxter. What can I do for you?" He proceeded down the line, shaking each man's hand in turn.

They each gave him their names, all of them either members, scouts, or leaders of the newly arrived wagon train. The last man in the line—the one with long white hair and beard, who also held a paper and two arrows in one hand—spoke now.

"Name's Caesar Cranston, colonel of the wagon train just yonder." He thrust a blunt finger toward the window and then swung it toward the blond man with the paper. "This man here is Parson Adam Houston."

Boone glanced back toward the minister, whose hand he had already shaken.

The man narrowed his eyes and tilted his head, assessing him like a snake beneath his boot. So his intuition had been correct. His no-account brother had struck again. Boone retreated behind his desk, weary with the burden of sharing a name with that wastrel.

The parson spoke cautiously. "I confess we didn't know your name, sir. We asked to be directed to the colonel's office and were sent here. So, it is with some unease that we learn your name. You know a man named Brad Baxter? He any relation of yours?"

Boone sank wearily into his seat, propped his elbows on the blotter, and laced his fingers. "It is with a portion of regret that I confess to being his brother. What has he done now?"

After another exchange of glances and a few nods, the parson and the wagon master stepped forward. As the wagon master laid his two arrows and a paper on the desk—a paper that contained words—the parson spoke. "Five days back, we came across a wagon train that had been attacked." He laid his paper face up on the desk.

Boone felt a chill sweep down his spine as he stared at a near-perfect sketch of his brother.

The parson continued with a gesture toward the letter. "We've written down our account for you, but I'll tell you what it says. The wagon train was still afire. The bodies still warm. Some supplies from the wagons were stacked in neat piles as though someone had planned to come back for them. Arrows like those, which you can see are not made by any local tribe, were wrapped in flaming rags and stuck into some of the wagons. We surmise that we interrupted the marauding. But that is beside the point now. In that wagon train were some children, hidden by their father in a compartment in the base of their wagon. One of those children is quite an artist, as you can see from this sketch. He swears this is the man he saw shoot his mother in the back."

Boone's hand trembled as he lifted the sketch and drew it with him as he fell against the slats of his chair.

The parson shifted and swept his hat through his fingers. "I can see from your expression, Colonel, that you are familiar with this visage?"

Boone felt all hope of saving his brother leave him on a sharp exhale. "Yes. This appears to be my brother."

"My wife swears that not more than a few minutes ago, she saw him down in the mercantile. One of the children also identified some tableware as having belonged to her aunt, a member of the attacked wagon train, though the child is not more than a mite."

Boone continued to stare at the sketch in his fingers. He must act. And yet how could he move when it was certain to make him the executioner of his own brother?

He fought the memories of them as boys. He, and Barron, and Brad swinging in the tops of the spindly birches that grew along the banks of the creek. Brad had always been the most daring of them all, willing to leap the farthest, swing the fastest, fall the hardest. He thrived on the thrill of adventure.

For a time, after they'd lost Barron to consumption, Boone had thought that Brad might come around to being the upstanding citizen they'd all been taught to be. Yet here he was, willing himself not to tremble like a greenhorn as he stared down at his brother's face on this sketch. A sketch said to be of the man who had attacked a wagon train.

"Colonel?" The parson interrupted his thoughts.

Boone lifted his gaze to the serious men before him. "He left my office scant minutes ago. My men and I will find him, and we will inquire into the situation. Please return to your wagons and wait to hear from us. If there are those who have witnessed ... crimes ..." Had Brad really shot a woman in the back? It seemed unfathomable. "We will want to hear their testimony."

The minister's hat continued to spin through his fingers. "Children, sir. Three children who are the only survivors. They are currently in the care of my wife, Eden."

Boone rose, willing strength to his legs. "Are they old enough to be certain of what they saw?"

The minister nodded and swung his hat toward the sketch. "Old enough to have created that sketch."

Boone lifted his hat from its peg on the wall. "Then they are old enough to testify to what they have seen. I will fetch my brother. A trial will commence on the morrow at eight sharp. Please bring the children to the church by that time."

"If I may, sir?" The minister held out one hand. "What is the common practice with children such as this? Children who now find themselves without family?"

Boone settled his hat on his head. "If there is no family willing to take them in, my men and I will escort them back to Independence. From there, they will be transported to New York. There is a new organization called The Children's Aid Society there."

"The children say there is a neighbor that might take them in?"

Boone settled his gaze on the man. He looked hopeful. Was he really so naïve? "Are the neighbors related?"

The man shook his head. "No. Not to my understanding."

"Families who live in shantytowns rarely have enough to care for their own children, parson, much less someone else's. The Children's Aid Society will care for the children until families can be found to care for them."

"Families? What kinds of families?"

Boone grew weary of the questions. How should he know what kinds of families? "There are plenty of families who need children who are willing to work, parson. I'm sure the Society makes sure the children are fed and sheltered. Fear not. Now if you'll excuse me..."

With that, he exited the office, leaving the men from the wagon train to trail after him.

He felt as though every ounce of his strength had been sapped. Brad was the last of the Baxters. Betsy, Barron's widow and the owner of the mercantile, was also family, but she was merely a Baxter by marriage. If Boone ordered the execution of his brother, he would be the only Baxter left.

His hand trembled as he laid it on the doorknob at the bottom of the stairs. He had no wife, just Deliverance—his very own little Delilah. And he couldn't leave a legacy of Baxters through her. Even though she was carrying his child, it wasn't the kind he could claim. The thought of Del's baby stirred something warm in him, but it wasn't enough. He wanted descendants he could be proud of—those others would look up to and respect. And Del's child would never be that.

With a grunt, he pushed through into the bustle of the mercantile and then forced himself to walk through and step onto the boardwalk. He must find the strength to arrest his brother on a charge that was sure to be the death of him.

Maybe the death of them both.

For the grief just might do Boone in.

Old enough to have created that sketch.

Brad eased away from Boone's door and slunk down the stairs, heart in his throat.

It sure was a good thing he'd gone up to say goodbye to his brother! He'd been coming back to do just that and had known he was too late when he'd arrived in time to see the door closing behind a troop of men from the wagon train.

His first instinct had been to turn and run, but his second had told him that he'd better take a moment to listen at that door.

Now as he trotted down the stairs from Boone's office, anger burned like a hot coal beneath his breastbone.

Some kid had seen them? He would have said that was impossible! Where had he been hiding?

That didn't matter now. All that mattered was that he stop the witness from ever speaking to anyone else. A sketch could be explained away—especially one drawn by a mere child. But a scrawny little innocent witness? That was harder to brush aside.

The man he'd overheard speaking had been introduced as Parson Adam Houston. The lady in the store had said she was married to a minister. That couldn't be a coincidence, could it? Would there be more than one minister in the same wagon train? Possible, he supposed, but it at least gave him a place to start. He'd seen the wagon she stopped near earlier.

As he breezed through the store, he lifted a hand to Betsy at the front counter. "Riding out, Bets. Good to see you again!"

She lifted her head and offered that kind smile she always had for him. "Bye, Bradley. Stay safe and bring me some baby chicks on your next trip, would you? Coyotes got almost all of mine this year right through the fence of the coop!"

He waved a hand. "I'll see what I can do."

With that, he was out the door and motioning his men closer.

After a few brief instructions, he would implement his plan. It was a good thing he was fast on his feet.

Time was of the essence.

Eden heard the crunch of footsteps outside the wagon and felt her heart ease with relief. The men had returned sooner than she'd expected! She hurried to the back canvas, speaking even before she swept it aside. "Oh, good. You've returned! What did you discov—"

On the other side of the canvas, Brad Baxter stood with a gun in one hand and that black bandana pulled up to just below his eyes. Eyes that glinted as he motioned with his gun for her to get down from the back of the wagon. "Not a word now." He spoke quietly. "Or you and—" He peered past her shoulder. "—these children are done for."

Eden hesitated, feeling a shock of horror sweep through her. In that moment, she knew that whether she went silently or not, she and the children were done for.

But if she called out, they might stand a chance!

She glanced toward the closest wagon, which was Mercy's, and immediately felt the sharp pain of defeat.

She gave her head a little shake. She couldn't live with herself if calling out brought others into danger. Mercy had two boys of her own to care for.

Eden's headache returned like her skull was steel and a blacksmith was trying to pound her into shape.

Brad cast a quick look of assessment toward the fort and then stepped sharply toward her. He reached in and grabbed her arm, giving her a yank. "Move woman, if you know what's best for you!" His whisper was a sharp hiss. "And get those kids out here too."

Oh, Lord. Oh, Lord. Oh, Lord.

Eden turned to the boys and motioned them forward. Was she dooming them to their deaths? It would be certain death *now,* however, if she didn't comply.

Wyatt's eyes were wide and searching as he swept her with a look. Afton had fallen fast asleep while they read from the storybook. She lay sleeping on the pallet at the back of the wagon.

Did the man know how many children there were? Would he notice if she didn't bring her? He'd seen her in the mercantile. And yet from his angle, Afton would be completely hidden by the rumpled quilt.

Eden had to try.

She motioned Asher and Wyatt closer, willing them to read the caution in her eyes. She wasn't sure what had brought Brad Baxter to their wagon, but knew it didn't bode well for Wyatt. Had the man seen the sketch?

Wyatt glanced toward Afton and then back to her. Eden widened her eyes, hoping he could read the warning in her gaze.

"What is taking so long?" Another hiss. "Get out here! This is your last warning."

Eden nudged Asher out first. Helped him descend. Then Wyatt. And then she swung a leg over the tailgate.

The outlaw was next to her in a heartbeat with his gun shoved into her ribs. "Where's the girl?"

Eden continued her descent, bracing for the bullet that would surely end her life at any moment. "The child you saw me with in the mercantile was not mine. I was watching her for her family while they took care of their animals. She's with them now." She had no qualms in offering the lie to a man such as this.

Both Wyatt and Asher shifted, frowning from the man with the gun, to her, and back.

When Eden's feet hit the ground, Brad flicked aside the canvas and scanned the interior of the wagon. Just as Eden had hoped, he didn't climb inside to verify her story. "Fine." He twitched the canvas closed again and motioned with his gun toward the trees along the riverbank in the distance. "She's not old enough to be a witness anyhow, and I'm no baby killer. Start walking. And be quick about it."

Baby killer . . . *Killer!*

Terror washed through Eden, as she tugged Asher close and rested a hand on Wyatt's shoulder. She had to be strong for the boys.

Surely one of the other women would look out of her wagon at any moment and raise an alarm?

No. They'd all been instructed to stay in their wagons until the men returned or they heard fighting.

Brad had been quiet.

Most of the women were probably taking advantage of the rest and were either sleeping or entertaining their children with stories as she had been. They wouldn't be listening to what was happening outside.

She hoped the boys could not feel her quavering as she pressed them forward. None of them said a word. But as they took their first steps, a shiver of fear swept down her spine.

Please, Lord, bring Adam to save us before it's too late.

Fast on the heels of that prayer was the realization that if Adam came for them, he could get hurt. She didn't want that either.

Oh Lord, You know I can't choose between them. We are in Your hands. I rest in You. Give me wisdom and if possible, grant me the lives of these I love.

She swallowed the dryness from her throat.

These that she loved. She suddenly knew without a doubt that she would do everything in her power to save Wyatt and Asher.

But would it be enough?

Chapter 17

Brad felt quite proud of himself as he strode behind the woman and two boys away from the wagon train. He'd thought quickly and acted even more quickly. His swift actions were going to save his life.

One of these two boys had to be the one who had drawn the sketch, right? How old were these kids? The oldest wasn't more than ten, surely. As he'd thought, it couldn't be that good of a sketch. He hadn't seen it, of course, but how good could one ten-year-old draw? Maybe good enough for Boone to recognize him in the drawing, but likely not good enough to condemn him in a court of law!

Either way, he now had the pretty blonde, and what better hostage than that? Hers was certainly a face that people would be willing to trade for—if it came to that. Meanwhile, it certainly wouldn't hurt his feelings to spend some time with her.

He hadn't quite expected *two* boys to be with her, however. No concrete number had been mentioned by the men in Boone's office.

If only he hadn't been in such a hurry, he would have investigated further about the little girl. But the wagon had been empty. So if the little girl really was related to these, she must have been off with a friend in another wagon.

The boys though ... He studied them from behind, prodding the trio to a quicker pace.

As soon as the first of the trees stood between them and the fort, he nudged the woman to the right. He felt relief to be out of sight of the fort.

He shoved the oldest boy toward Donnigan's horse. "Get up there." He didn't bother to keep his voice down now. The other boy he tossed onto the saddle in front of Killingbeck. "You"—he took the woman by her arm and smiled down at her—"get to ride with me."

He boosted her into the saddle and then swung up behind her. Thankfully, his horse was a good strong beast that would tolerate the extra weight for the miles they would need to lose themselves in the forest. He knew a spot on this river that would be a likely place to camp tonight. Then maybe tomorrow they'd cross the river to the north and disappear into the country beyond.

Boone had one of the best trackers around, but Brad's men knew how to brush trail. They'd be fine.

Relief washed through him. He'd done it.

Now all he had to do was work up the courage to kill a kid—two of them. Killingbeck would do it. Maybe not without qualms, but he would do it if ordered to. However, Killingbeck had been angling for his position as the leader of the gang for quite some time. If Brad wanted his men to continue respecting him, this was a job he ought to do himself.

As for the woman, she certainly felt soft and warm, seated here in his arms as she was. He smiled. No matter how appealing she was, he would likely tire of her soon.

Killing her would be easier. He would hide the bodies well, and then he'd be free of this whole sorry mess with no proof against him.

Or maybe he'd let the woman live. Leave her somewhere that she would be found.

People would be grateful for that. Grateful that his kindness kept the woman alive. And that would be one less death on his conscience.

He could decide later.

For now... He motioned to Malkovich. "Hang back and brush our trail."

"Yes, boss." The man turned his horse to follow orders and Brad felt satisfied with his morning's work.

Everything was going to be fine.

***

Eden tried to hold still, but sitting sideways as she was, the saddle horn kept jamming into her thigh. Each time she moved, she could feel the brush of the outlaw's arms penning her in front and back. Sense him leering at her, though she refused to look at him.

A covering canopy of tree branches and green leaves prevented sunlight from penetrating to their path. The forest floor grew dim as they made their way through trees that grew so thick that she could have reached out and touched the trunks several times if she had wanted to. She beseeched God with constant prayers and willed herself not to despair, and yet despair was practically the only emotion she could seem to dredge up at the moment.

Despite that, she determined that she would be strong. Strong until her very last breath. She would not fail these boys in their grief and fear as she had failed Adam when they'd lost their son.

Lord, please grant me the mercy of strength in this dark hour. Help me to think past this pain in my head. You promise not to give us more than we can bear, so if You could just take the pain away, I would ever be grateful. I want to be strong for the—

As though someone had poured a warm balm over the crown of her head, the stabbing pain that had plagued her for weeks dissipated.

It took her a moment to register the healing, and then she almost sobbed in relief.

You, Lord, are good, and ready to forgive, and abundant in mercy to all those who call upon You!

The words from the eighty-sixth Psalm poured from her in gratefulness.

Thank You. Oh, thank You. Please send Adam in time. Keep him and all those with him safe.

She refused to give lodging to the despair that came knocking.

Yay, though I walk through the valley of the shadow of death, I will fear no evil.

She couldn't imagine that the men planned to let her and the boys live. But she would cling to the promises of scripture. She had a big God, and she would trust Him, no matter what He planned to let happen here. If He let her live, she would live for Him with every fiber of her being. If He let her die, she would gladly go to the rest and beauty of heaven, where she knew without a doubt that she would find her son. And yet... These boys still had so much life left to live. For that reason, she turned her prayers to requests for rescue.

Save us, Lord, please? For the boys' sake.

What was Brad's plan? Did he even know that the boys had witnessed the attack on the wagon train?

Surely he'd come after them for that very reason?

"What made you come after us?" The question popped free before she thought better of conversing with her captor.

He snorted. "Knew from the moment I laid eyes on you in the mercantile that something was wrong. Most women..." He raised one hand to stroke the backs of his fingers along her jaw. "... are flattered when I stop to speak to them."

Eden flinched away from his touch and swung her elbow on instinct.

A sharp *crack* shot through the air when her elbow connected with his nose.

"Woman!" He had her throat in the gouging grip of his fingers before she could blink. Breathing hard, with blood dripping over his lips, he glowered into her face. His bloody lips snarled like an angry wolf.

Don't cry. Do not cry. She didn't want to give him the satisfaction of seeing her fear. Men such as this thrived on fear, she felt certain. So despite the fact that his fingers had clamped off her windpipe, she held her breath and tried to remain calm. She glared at him, waiting for either death or release.

But he was patient. He maintained his grip on her throat and calmly glowered into her face with that snarl remaining in place.

Her lungs begged for air, spasming fire through her chest. Black spots floated in her vision. Her body betrayed her and gasped for air that was not available to her. She clawed at the hand around her throat, uselessly.

Felt the blackness seeping in from all sides of her vision now.

Suddenly, he released her with a chuckle. He swiped a hand at the bloody stream seeping down his face and purposely wiped the blood on her skirt.

Eden concentrated on breathing. Her heart thundered her failure in her chest. Both here and back at the mercantile. Had he really been able to read her fear of him so easily?

"Of course"—he continued their conversation as though they hadn't just had a lull where he'd tried to kill her—"when I went upstairs and overheard the men from your wagon train discussing my demise with my brother, I knew I needed to hightail it right on out of town. But I couldn't leave witnesses who could identify me, now could I? Which of those boys drew that sketch? Hmmm? Can't have been that good, is my guess. But good enough that my brother was apparently able to recognize me. However, once the kid is snuffed..." He pinched his blood-stained fingers at the air as though extinguishing a candle flame. "Then I'll meander west. Sadly, I'll never be able to see my brother again, and that vexes me. Sorely vexes me."

Eden drew a shuddery breath through the pain in her throat. "Your brother is a good man, is he?"

Brad made no reply for a long moment as they followed the curve of the path through the trees and the horses clambered down into a shallow creek bed and up the other embankment. Then he said, "Boone would want me to say that he's the very best. A conformer. A great leader of men!" He shouted the last words mockingly, as though the reasoning behind such a virtue escaped him.

"I suppose he'll never stop looking for you then." Eden tucked her lip between her teeth. Hadn't she learned her lesson? She oughtn't poke the bear.

Just as she'd feared, he rapped his knuckles along the side of her head. "Shut yer mouth. No more talking."

Eden gladly complied.

Adam felt a mixture of consternation and relief as he hurried with the rest of the men from the fort to the wagon train. The colonel seemed to be a reasonable man. The meeting had gone peacefully. None of them had even needed to raise their voices to be heard.

And now the colonel was off with his soldiers, looking for his no-account brother, as he had labeled the man.

When Adam had first learned that the men shared a last name, he'd been trepidatious. But he felt marginally better about the whole thing now that he had met the colonel. After all, one didn't rise to the position of colonel of a fort without having some strength of character. Even so... a small part of his mind lingered in worry. Could the man be trusted?

An even greater portion lingered in concern over the children. *Families who need children who are willing to work... Fed and sheltered.*

He swallowed. That was no way to talk about caring for a child. They had needs beyond mere food and clothing. Needs like love, nurturing, discipline, spiritual teaching. Children needed a home. Not a structure, but a community of people working together for the betterment of each other.

He gave his head a shake. They could decide what to do after the trial. And if they decided to keep the children? Who would there be to protest such an action? According to Wyatt, no one was left to even know that they were in need.

He had just determined to push thoughts of the children from his mind when he heard the crying.

Afton.

He hurried his steps, feeling sure that Eden was more than ready for a break from the children. He hoped she hadn't overtaxed herself with this whole situation.

At the back of the wagon, he climbed up. Thrust his way through the canvas. Froze.

Afton sat on the pallet at the back of the space, eyes glassy and red, and curls spiraling from her head in every direction. She sniffed. Scrambled off the bed and toddled toward him, arms raised.

"Hey there, moppet." Adam lifted her up, rubbed her back, and scanned the remainder of the wagon with his heart pounding against his ribs.

Empty.

Afton flopped her chin onto his shoulder and wrapped her stubby arms as far around him as they would go.

He swallowed and closed his eyes, allowing himself the briefest of moments to relish the feeling of having another trust in him so completely. "It's okay. I've got you now." He mumbled the words mindlessly as he frowned.

Eden would never go off and leave this child alone! Where were she and the boys?

Terror clawed through him.

God of all mercy, please . . .

He spun and climbed out—an awkward maneuver with a child in his arms. He scanned the area but saw no movement other than the other men who were just reaching their wagons. A few swift strides took him to the rear of Micah and Mercy's.

"Excuse me?" he called. "May I speak to Mercy for a moment, please?"

Micah swept back the canvas and peered down at him. He held a hammock, of all things, in one hand. Mercy stood right behind him in the narrow aisle between their supplies that were stacked high on either side. Humor danced in Micah's eyes—over some shared joke with his wife, perhaps—but the moment Micah assessed Adam with Afton in his arms, all humor faded. "Of course." Micah set the hammock on top of some crates and descended. He turned and helped lift his wife to the ground.

Adam spoke before they were both settled. "Have you seen Eden? The boys?"

"What?" Mercy turned on him, eyes wide. "They aren't in your wagon?"

Adam's heart sank at the surprise on her face. He'd hoped she would know something. Maybe one of the boys had needed a quick trip into the brush, or... No other logical explanation came to mind.

He scanned the vast emptiness of the plains, the horizon, the circumference of the wagons stretching in a circle. No Eden. No Wyatt. No Asher. Only a few trees a ways off to the north—along the river maybe.

He swallowed. "Mercy, did you hear anything out of the ordinary?"

Mercy hung her head, and Micah swept his arm around her shoulders, tugging her close. She swept a dark lock of hair behind her ear. "I'm sorry. The children and I fell fast asleep, and Micah woke me just now as he returned. But surely if—" She frowned. "—something had happened, I would have heard a commotion?"

The words hit Adam as surely as though she'd swung a bat. He patted Afton's back, even as he took a bracing backward step. He felt as though he had to pull every thought from deep mud. "She's gone. She and the boys are gone."

Micah touched his shoulder, then swept past. "I'll fetch the others, and you can tell us all at once."

Mercy stretched out her arms. "Please let me take the little one. She can rest with the boys inside."

Adam hesitated, suddenly reluctant to release the girl into another's care. What if something happened to her too? Then he'd have no one again.

Guilt slammed home. He closed his eyes. *Yes, Lord. I know I will always have You and Your Word says You will never leave me nor forsake me.*

And this child wasn't even his.

"I'll keep her in my sights at all times."

Mercy's words opened his eyes. She stood before him with arms outstretched.

"Thank you." She was right. It was only logical that he leave Afton here while he and the men tried to find Eden and the boys. But my, how his arms felt barren after he'd passed the little girl over to Mercy. "Thank you so much." He motioned to her wagon. "Here. Let me help you climb up."

She nodded, and he took her elbow and steadied her as she climbed into the back of the conveyance with Afton clinging to her neck. The poor child seemed content to be held by anyone so long as she wasn't alone.

Mercy cradled the girl as she turned to look down at him. "I'll be praying, Parson."

"Thank you." Adam dipped his chin.

Men were already gathering around him as Mercy disappeared behind the canvas.

Striker Moss approached, stark concern etching his features. "Tell us what's happened?"

Adam wagged his head. "I don't know. When I arrived at the wagon, Eden and the boys were not there, and Afton was all alone." Adam scanned the surrounding area one more time, trying to quash the illogical hope that begged for Eden and the boys to appear out of thin air. He gripped the back of his neck. "Eden would never have left the little one alone like that unless . . ." He couldn't bring himself to finish that sentence.

Adam felt a hand on his shoulder and turned to find Micah. The man gave him a nod before releasing him. "We're going to help you find them."

"Yes." Striker raised his voice. "Here's what we are going to do. You three . . ."

Striker's words faded into a blur. Adam felt relief at having someone else take charge of a situation he felt so ill-equipped for.

What was he going to do if he lost Eden again? More than that, he now had the worry over the boys, too. He'd realized when Wyatt went missing the other day, with that herd of bison looming, that he was fighting a losing battle against growing too attached to the children. But it surprised him how much concern filled him for them as well. He'd gone and done the very thing that he'd been praying Eden wouldn't do—fallen in love with those children.

Adam swallowed. *God, please . . .*

"Right, we meet back here in ten minutes," Striker said.

Adam blinked, realizing he didn't know what he ought to be doing.

It was Micah who came to his rescue again. He thumped him on the back. "You're with me, Parson. We follow Cody Hawkeye starting at the back of your wagon. First, we need to get our horses."

Adam nodded, once again relieved to have another making decisions for him.

At least his heartbeat wasn't hammering so rapidly against his sternum now.

Chapter 18

In the dark basement beneath the Fort Kearny mercantile, Deliverance shivered. The warmth of spring had not yet reached this cold, dank room. The chain's cuff cut sharply into her wrist, and she gritted her teeth and propped that arm on her head to ease the pressure on the joint. The sole light that filtered into this basement room came from a six-inch window in the foundation near the stairs that led up to the mercantile. All the supplies for the mercantile were stored down here.

Master had insisted that this would be her life for some time now. Her own fault, he had said, because he couldn't trust that she wouldn't run off. She puffed a sharp breath. He was right on that count. If she could just get loose of these chains, she would have a whole day's head start on her escape.

But the cuffs were tight. And lands, her arms hurt, chained to the ring in the wall above her head as they were.

Her belly grumbled too, but naught would be done about that till evening, so she may as well disregard it. Back on the plantation, at least she'd had work to keep her mind off her hunger. She'd had the warmth of the sun streaming into the office where she'd kept the books, and the songs that the palm leaves had sung in the breezes just outside the open windows. But chained here like a dog to a tree, the hunger pangs ate at her, especially pestered as she was with the scents of coffee, pickles from the barrel to her right, and the grainy scents of beans and sacks of wheat.

Thinking about such things would do her no good. Master kept the chains short enough to ensure she couldn't reach any of the foodstuffs.

Instead, she turned her focus on the bolt her chains were looped through. She might not be able to get her cuffs off, but if she could get that bolt unscrewed from the wall...

Now there was a task to keep her mind off her hunger.

The problem was, she'd tried day in and day out to unscrew that bolt, but had never succeeded. The bolt was nigh on half an inch thick and her hands were not strong enough to unscrew it from the hardwood of the log it had been driven into.

Despairing of trying again today, she shifted to try to find a more comfortable spot and her skirt tugged against something.

Metal clattered loudly against the floor.

Del's heart jolted, and she spun to face the mercantile door. She wasn't sure what she'd bumped against, but surely that clanging had been heard above stairs? She was sure to get it now! Yet after two minutes passed with the door remaining closed, she turned to study the shadows near her feet. What had she knocked over?

Whatever it was, Master must not have seen it in the darkness of the basement when he'd brought her down today. Always, she was out of sight before the doors of the mercantile opened for the day. One day, she'd tried yelling when she heard the floorboards creak with the footsteps of a customer overhead, but only a moment later, Master had appeared. His fist had split her lip and knocked her out for most of that day. Her head had ached something fierce for days afterward, and she'd spent most of those days in a drowsy half-sleep—as much sleep as she could get chained to a wall with her arms above her head. That had been weeks ago, and she hadn't relished the thought of what he might do to her if she tried again, so she'd never called out a second time. She'd been biding her time.

Her eyes adjusted to the shadows, and she found the object. A pry bar! They used it sometimes to adjust the gears of the small grist mill in the mercantile. She hadn't even seen it herself at first, leaning against the wall in the darkness as it must have been.

But now her heart soared, because she knew the Lord had answered her prayers.

She stretched out her leg and used the toe of her boot to scoot the bar closer. The problem was that her chains were short enough that she couldn't bend all the way to the floor to pick the bar up. But maybe if she could balance the bar on the toe of her boot and lift it close enough to her hands...

She rolled the bar until it clunked against the wall, snatching glances at the mercantile door. Master Boone would be up in his office now, but what about Miss Betsy? If the proprietress caught her, would she inform Boone? The woman surely didn't like her warming the master's bed. Deliverance had seen her frown on more than one occasion when Master Boone fetched her from the basement of an evening. But the woman always had a hot plate ready for her, and for that Del would ever be grateful. Many a woman she'd known would have made her fend for herself in the kitchen.

After Betsy's husband had passed away, had the woman set her sights on Master Boone? She'd certainly been none too happy when Master returned from that trip to Georgia with Del in tow. And yet, despite her frowns, the woman had treated her decently. Well, except for the fact that she seemed to make no protest about Master Boone chaining her in the basement.

Deliverance twisted her lips grimly at that thought. No. She couldn't rely on that woman.

Seeing the stairs remained clear, Del stepped on the sharp end of the pry bar. This lifted the other end just enough for her to get the toe of her boot beneath the bar. She worked her foot to the middle of the bar and, with the help of the wall, balanced the tool on her foot as she attempted to lift it near enough to grab. This was complicated by the fact that to lower one hand, she had to raise the other. And the higher she raised her foot, the more awkward her balance.

With her left hand thrust high, she leaned to the right to reach for the bar, but her balance was thrown off, and the bar tipped and clanged back to the floor.

Heart in her throat, Del spun to look at the stairs. If this noise continued, she would surely catch another beating.

The door remained closed, however.

Del repeated the process, balancing the bar, leaning to her right. Her fingers grazed against the cool metal. She nipped her tongue between her lips. Just... a little... more!

At last, she had the pry bar in her grip. Her eyes fell closed as she relished the heft of the thick metal against her palm.

Lord, Your graciousness is forever true. Your kindness to this daughter never fails. I have tried to serve my master faithfully, as Your Word says. But now You know that I got reason to run. Go before me, please, Father of Mercy. Lead me. Provide a way of escape.

She reached up and slipped the bar into the eyebolt. It wouldn't go all the way through because of the chain that was also in the bolt, but it slipped in far enough to give her leverage. She worked both hands to the farthest end of the bar and used her weight to pry downward.

The bolt twisted! Elation surged. She clamped her teeth against a cry of excitement. Gathering herself, she inserted the end of the bar into the bolt at the new angle and twisted again.

As the bolt continued to loosen, her heart hammered harder and harder. She would have to escape with the manacles still on her wrists, because the pry bar would do nothing to help her with those.

How would she get out of this basement without being seen?

She paused the turning of the bar.

She must think. Be smart. Plan.

For she would only get one chance at escape. And she needed to make it.

Please, Lord. I'm begging for the life of this child that You know I didn't have no choice in creating.

Tamsyn stood at the tailgate of her wagon, brushing away crumbs from the biscuits Edi had eaten rather messily. "Edi, when you make a mess, you have to help me by cleaning up after yourself, okay? All you have to do is brush these crumbs onto the ground."

"But then—" He gestured to the ground. "—crumbs in the dirt."

"Yes, I know. But the birds or bugs will eat what they want, and the rest will melt in the rain."

"Okay. Edi do better next time." He slumped over to sit on one of the rocks she'd rolled near their fire. He picked up the stick he'd been whittling.

Tamsyn smiled at her brother's back. At least he was willing to say he'd try—whether he would remember, only time would tell.

Tamsyn felt weary at the prospect of the future that lay before her. She loved her brother. Wouldn't want anyone else caring for him. Yet the dreary years of cleaning up after him stretched into the distance. Dreary years of loneliness because she wouldn't want to burden anyone else with this life. She frowned at herself and shook the thoughts away. This was all Striker Moss's fault! Before she'd met that man, she'd been more than content to think of taking care of Edi and it being just the two of them.

But . . . She gave herself a mental shake. She wouldn't dwell on what her brother might cost her when it hadn't even been offered to her. Striker was a kind man simply doing his duty to those in their party. When he brought her meat, he brought it to many others also. A few days back, when he had helped her soak her wheel which was getting too dry and coming loose from the rim, he'd helped Hiram Hawthorne, too. And yet, the way he looked at her . . . The warmth of his fingers that sometimes lingered around hers just a little longer than propriety allowed . . .

No. Stop.

She was tired. That must be the reason dreams were leading her on a fanciful chase. While they were here at the fort she would try to rest. She'd been to the mercantile and purchased the supplies she and Edi could afford, which hadn't been much. A little more coffee for Edi. And a small packet of sugar.

Despite her thankfulness for the rest, she hoped this stop at the fort would not take them long. She wanted to get Edi to their property in the Oregon Territory and get on with the rest of their lives. The sooner they were settled and in a routine, the sooner the routine with Edi would be easier.

Striker rounded the end of the wagon, and almost made her gasp.

Confound it. She'd only just managed to stop thinking about him.

He held his hat in his hands and looked far too handsome for her good.

Suddenly, she registered his expression and straightened. "What is it?"

"Eden and the boys have gone missing—"

"What?" Shock sagged her against the edge of the tailgate. She was selfish to her core, hoping he'd come to talk to her when he'd come to tell her of a tragedy. "Wait, you said 'boys.' What about Afton?"

Striker pointed to the Morrans' wagon. "She's with Mercy at the moment."

Well that was something at least.

"Is she hurt?" When she lurched upright, he thrust up one palm.

"She seemed fine. We're about to ride out to get the others back."

"Get them back? Did someone take them?" Someone from the fort? Why would anyone want to harm dear, sweet Eden? Had it been discovered that the children were witnesses?

He merely lifted a shoulder. "I just wanted you to be aware that your doctoring might be needed if—when—we return."

"Who has them?"

He frowned and scanned the prairie surrounding them. The trees in the distance. "We don't rightly know. But Eden told Adam that she saw the man from Wyatt's sketch—the man who attacked the Slade party—in the mercantile. We went to report this to the colonel, and when we got back . . . She wasn't in their wagon." A grim note of worry rang in Striker's voice.

Tamsyn tugged at the small ribbon at her throat. "You think he has them." And Striker would be riding right into the heart of the conflict with a cold-blooded murderer.

"Likely." He withdrew a step, the brim of his hat curled in one hand. "I have to go."

"Be careful." Tamsyn lowered her gaze to the tailgate and frowned at herself. She had no right to tell the man to be careful. She rushed to add, "I'll double-check my herbs and keep water on to boil in case there are wounds to tend."

Edi shifted from his seat near the coals of the fire. "Edi see that man."

"You what?" Striker's voice rang sharp with excitement.

Edi seemed taken aback for a moment, and Tamsyn rushed to reassure him. "It's okay, Edi. Mr. Moss is happy that you did. Can you tell us what you saw?"

Edi pointed toward the Houstons' wagon, then seemed to change his mind and pointed to the tall grass next to their own. "Edi lay there."

Tamsyn could see the indent where Edi had apparently been resting in the grass.

He pointed at the sky. "Clouds make pretty pictures." Now his finger swung back toward the Houstons' prairie schooner. "Ms. Eden and the boys, they walked away. With a man."

"Only one?" Striker seemed to have purposely gentled his voice for her brother's sake.

Edi lifted one shoulder. Nodded.

"Can you tell me which direction they went?"

Edi swung a finger toward the north. The Platte River would form a barrier not too far out there. Hope filled Tamsyn for the briefest of moments, but then dread rushed in on its heels to chase it away. Just as the river might keep the kidnappers from going too far, it also might hasten Eden and the boys' demise.

Striker clapped his hat onto his head. "You're a good man, Edi. A good man."

"Miss Acheson!" One of the oldest Hawthorne girls rushed toward them. "Please come. It's my ma. I think her time has come!"

Striker retreated a hasty step, looking as uncomfortable with this new information as an ox in a milking pen. He withdrew another stride, shoving his broad, blunt fingers through that mass of wild hair. "I— I'll just let you deal with that." He swung his hat toward the blonde girl, then plunked it on his head, tugged the brim in Tamsyn's direction, and hurried off.

Tamsyn bit back her humor as she watched him flee. *Lord, bring him back safely. Them. All of them.*

She forced herself to calmly take up her bag of herbs and wrapped one arm around the girl's shoulder, directing her back toward her mother's wagon. "Are you Wren or Whitley?"

"Wren, miss."

"Right, Wren. Let's see about helping this new sibling of yours into the world, shall we?"

"Siblings. At least... all us kids are laying odds toward that outcome."

Tamsyn smiled, tamping down her trepidation over bringing multiple babies into the world. "Won't that be grand? Do you know how long ago your mother's pains started?"

She glanced over her shoulder toward where the men were mounting up. Striker, who was already seated on his big red horse, offered her a bold grin and another tug of his hat brim. She dipped her chin quickly, then snapped her attention back in the direction of the Hawthorne wagon. Had he been watching to see if she would look back?

She felt heat prickle along her neck beneath her collar. And drat if she didn't suddenly realize that Wren had responded to her question about the beginning of her mother's labor, but she'd missed the answer.

She would not think about Striker Moss for one more moment. She simply wouldn't.

The sound of slow-flowing water grew stronger as the horse emerged from the forest, and Eden could see a low, flat river drifting between shallow riverbanks.

When Brad called his men to a halt, Eden knew she and the boys didn't have much time. Brad swung down and then reached to pluck her from the back of the horse.

She almost groaned from the tingling pain in her lower extremities. Her legs and back were stiff and sore from balancing sideways as she had been.

Brad motioned to one of his men. "Get a fire going. Got a hankering for a good meal. So before we . . . take care of business." He curved a hand around her upper arm and leered down at her. "You can cook, can't you?"

Eden nodded.

"Good." He thrust her toward the man who was laying rocks in a circle. "As soon as Killingbeck has a fire going, you're going to cook us a meal." Brad stalked off, leading his horse behind. "Donnigan, set up a corral!" he snapped. "Malkovich, get in that maple and keep an eye out."

The lone tree stood apart from the other trees on the riverbank, and would give anyone in its branches a good advantage for miles in several directions. Only the forest they had come through between the fort and the river would offer any concealment.

Both Asher and Wyatt had been set on the ground as well, and as the outlaws all moved to unsaddle their mounts, they looked at her wide-eyed. Eden stretched her arms to them, and both boys ran to her.

Eden pulled them close, relishing the feel of their warm little bodies full of life as she wrapped them in her embrace.

Wyatt looked up at her. "That's the man... these are the men who—"

She touched his cheek. No matter how much she wanted to reassure him, she couldn't lie. "I know. We must stay calm. Adam will come for us just as soon as he discovers we are missing."

Wyatt glanced back the way they'd come, worry filling his expression. "We rode a long time."

Eden knew the worry filling his eyes stemmed from the fact that Adam and the men from the wagon train might not reach them in time. She pulled Asher tighter into her side and touched Wyatt's chin. "The Bible says that God knew all the days ordained for us before we were even born. We will trust Him, okay?"

Asher nodded, but surprisingly it was Wyatt's eyes that filled with tears. "But what about Afton?"

Eden snatched him in tight again and rested her chin atop his head. The boy's life was in danger, and yet he was worried about who would take care of his little sister. Eden pressed a kiss into the mop of his hair. "Adam will take good care of her, I promise you that."

"But he doesn't even want us."

Eden's heart felt like it might crack in two. She eased back enough to touch Wyatt's chin. "Sometimes, when a person has experienced a tragedy that almost broke them, the prospect of facing that same situation again seems more than they can bear. Adam has a big heart. No matter the words that he's spoken. He'll come for us. Not just for me. For us."

Wyatt dashed the hem of his sleeve at his tears. "Okay."

Asher tugged at her skirt and thrust a short finger at the ground.

Eden glanced to where he had pointed into the shadow that lay on the shady side of a long white piece of deadwood. Her eyes widened. Growing in the shade were several mushrooms, bright red with white spots on the caps.

"Oh, we mustn't eat those, they are likely poisonous."

The little boy only nodded, then glanced toward the fire being built.

Eden's heart pumped hard in her chest. "Asher, you're a genius!" She strode over and sank onto the log, spreading her skirts and patting the space on either side of her for the boys to sit. She leaned down and felt for the mushrooms as she spoke to them. "You see? The Lord is providing for our safety already." She slipped one mushroom into the pocket of her skirt and reached for another. She ignored the pang of guilt she felt at the words. Would the Lord really provide for the harming of someone, even if they were the lowest kind of men imaginable?

"What are you three doing over here?" Brad's footsteps crunched through the brush behind them.

Eden snatched her hands into her lap and folded them. She glanced over her shoulder at him. "Just waiting for the fire to be built so I can start cooking."

Her heart hammered. She'd only managed to pick one mushroom. How many would it take to render these men inert?

Horror swept through her at the thought of what she was about to do. Was that God trying to warn her not to follow through?

She didn't want to kill them! How many mushrooms would it take to kill a man?

Yet, what were the chances that Brad would have set her down and commanded her to cook, and they'd have looked down to see a patch of mushrooms? She had to think that the Lord had provided just such an escape, and she must fight for the lives of these children. *Lord, You know that I've no desire to harm these men. Please help me and guide me.*

The bright red mushrooms would need to go into a stew if they were to be disguised. "What exactly is it that I'm to cook for you?"

She held her breath, waiting for his answer even as she felt Asher's little hand slip into the pocket of her skirt and then slip back out again. She wanted to warn him not to put his fingers anywhere near his mouth until they could wash, but with Brad leaning over them now, and the fact that Asher had been the one to point the mushrooms out, she could only hope that the boy already knew that.

Brad thrust a pot that contained a long spoon into her hand. "Fetch water." He waved a hand toward the drifting river. "Donnigan is getting us a hare right now. And here—" He slapped a small bag into her palm. "—is the rice you'll need. Always been partial to rabbit and rice soup." He leered at her. Swept her with a glance. "After we eat, maybe you and I will have a little fun back in the trees for a few minutes."

Horror crashed over Eden.

When he stalked away, she snatched up two more large mushrooms and dropped them in the pot. Both the boys added another mushroom each.

Gracious heavens! Were they going to kill this whole group of outlaws?

Eden stood and glanced down. They'd plucked all the mushrooms from the patch, and grass had filled in where the stems had been. Only because she knew the mushrooms had been growing there a moment earlier could she tell that something was missing.

"What are you waiting for?" Brad bellowed at her from where he was brushing his horse down with a handful of grass. "Get that meal cooking and don't try running off. I'm keeping an eye on you!"

"I'm going now." Eden motioned for the boys to join her as she hurried toward the Platte. "Rinse your hands carefully, both of you. And whatever you do, do not eat even one bite of this soup, understand?"

They both nodded.

Chapter 19

Adam and Micah had just returned with their saddled mounts to meet Cody at the back of the wagon when Striker trotted up on his big Morgan.

He pointed toward the north. "Cody, concentrate in this direction. Edi says that he saw Eden and the boys walking away with a man and that they headed this direction."

Just like that, Adam's heart was pounding again like a blacksmith working an anvil. But this time his thinking was clear. He swung into his saddle, impatient to get moving. Were they going to have to wait around for Cody to hunt up a trail? Where was the man's horse?

Cody broke into a long-legged lope, his gaze firmly fastened to the ground. He waved over his shoulder for them to keep up. "Been scouting already. Edi's right."

Adam exchanged a look with Micah as they reined their horses in behind Cody.

"You think he's going to slow us down without a horse?" Micah asked Striker.

Striker smiled and nudged his mount into a trot in Cody's wake. "I've seen Cody run at that speed all night before."

Adam shared another look with Micah. He was suddenly thankful to have the man helping him find Eden. It was much easier to follow sign from the ground than from horseback. He might not be the best of trackers, but even he knew that much.

They'd only been trotting for about five minutes when Cody shot up one fist. "They mounted horses. Wait here so you don't mar any tracks." They halted and waited as Cody moved cautiously into the shadows of a thick forest. From his saddle, Adam could see tall oaks, shorter hickory and walnut trees, and low-growing, scrubby ironwood. The path Cody had entered was narrow, and judging by the thickness of the canopy, it would be dark in there.

He swallowed. He didn't want to ride these men right into an ambush.

But neither could he afford to delay. Eden and the children's lives depended on it. His impatience grew.

After a few anxious moments, Adam called into the woods, "What's the hold-up?"

Cody stepped back into the sunlight with a glower. He held up a hand for silence. He silently jogged the paces back to the mounted men and spoke in a voice so quiet Adam almost didn't make out his words.

"They brushed their trail, but I'll find it." With a press of his finger to his lips, he said, "Voices carry across these plains." Then he disappeared into the forest again.

Adam felt his impatience rise as he and the men sat on their horses and bided their time. His horse shifted beneath him, apparently having sensed his tension. Back in the darkness of those trees, anything could be happening to Eden and the boys!

Striker eased his mount closer and kept his voice to a whisper when he spoke. "If anyone can find these crooks, it's Cody."

As though to prove him right, Cody appeared and waved for them to join him. He started forward in that long lope of his again.

Relief surged through Adam, and he was the first to heel his horse into the shadows of the forest path. At least they were moving forward.

Eden hunkered down next to the trickling creek and let water fill the pot. The mushrooms inside floated to the top. She gave the water a quick swirl, dumped it off, and then filled the pot again. With a quick glance over her shoulder, she pulled a mushroom from her pocket, gave it a quick rinse in the creek, and then broke it into little pieces in the pot. Another glance, and another mushroom fell to pieces beneath the ministration of her fingers. After a quick swirl in the creek to rinse yet another, she realized the irony over the fact that she was rinsing mushrooms that she hoped would harm the men who were about to consume them. After that, she set to rapidly breaking up the red caps, and soon, they were all broken into little bits and waterlogged enough that they had sunk to the bottom of the pot.

She stared at them. Was this the right thing to do? Beside her, Asher shifted, and she glanced into his blue eyes. One of his curls fell across his forehead, and Eden reached to swipe it back. His hair was such a unique color, mahogany at the roots, but sun-bleached gold at the tips. His head was warm and full of life beneath her hand. On her other side, Wyatt looked up at her with the same blue eyes his brother had, but with golden hair instead. If she didn't fight for these boys' lives, each made so unique in the image of God, who would? There was no one else here to do it.

Decision made, she emptied the measure of rice into the pot on top of the mushrooms and felt satisfied to see that the rice completely covered the bits of red.

"What's taking you so long over here?"

Brad's voice coming from directly behind made her gasp. The burbling of the river must have kept her from hearing his footsteps. Had he seen anything?

She stood slowly, bringing the pot with her as she turned to face him.

"Well?" He glanced suspiciously from her to the pot in her hands and back.

She lifted her chin. "Do you think I'm in a hurry to cook what is likely to be my last meal?" She would not cry. "What is likely to be these children's last meal?"

Brad clapped a hand over his heart. "Aw. I'm touched. You're right. I should really just let you all go."

Unlikely hope flared. She searched his face only to see his lips twist into a mocking smile. With a little shove, he urged her toward the fire. "The hare is skinned and waiting for you."

Eden was suddenly worried about the taste of the mushrooms. Would the men be able to detect them with the first bite? She'd tried to break them into small enough bits that they would fade into the texture of the rice. But maybe . . . "Do you have any salt or spices? A stew is always better with a hint of flavor."

"Fresh out." He pressed one hand to the middle of her back and thrust her forward. "We'll just have to make do."

Eden glanced into the pot and caught a glimpse of red peeking through the grains of rice as the water sloshed with her steps. Her throat felt as though it were gripped in a fist. What if the mushrooms turned the stew red? Would the men notice something like that?

She stumbled forward, feeling the noose of their time on this earth slipping over her head.

It would be a miracle if she could pull this off. *Lord, please, for the children's sakes.*

Deliverance wanted to give a shout of victory when the bolt finally came loose from the log above her head. Her arms ached something fierce as she finally was able to lower them to her sides. She almost cried with the relief of it.

But her chains clanked too loudly in the darkness of the basement. With each movement, it felt as though a bell were clanging to announce her escape. How was she ever going to get away with all that noise following her every step?

She despaired at having made it this far without a way to attain full freedom. Besides, how was she going to get out of this basement without having to go through the store upstairs? Even if there were no customers, Betsy would still be there behind the counter, and the basement door opened just beside the counter. She'd never be able to move in these clanking chains without drawing Betsy's attention. And then Master Boone would be just up the stairs in his office.

She needed to ponder and think. Come up with a plan. For, to run without thought would certainly be the death of her.

Lord, You surely didn't allow me to find that pry bar near to hand and make an escape without forethought. Please help me to be calm and clear thinking. You know I don't ask that for myself.

Her stomach rumbled as her hunger prodded for recognition.

Del glanced around the basement. To her right was the barrel of pickles. On a shelf to her left, strips of jerky were stored in jars. Tins of hardtack sat next to the jerky. And a crate of oranges sat in a shaft of light that filtered through the tiny window.

Her mouth watered at the thought of one of those oranges.

Master Boone ate one every evening after he brought her upstairs, but all she was ever allowed was whatever plate Betsy had fixed for dinner and a bowl of oats and a glass of milk in the morning.

Despite her hunger, she feared moving. Could she reach the oranges without alerting anyone upstairs? Would Betsy notice an orange missing when she came down later to fetch Master Boone's?

Del assessed her chains. The one between her feet was short. If she pressed her legs wide enough, she could keep enough tension on that one to keep it from making too much sound. The ones on her arms were longer to keep her tied to the bolt high above her head. However . . . As quietly as she could, she gathered them close and tucked most of the links into the crook of her left arm, leaving herself only enough free chain so that her right arm could move a little.

Feet pressed wide, she pigeon-walked her way across the cellar to that crate of tempting fruit, wincing at each tiny clank the chains made. She bent and reached for an orange. One of the chains in her left arm tumbled free and clattered against the edge of the crate with a loud clang.

Del froze and jerked her gaze to the door just up the stairs. If anyone opened that door, they would immediately see her standing here. After several heartbeats, it seemed no one was coming. Maybe they couldn't hear the chains as loudly above stairs as they sounded in her ears here in this enclosed space?

Del took up one of the oranges, moved to the jars of jerky, and opened one to extract a thick piece of meat. She also opened a tin and took a small piece of hardtack from within. She debated on a larger piece, but hardtack always made her dreadfully thirsty, and a quick scan around the remainder of the shelves didn't reveal any canned juices, so she held herself to one small piece.

She ought to stay close to her proper position in case she needed to move quickly to make it seem like she was still chained to the wall. With that thought, she returned near to where she was kept chained and sank onto a barrel, piling her pilferings atop the chains in her lap.

She lifted the orange and inhaled the scent, long and slow. Her stomach rumbled again. Her hands shook as she went to work peeling off the skin of the fruit in one long spiral, like her mama had shown her back on the plantation. They used to see who could form the longest spring of orange peel. Just the memory of that brought tears to her eyes. Was Mama still working for Master Hampton? Or had she been sold off to another by now?

If she could escape, maybe she would go back home to find out. But it did seem rather foolish to try to travel through the South as a single black woman. As she nibbled on one section of the orange, savoring the burst of citric juices across her tongue, she also fought despair. Even if she escaped from here, where would she go? Where *could* she go?

She made herself set the orange aside and eat the hardtack first. Then the jerky. Finally, she allowed the juicy sections of fruit to quench her thirst.

She tilted her head back against the wall and whispered, "I cried out to You, O Lord: I said, 'You are my refuge, my portion in the land of the living.'" She let the reminder from the one hundred and forty-second Psalm wash over her.

She would fight to live. But if she didn't make an escape, she would take comfort in the Lord and rest in Him.

With her belly finally full—how long since she'd felt this satiated?—weariness washed over her. She tipped her head against the wall and closed her eyes.

Sleep overtook her before she could think better of it.

With the hare immersed in the water, Eden hefted the pot over the flames and rested it onto the tripod of rocks that one of the outlaws had placed in the center of the flames.

Her stomach rumbled, and she almost chuckled. She would not be satisfying her hunger with the stew in this pot!

That thought raised a concern. What were she and the boys going to do if the outlaws noticed they weren't eating?

As the water heated she kept an eye on the stew, concerned that the red of the mushrooms would give them away, but once the water was boiling, the brown of the rabbit meat darkened the stew and when she trepidatiously gave it a stir, she was relieved to see that the bits of mushrooms had faded and blended into the rice. Nearby, she found a patch of wood sorrel with its bright yellow flowers just coming into bloom. She plucked several handfuls and tossed them into the stew.

"What did you just put in there?" Brad demanded.

Eden willed herself to be calm as he walked over and stared into the pot. "That is wood sorrel. It will add a lovely flavor to the stew."

Brad pinned her with a glare. "You think I'm stupid?"

"No. Why would you ask that?" She willed herself to continue stirring the stew calmly.

"You trying to poison us?"

Eden strode back to the patch of wood sorrel and plucked off several of the leaves, then stuffed them into her mouth and set to chewing. Once she had swallowed, she asked, "Satisfied?"

Brad was still frowning, but he did stalk away toward the river. As he did so, he snapped his fingers at the man he'd called Killingbeck. "I'm going into the brush. Keep an eye on her and make sure she don't add nothing else to that pot."

Eden breathed a sigh of relief. The sorrel would add more color to the stew and darken the broth. She wanted these men to get as much of this soup into their gullets as possible before one of them might notice something amiss.

Please, Lord. Bring Adam to us quickly.

It had been her constant prayer since she and the boys had been marched away from the wagon train.

How long had they been missing? Adam had been at the fort. Had anyone even noticed their absence yet? Had Afton woken? Eden pushed away that worry. She wouldn't be able to live with herself if anything happened to that child because she'd been trying to save her. Of course, she might never know one way or the other until she reached heaven.

To live is Christ. To die is gain.

Eden's gaze moved to the boys, once again. They huddled on the ground, with their backs to a log. Wyatt had his arms around his brother's shoulders, and he glowered fiercely at any of the men who stepped into his line of vision. Asher had tears tracking his cheeks.

Eden strode to them and sank down beside Asher. She reached one arm behind him until she had settled her hand on Wyatt's far shoulder and drawn him close. Sandwiched between them, Asher looked up at her with soulful eyes. Eden took one of his little hands in her free one. "I know you are scared." She squeezed Wyatt's shoulder. "We're all scared."

Wyatt shook his head vehemently. "I'm not scared."

Eden let the lie pass. She knew he was scared. But there was more too. And how well she knew that dark anger that accompanied the terror of the unknown. The terror over wondering how to go on living after so much loss. The terror of wondering if life would ever feel good again. And now the fear for their lives.

How did she help him? Words certainly wouldn't have reached her during the peak of her anger.

The hymn came to her unbidden, and she was singing before she thought better of it.

> *"Sweet hour of prayer! Sweet hour of prayer!*
> *That calls me from a world of care,*
> *And bids me at my Father's throne*
> *Make all my wants and wishes known.*
> *In seasons of distress and grief,*
> *My soul has often found relief,*
> *And oft escaped the tempter's snare,*
> *By thy return, sweet hour of prayer!"*

Wyatt had seemed to relax beneath the stroking of her hand across his shoulder, and he dropped his head onto his knees.

She'd meant to stop singing, for fear the men would get upset with her for the sound. But seeing how it had eased Wyatt, and Asher too, who had relaxed into her side, she searched for the next words. None would come to her, save the last verse.

> *"Sweet hour of prayer! Sweet hour of prayer!*
> *May I thy consolation share,*
> *Till, from Mount Pisgah's lofty height,*

I view my home and take my flight.
This robe of flesh I'll drop, and rise
To seize the everlasting prize,
And shout, while passing through the air,
'Farewell, farewell, sweet hour of prayer!'"

Eden felt a shudder work through her. Was she about to experience that dropping of this robe of flesh? Were these children?

When she opened her eyes, Brad stood before her, a sardonic smile on his face. "If you thought your little hymn-sing would make me change my mind about my plans, you thought wrong."

Eden's heart hammered even as horror and distress clambered through her.

"Up!" He snapped, tilting his head toward the dark shadows beneath the trees. "We have an appointment to keep."

When Eden didn't move, he did. Like a striking rattler. He snatched a handful of her hair and hauled her to her feet. His breath was fetid as he spoke mere inches from her face. "When I say move, you do it, little lady."

Even with her head yanked back as it was, Eden refused to cower. She met him glare for glare. "Your day will come too, Mr. Baxter. The day when you stand before the Almighty. And what will He say to you about your actions on this day?"

Brad laughed. "I highly doubt I'll be standing before any almighty anything come my time."

"You're wrong. At any rate, if I don't stir that stew, thick as it is, it's going to start burning to the bottom of the pot." *Please, Lord.*

Brad's lips twisted into a snarl. He shoved her toward the fire. "Fine. See to your stew. But don't think that's going to save you from spending a little time with me before . . . Well, let's just say that your cooperation might determine how long you and these boys get to stick around."

Eden moved on legs weak with relief, and trembling with dread. She took up the long spoon she'd been using to stir the stew. She could delay a little longer, but more than delay, she wanted these men to eat. Now. "This is ready. Bring your bowls."

She suddenly had no qualms about the mushrooms in this stew. How soon would they take effect? She had no idea!

She could only hope it would be soon enough that Brad's plans for her—and for these sweet boys—would be foiled.

Chapter 20

Adam's head snapped up as the first notes of Eden's mellow contralto singing "Sweet Hour of Prayer" drifted through the trees. To a man, they broke into a trot.

Adam felt a tremor of anticipation work through him. They had found them before it was too late!

The sound of her voice drew them into a shallow gulch that likely was filled with river water when it ran high. But for now, thankfully, it was merely damp enough that the horses hooves made slight sucking sounds as they walked. The low-sloping sides of the gulch made their path easy. There was only one way forward. Adam willed himself to breathe and hoped the horses wouldn't make too much racket as he rode directly behind Striker, who followed Cody. The other men were in line behind him.

Cody's long legs ate up the distance as he led the way. He leapt over brush and boulders, continuing to scan for sign and waving to them over his shoulder to keep up.

They were moving fast with the aid of Eden's voice. However, all too soon, that sweet sound ceased, and if it weren't for the men before and behind glancing back and forth at each other in grim concern, Adam might have surmised that he'd imagined it.

Ahead, Cody slowed, searching the ground more thoroughly now. He kept glancing up toward the trees that grew on either side of this shallow gully, and Adam suddenly realized how exposed they were down here, where only low brush and grass were now growing. Anyone up in the trees would have the drop on them.

But that realization wasn't what had terror clawing through Adam's chest. Had Eden stopped singing because some harm had come to her?

Father, Your Word says that though we live in the world, we do not wage war as the world does. The weapons we fight with are not the weapons of this world. On the contrary, they have divine power to demolish strongholds. If You can demolish divine strongholds, then a manmade stronghold is nothing to You. Demolish this one, Lord. Please, for Eden. For those children. Get us there on time.

When they came abruptly to the end of the gully, the only way forward was to clamber out into the sunlight of the riverbank. Cody shot up one hand formed into a fist. He glanced up at Striker and shook his head.

Striker's shoulders slumped.

Adam caught his breath and moved so that he could better scan the sun-bathed shore of the Platte River in the distance. There was a long stretch of flat land before the river. Grass grew in long, swaying tufts, and here and there he could see waterways that cut through the grassland. He scanned the shore as far as he could see, both east and west, but he couldn't see any of the outlaws, nor Eden or the boys. Where were they? Her voice had sounded so clear a mere moment earlier! Surely, they had to be right here!

Yet, if they could not see the outlaws and stepped out into the open, they would be leaving themselves at risk of being shot before they could even find a target to shoot at. With the long grass and low-growing shrubs that lined the riverbanks, there were any number of places for the outlaws to lie out of sight!

And yet...

"The risk is worth it." Adam was thankful he'd had the presence of mind to keep his voice low. His horse shifted beneath him. He motioned forward. "We have to save Eden and the boys!"

Striker shook his head and pointed at the open space out in the sunlight. "We step out there and we'll be like fish in a barrel. Our eyes will need a moment to adjust to the light and . . ." He swept a hand to all the hiding places along the riverbank. "They surely have a guard posted. He'll be hidden. We'll be picked off one by one just trying to move forward."

Adam felt despair sweep through him. He nudged his horse forward a step. "Let me go then. I'll take the risk." He started to walk his mount past the scout, but Cody grabbed his reins and blocked his path.

The man's voice was quiet and calm when he spoke. "You want to live to see your wife again?"

Adam took a breath. Nodded. Of course he did.

"Then we go back. We split up. We flank them." Cody pointed up and down the river. "Two points of approach are better than one."

Adam wanted to bowl the man over and barrel past him. He would barge headlong into any danger to save Eden! He drew a breath, willing himself to remain calm. "By the time we circle around, we might be too late!" He thrust a finger toward the river with terror pumping through his veins. If they all burst from the trees at once, surely they would have enough men to . . . And yet, he didn't want to risk the life of even one of these friends.

Cody shook his head. "We waste time arguing." He stepped past Adam and pointed to Cranston, Striker, and Hawthorne. "You three upriver with me. Jeremiah." He thrust a finger downriver and swept a gesture to indicate the remaining men. "Wait for my signal." He turned then and loped in the other direction with the men he had named following him.

Micah, Gideon, and Jeremiah stared at Adam. They seemed to know that he was still considering barging into the open.

Micah clapped him on one shoulder. "You'll do her no good by getting yourself killed." He motioned with a nod that they should follow orders. Jeremiah reined his mount downriver.

Micah's gaze was all seriousness when he said, "If you go out there, I'll come with you, but I think we should listen to the scouts."

"I'm with you, too." Gideon's feet shuffled as he divided a longing glance between Jeremiah's retreating back and Adam.

Adam could tell by their expressions that both men would rather stick with the plan, however it did his heart good to know that they would stand with him despite their feelings.

He felt the pressure of his decision like a vice. These men had families of their own. Families who were counting on them to come home. Sure, he wanted to rescue Eden. It was one thing to risk his own life, but to risk the lives of others?

With one last glance at the temptation of the riverbank where he would surely be able to find Eden soon, Adam conceded that what Jeremiah and Cody had said was true. The outlaws would be fools not to post a hidden guard in such a place. Any man could be lying in wait with a rifle to pick them off. And the sound of a shot would alert the other outlaws that they were close.

Lord, please keep her and the boys alive until we can reach them!

Adam had never felt so helpless as he did in that moment as he turned his horse and trotted away from Eden and those kids.

He heard Micah's and Gideon's horses keeping pace behind him— the pace to a percussive song that pounded his failure repeatedly.

Deliverance woke with a start to find Ms. Betsy leaning over her.

She flinched and cowered against the wall with her arms curled over her head. The chains rattled as they cascaded all around her. Caught! The sounds must have alerted the woman after all!

But to Del's surprise, the woman gently touched her arm. "Hush now. You're safe with me. I see you must have found the pry bar I left for you?"

Del uncoiled just enough to peer at the woman through her arms.

She made soft clicking sounds of apology with her tongue. "Such a horrible thing to keep another human being chained like a dog. Here, I've retrieved his keys." She set to undoing the manacles around Del's wrists, and then her ankles.

Del tossed a fearful glance toward the stairs. Was this a trap? Would Boone be pounding into the basement at any moment on the woman's heels?

As the chains clanked free, Betsy offered, "I hope you helped yourself to some food? I brought you some biscuits and vittles." The woman squatted before her and lifted a small plate and glass from a tray on a nearby barrel.

Del eased a little more and rubbed feeling back into her wrists. Still, life had taught her to be cautious, and she prepared herself in case the woman's kindness was a ruse of some sort.

"Tha—" Her voice broke from disuse. She tried again. "Thank you, kindly, ma'am."

Betsy flapped her hand to indicate she wanted no gratitude. "Please, don't thank me. You've been here for weeks already, and I didn't know how to help you. But now, you must eat quickly, because this is a good chance for you to escape. I didn't know Boone would be called away today, but he has been—thanks to the *other* no good Baxter." As she spoke, Betsy bustled around the cellar, stuffing a little of this and that into a rucksack.

The word *escape* sent such a shock of surprise through Del that she almost choked on the bite of biscuit in her mouth.

"It's not right, what that man is doing to you. He may be my brother-in-law by marriage, but I'll not stand by and see him treat you like a dog—and a poorly kept one at that. And like I said, I'm just sorry it's taken me this long to figure out how to help."

Del wished that her sleepy brain was doing a better job of keeping up with this conversation.

"Boone has been called away to search for his brother—a blessing from above. I'm sure Boone and his men will be out all night and likely won't return till sometime tomorrow. That gives you a day's head start. I wish I'd a horse to give you, but on the open prairie, they'd be able to see you for miles if they gave chase, and you know Boone's tracker is second to none. But never fear. I've thought of a different plan. We can't have you leaving footprints. We'll get to that in a moment." Betsy shoved a whole tin of hardtack into the bag, followed by two jars of the beef strips. A small pot, a plate, a spoon, a pound of coffee grounds.

Del gave her head a little shake, trying to process the woman's words. Not leave footprints? Did the woman expect her to float away on a cloud? Caution called for her attention.

"Eat. Eat." Betsy waved at the tray on the barrel, which Del now saw held another plate filled with a thick piece of chicken, a couple of hard-boiled eggs, and a whole mess of greens.

She rose to her knees beside the barrel. She set to eating the best tasting meal she'd had in a month of Sundays, despite how good that jerky and hardtack and orange had tasted earlier.

Betsy gave a nod of satisfaction. "Good. Now. I've thought of a plan and I think it's a good one. There's a new wagon train in town. I don't miss much since most everyone who stops by has to come into my store at one time or another." She thrust a packet of tea into the rucksack. That was followed by a jar of dried apricots.

Deliverance fleetingly wondered how heavy that bag was going to be and if she'd have the strength to pack it. With little food and little exercise for months now, she knew her stamina was limited. When she'd first found herself chained in this cellar, she'd made herself do exercises. Squatting repeatedly to strengthen her legs. Or pushing herself off the wall to strengthen her arms. But as day after day had passed, her hopes had flagged and she'd given up the practice. Why had she given up?!

Betsy continued to ramble as she filled the bag. "One of those scouts, well, he's a man of color like you. A free man. A respected man from the way the other men of the wagon train treated him. I've watched carefully and believe I know which schooner is his."

A swallow of chicken stuck halfway down Del's throat. She coughed. Surely the woman didn't plan for her to—

"You'll get in his wagon and not come out until you are miles from the fort. He seemed a kind man. Even bought some penny candy for a passel of look-alike children to share. I don't think he's the kind to turn you out. I know I'm bossing you a bit. But Boone won't suspect that you simply dashed over there and hid in a wagon. He'll look for you to have run to the west. Or even back east. Once you are far enough away to ensure your escape from Boone, you can make your own choices."

Del pushed the plate back, certain she wouldn't be able to swallow another bite. This sounded like an awful plan.

"There!" Betsy set to buckling the rucksack closed as she continued her chatter. "This bag has enough supplies that you should be set for a couple of weeks on your own. You save these supplies until you need to strike out alone. That man won't begrudge you a few shared meals. Are you ready? Do you need to use the necessary before we go up to the wagons?"

For the first time since she'd come down the stairs, the woman ceased her chatter, and Del found she had no words to fill the silence. Ready? No. She certainly wasn't ready. However, she did nod at the offer of the necessary.

"All right, then." Betsy gave a sharp dip of her chin as she led the way up the stairs, speaking quietly. "Most of the soldiers are off with Boone hunting down Brad. And I'll send the one standing guard in the store on an errand. Here." She thrust the rucksack into Del's hands. "Hold this and stay right here until I return for you."

With that, the woman disappeared into the store, leaving Del waiting in the semi-darkness at the top of the cellar steps. She blinked and gave her head a little shake. Was she truly awake? Or was all of this a dream that she'd wake from in a moment?

Eden willed her hands not to tremble as she ladled bowl after bowl of the poisoned stew into the outlaws' outstretched hands. The first to get his meal had already wolfed down several mouthfuls, and as she filled the next man's bowl, she watched the first.

Would he keel over before any of the others could take their first bite?

The man continued to eat as though nothing were out of the ordinary. In fact, he downed the complete bowl as she served the others and then took a spot behind the last man in line for another bowlful.

He gave her a friendly nod as she scooped him out another portion. "Best soup I've had in a long time, ma'am. Thank you, kindly."

Eden murmured, "You're welcome," even as guilt washed through her. Here she was hoping for the man to collapse—but not too quickly, mind you—and he was thanking her for the food.

The mushrooms had to work. Everything she'd been taught about them said that these ought to be poisonous! Maybe they were just acting more slowly than she'd expected? That wasn't such a bad thing. It would give all the men time to eat a whole bowl before any of them started showing signs of illness.

She turned her attention to the man on guard in the tree. If the men of the wagon train came, they would approach through the forest the same way Brad had brought them. If she could eliminate even one more obstacle to their rescue, she must do so. She filled a bowl and started toward the tree.

"Where are you going?" Brad's hand came out of nowhere and knocked the container from her hands.

Eden gasped. Soup sprayed everywhere, and the enamelware bowl clattered against a stone in the grass. "I was just taking a bowl of soup to the guard."

"You don't go anywhere unless I say you can." Brad, who had yet to take a bite, stomped over and sat on a log near the boys.

Eden wiped her trembling hands on her apron and bent to pick up the bowl. So much for eliminating the guard. *Just eat the blazing soup!*

Eden wanted to rush over there and snatch the children away from the man, but she made herself remain where she was near the fire. She curled her hands into the folds of her skirt.

Brad waved his spoon from the boys toward her soup pot and back. "You boys can get some soup if you like. Never say that I sent anyone to their grave hungry."

Wyatt went a little pale and swept an arm around Asher to tug him closer. "No, thank you. We're fine."

"Suit yourself," Brad shrugged. He slurped a spoonful of the stew. "So I hear one of you boys is some hand with drawing?"

Wyatt angled him a squint, but didn't respond.

"It's you, is it?" Brad prodded, swallowing down a second bite. "I hear you're quite good. See that white rock right there by your boot?" He pointed with his spoon. "Pick it up and draw me a . . . horse on that tree trunk there." He swung his spoon to a large river birch that shaded the area where they sat. When Wyatt hesitated, he barked, "Go on, boy! When I tell you to do something, you move!"

Tugging Asher with him, Wyatt picked up the white rock and moved to the tree trunk.

Eden felt frozen in place. Had Brad not seen the sketch of himself? Maybe if Wyatt drew a poor likeness, Brad would let them all go? She huffed. His letting them go was a slim hope and unlikely. At any rate, she couldn't very well speak the thought out loud. But maybe Wyatt would realize?

As Wyatt sketched the first sleek strokes of a horse onto the bark, Eden realized that the boy hadn't made the connection that his talent was what might get them all killed. Only a few strokes in, the animal was already coming to life. Wyatt likely couldn't create a lousy drawing if he tried!

Eden turned her face to the sky. Did the Lord see them all down here? She knew that He did. Why would He allow this to happen to these sweet children? Why would He allow the attack on their families in the first place? The Word said that God worked all things for the good of those who were called according to His purpose. Was the death of the children's parents for their own good?

She remembered Adam's words about trusting that their son was in heaven with the Lord. She supposed that if she thought of the attacks in the light of eternity, instead of merely seeing them from the earthly aspect, they could be seen as for the good of those people. Here one moment, and in heaven for eternity with the Lord the next.

She glanced at the men who had mostly consumed their soup now. Even Brad was nearly finished with his bowl and all of them seemed to be doing just fine. Maybe those mushrooms weren't poisonous, after all. Bright red as they were, she'd thought surely they would be.

At least she wouldn't have all their deaths on her conscience.

What would it be like to travel to eternity? She dreaded the pain of death, certainly. But she knew with sudden clarity that those were just pangs like childbirth. Something to be passed through to get to something better. She would get to see her son. Better yet, get to see Jesus, the One who died to set her free.

Peace washed through her so strong and sweet that she drew in a long breath, almost able to smell the fragrance of serenity. *Okay, Lord. If this is Your plan for me, help me to be strong for these boys to the end.*

The clatter of Brad's spoon against his bowl drew her gaze.

Brad's eyes were a bit awed as he took in the strokes Wyatt was still making against the tree trunk.

Eden glanced at the drawing. She could almost see the horse's mane blowing in the wind, the ripple of strong muscles beneath a shimmering coat. There was even a glint of light shining off the horse's eye.

Asher pointed to the horse's haunch. "Draw a fly right here."

Wyatt smiled and complied with his little brother's request.

Brad shifted uneasily on his log bench. "How many times have you drawn that exact horse?"

Wyatt frowned. "This is the first time."

Brad tugged at his collar, seeming to suddenly feel it too tight. "You can just draw like that? Without even needing an animal to look at?"

Wyatt pointed to the horses penned into the rope corral just a few paces away. "I've seen horses plenty of times."

Brad pursed his lips. "But you didn't look that way even once whilst you were drawing."

Wyatt frowned. Shook his head as though confused by the comment.

Despite their circumstances, Eden tucked away a smile. It did her heart good to see Brad squirming a little.

"Draw Killingbeck there." Brad jabbed a gesture at a man seated on a rock not too far away.

Wyatt searched the area and tugged Asher with him to another tree a few feet from the one with the horse on it. He looked at Killingbeck for a few seconds.

Eden could almost see the boy calculating the strokes of each feature. "Take your time, Wyatt." She guessed if he'd already revealed the depth of his talent, that he might as well extend their time a little by drawing more slowly. And maybe he could put the fear of God into these men while doing so.

Wyatt glanced at her and gave a nod. Then he turned back to the tree and started drawing. His strokes were calculated and delicate this time. First, he outlined a face. Then added the rough strokes of eyes, nose and mouth with measured slashes. The man's hat came next, followed by the swoops of his longish hair. After that, he set to filling in details. Killingbeck's eyes came to life. As did the scar that prevented his beard from growing near his chin and the slight bump where his nose must have been broken at some time in the past.

Despite Wyatt's slow, deliberate strokes, it took him no more than fifteen minutes to shade in the planes of the man's face and sketch in his beard. He added a few more strokes beneath the man's eye.

All the while, Eden waited with bated breath for one of the outlaws to collapse from her soup. But none of them even seemed to feel queasy.

Perfect. She'd found the one patch of bright red mushrooms in the world that weren't poisonous? Now what?

Wyatt tossed his chalky rock aside and dusted his hands. He tugged Asher close again and hung his head as though waiting for his demise.

Eden pressed a hand to her heart and blinked back tears. She wanted to dash over and snatch the boys into her arms. Hustle them off to safety. She remained where she stood, not wanting to cut this brief reprieve any shorter than it already would be. At least Brad's attention was fixed on something other than killing them for the moment. Where were Adam and the men from the wagons? Would they even be able to find them this far out through that forest and near the river as they were?

Eden despaired. Not likely. And she didn't know any other way to protect these boys than to remain quiet and hope Brad continued to delay the inevitable.

This was an impossible situation they all found themselves in.

Brad set down his bowl, his face pale as he glanced from Killingbeck to his likeness on the tree and back again. "That's you right down to the scar under your eye," he said.

Killingbeck grinned lazily and scooped up the last of his stew. "Think he drew you that good, boss?" There was a bit of a taunt in the words.

Brad surged to his feet and stomped toward Eden.

She swallowed. So much for continued reprieve. This was it then?

Sure enough, there was a leer in his expression as he swept her with a lecherous glance. "Guess it's time for you and me to spend a spell together." He tossed his soup bowl on the ground nearby, offering her a grin that was more threat than humor.

Lightheaded, Eden stumbled a step back to catch her balance. She whipped a glance at the boys. Wyatt had one arm draped across Asher's chest as he pulled his younger brother against him protectively.

Eden covered her mouth with one hand. She had failed them. Could they see how sorry she was?

She closed her eyes, shuttering that one last glance of the boys into her heart.

A hand clamped around her wrist, and her eyes flew open. She tried to wrench free, but it was no use. His broad hand was like a manacle around her wrist.

Brad curled one lip, never taking his twinkling eyes off her as he said, "Killingbeck, you take care of the kids. I've got this one."

Killingbeck's spoon clattered into his bowl. "Me? Why do I gotta take care of the kids?"

"Just do as you're told!" Brad turned and dragged Eden.

Dejection sweeping through her, she stumbled behind him up the slope away from the river and into the darkness of the trees.

Chapter 21

Boone had brought the fort's tracker along, just in case his assumptions about where his brother was headed were wrong. But he hadn't needed to track his brother's sorry hide, just as he'd suspected would be the case. He'd known the moment he'd figured out that Brad was no longer in the fort, just where he would go. The man was nothing if not a creature of habit. And the fishing hole where Pa used to take them all as boys had good concealment that Brad would be craving. The forest grew almost all the way to the river's edge there.

As Boone and his cavalrymen rode through the forest, all around them the vibrant greens of spring drew his attention. He gave his horse its head, knowing it would follow the tracker through the woods.

Had he ever noticed how many shades of green there were before? Newborn ferns unfurled at their feet, not yet faded by the passing of time—a green brightened by undertones of gold. Moss grew on the shady sides of trees in soft sheets of jade and emerald. Lime colored leaves, newly birthed from buds, arched in a canopy above their heads, dancing with other leaves in shades of viridian, olive, and mint. Birds sang lustily, as though completely unburdened of winter's long silence.

Boone wished he could feel so carefree as those birds must be. Apparently, they weren't weighed down by irresponsible brothers who dragged their family name through the mud. He smirked at the thought.

Ahead, his tracker stopped. "Seven, maybe eight men trailing Brad and his crew. Shod horses."

Boone narrowed his eyes. The only other men who could want to find his brother were the men from the wagon train. He cursed.

He motioned for the tracker to continue forward. His enjoyment of the beauty all around him was marred by one thought that hammered at him relentlessly. The men who had visited his office had beaten him and would soon have the drop on Brad and his crew!

They must have a tracker almost as good as his?

Seven or eight? Likely, mostly the same men who'd been in his office earlier.

Why were they out here, though? Irritation swirled through him. He'd told them to return to their wagons! Told them he would take care of this. There was no reason for them to be here, unless Brad had—

Boone cursed again.

Brad always had his ear to the ground. Had he overheard something and gone after the kid who'd made the sketch? Brad was a fool of the worst kind!

Boone might have been able to orchestrate his escape! Lord knew he'd done so plenty of times in the past.

But this time there might just be too many witnesses. It was one thing to fix his brother's escape when solely men who were loyal to him were nearby. But with a large group of strangers?

Boone put his heels into his mount's sides. He nudged his horse past the tracker and set his mount down the trail at a trot. "This way!" he called to his soldiers.

There was no shortcut through these thick woods to the river. But the wagon train men would be slowed by the fact that they needed to find Brad's trail. He knew exactly where to go.

And it was imperative that he and his soldiers reach his brother first!

Adam wanted to bellow in protest at the slow pace they'd needed to adopt as they moved through the trees along the riverbank. Several minutes back, the underbrush had become so thick that they'd needed to dismount and leave their horses so that they could continue on foot. Jeremiah had a hatchet, but they needed to proceed as quietly as possible, which limited the hatchet's use to small bushes with softer trunks that didn't make so much noise. This had necessitated their skirting around larger obstacles on more than one occasion.

When every moment could mean the difference between life and death for Eden, it felt like torturous failure to even have to go a few feet out of their way to skirt around a large bush or small tree.

It seemed it had taken them an eternity to get this far. But it shouldn't be too long now until they could approach the river and get a better view of what lay below on the flats once again. Would Eden and the outlaws be there this time?

Adam carefully placed his feet where Jeremiah did as he walked in his wake. Once every couple of minutes, they would pause and simply listen to the sounds all around them. The clank of a tool, or jangle of a bit, would be an odd sound out here in the wilderness that would give away the outlaws' location, but they heard nothing.

Adam willed himself not to give up hope.

The scent of food and smoke drifted to him. He shot out a hand and clamped it on Jeremiah's shoulder. They came to a stop along with Micah and Gideon behind them.

"What is it?" Gid whispered.

"Did you smell that?" Adam tested the air again. But whatever current had brought the scents to him must have blown in another direction, for he sensed nothing now.

His three companions didn't seem to sense it either.

What direction was the wind coming from?

He tilted his head to listen, but all was still save the tumble of water in the distance.

Which way was the breeze coming from? He closed his eyes and held out a hand, palm facing upriver, the backs of his fingers downriver. The breeze should cool the side of his hand that it touched. But the air was so still, he couldn't tell.

Frustration coursed through him as he wiped his sweaty brow with the bandana in his pocket and assessed the area. He glanced back in the direction they'd just come. Surely the cook fire lay ahead of them? They would smell it more strongly if they were near it.

Reluctantly, he nodded for Jeremiah to proceed.

The scout slowed even more now as they moved forward through the brush, and Adam bit back his frustration.

Despite his impatience, he knew that any snapping twig or crackling of branches could alert the outlaws to their presence. Yet none of them were expert trackers. Each of them at one point or another had misplaced a step that had created a noise of one kind or another. Adam could only hope that the sound of the gently flowing water of the Platte would disguise their approach.

He drew in a calming breath, praying without ceasing for the safety of Eden and the boys. The scent of smoke was a good thing, right? And food? That meant the men had stopped to eat. But had they done so before or after killing Eden and the boys?

His heart faltered.

Killing? Would they go so far?

Adam thought of the burned-out wagons and the women—one with arrows in her back. Yes. He knew without a doubt that if they didn't arrive in time, Eden would be lost to him.

Now his heart raced into an unsteady rhythm.

Oh God, please...

In that moment, no other prayer would come to mind. Just *please*. It repeated over and over in his mind as it had when he'd thought

Wyatt and the other boys were lost to the stampede. He willed despair to the recesses and tried to cling to hope.

Choose for yourself this day whom you will serve.

The thought crashed into him so suddenly that he stopped, and Micah bumped into him.

"What is it?" Micah whispered.

Adam brushed the question aside. Shook his head. Continued forward.

I choose You, Lord. Always and forever.

Jeremiah thrust up a fist and motioned for them to get down.

Swallowing hard, Adam hunched low and fell to his belly in a patch of tall grass beneath a vast river birch that must have been growing here for hundreds of years.

With his rifle clutched in one hand, he eased forward on Jeremiah's heels through the grass. Here, the bank of the river had been carved away by several feet in some bygone storm or quake. They lay on a shelf above a flat piece of prairie that was maybe an acre in size along the riverbank. Farther out, the river meandered past, still low and slow at this time of year.

This section of prairie was well concealed by the tree line to its south and the curve of the river north, east, and west.

Several men sat around a fire. It was clear from their casual manner that they felt safe in this place. Downriver, a temporary corral had been strung for the men's horses, and beyond that stood a large maple, and lying high on one branch, Adam could see a guard posted. Adam swallowed. The man probably had a clear view for hundreds of feet up and down the riverbank. True to Striker's words, they would have been easy prey for a man in such a position. Only thanks to the thick underbrush as they approached, and the tall grass they lay in now, were they likely concealed from the man's position.

He felt Jeremiah's eyes on him and gave the man a nod. Cody had saved his life back there. And those of Micah and Gid too, because they'd been ready to follow him. He wasn't too proud to admit it.

Adam returned his gaze to the outlaws.

Micah, who had been studying the area through a field glass, withdrew the monocle and nudged it toward Adam. He pointed toward a large tree trunk not too far from the fire.

Dreading what he might see, Adam peered through the glass and drew in a sharp breath. The tree contained a white drawing of a horse. *Wyatt's doing?*

Adam's heart pounded at the connotations that flitted through his mind. Why would Wyatt be casually drawing on a tree while being held captive unless . . .

Adam pressed his lips together and handed the glass back to Micah with a nod of thanks. His heart hammered in dread as he continued to search the prairie.

Besides the guard, he could see two other men lounging against their saddles near the temporary corral of horses, but nowhere did he see any of the faces that he longed to see. Adam snatched off his hat, hung his head, and raked an unsteady hand through his hair.

Beside him, Jeremiah reached over to squeeze his shoulder.

Adam resettled his hat and tried not to despair over the dreadful questions that pounded at him.

Where were Eden and the boys? Had they arrived too late?

Was God going to make him back his pledge? He tipped his face to the sky. Closed his eyes. He thought of Eden's declaration of faith. *Though He slay me, yet will I trust Him.*

Nodded.

I will keep praying, Lord, until I have an answer. Please, save Eden. Save these boys. But even if You don't . . . I choose You.

He didn't have any answers yet, but somehow he felt like a burden had been lifted. No matter the outcome of this situation, he would be okay, because Jesus had already conquered the greatest enemy. Death. And Adam would put his hope in that.

Willing herself not to fall to pieces, Eden tried to yank her wrist from Brad's grip, but she may as well have been trying to pull her hand from a vice. He dragged her closer to the forest, and that dreaded darkness under all those trees. Above them, a large tree leaned toward the river as though it had grown weary of that darkness and was reaching toward the light.

The ground beneath their feet transitioned from grassy prairie to layers of leafy loam.

"Where you gonna go, if you do get free?" Brad mocked her. "You gonna run off and leave those boys back there in my tender lovin' care?"

Eden fought even harder. He'd just told one of his men to kill the boys! She needed to get back there and try to help them.

Brad yanked her forward.

She stumbled over a rock and fell. Without the aid of her arms, and off balance as she was, her knees ground into the loam, and she felt the bite of one sharp root split the skin of her knee despite the padding of her dress and petticoat.

Brad did stop, but he never released his grip on her arm. "Get up." He gave her an impatient jerk.

She assessed the tear in her skirt as she breathed through the sharp agony. The roots were that sharp? Surely not.

She searched the ground and found the stone that her knee had landed on. A small, squarish rock about the size of her palm.

Maybe this was her chance!

Eden pressed her free hand against the ground to help her rise and, blessedly, found the piece of stone was indeed small enough to hold in her hand as Brad hauled her to her feet once more. She tucked that hand in close, heart hammering. Had he seen it?

He stopped abruptly and slapped her. "Drop it!"

Anger pulsed through her.

Eden swung hard instead. Right at the hand that gripped her wrist! The rock found its mark with a loud *crack*.

"Woman!" Brad released her and cursed, grimacing at the blood dripping from his fingers as he shook them.

Had she broken his hand? Split the skin certainly, but it was a shallow cut and likely wouldn't bleed long enough to give her much reprieve. She must act quickly!

Eden retreated from him, holding the piece of rock before her, ready to strike again if he got close enough. She mustn't lose her grip! She backed away, never taking her eyes off him. If she wasn't too late already, the boys only had moments to live! "Stay back. I mean it. I'll smash you again!"

Brad laughed short and sharp. "I knew I liked you. You've got fight." He swiped his bloody hand along the back of his leg and stalked after her.

Not broken then. *Dadgum!*

Holding her paltry weapon before her, Eden felt the prairie behind her with one foot, searching for a good place to plant her next step as she retreated blindly. She didn't dare take her eyes off this snake.

Brad sauntered toward her, slow and steady, keeping pace with her retreat. He seemed to be enjoying this game as he swept a gesture around them. "Where you gonna go? Huh? You and me, we're all alone out here."

"Boys!?" Eden called over her shoulder, desperate to know if Wyatt and Asher were still alive. "Wyatt? Ash?"

"You ain't gonna do them no good." Brad lunged at her.

Eden swung hard and fast.

A blow rattled through the rock, and she almost dropped it.

She'd connected with the knob of Brad's wrist!

With a sharp cry, he withdrew, cradled his injury, and glowered at her. "Now that's just downright unfriendly." A sheen of moisture dotted his face. He swiped at it with one sleeve, leaving a smear of blood across his forehead. He blinked hard a couple of times.

Eden studied him as she retreated a few more steps, calling again, "Wyatt? Ash?"

Silence rang loudly.

Despair clawed up from inside her. That same darkness that she'd felt all those years ago when she'd lost her son. But she battered it away. Refused to give up hope.

She couldn't be too late! She'd only left the boys moments ago.

Brad scrunched his eyes tight, then raised his brows and gave his head another shake before he continued to stalk toward her.

Adam was trying to decide what their next move ought to be when movement caught his eye and he came to an abrupt halt.

Eden!

She'd been hidden by a low-growing copse of shrubs, but now she backed into the open, holding something before her like a weapon.

Adam felt his heart go still.

Apparently also catching the movement, Jeremiah turned to look at what had drawn his attention. Beside Adam, Micah and Gideon also turned their heads.

Eden continued to retreat toward the fire. What was she holding before her? Something large enough that it seemed she was barely able to grip it in her splayed fingers.

From her stance, she was clearly under a threat of some kind, though he couldn't see who or what might be threatening her.

He had to get to her! But he didn't know where the boys were, and to dash out into the open would reveal their presence and might cause a fight they could avoid if they all worked together.

Where were Cody, Striker, and the others? Had they figured out yet that they had headed in the wrong direction and that the outlaws were upriver from them? It wouldn't hurt his feelings any to see them heading this way.

For now, Eden seemed to be holding her own, and he needed to think. They needed a plan.

Micah and Gideon looked to him, grim with concern. Jeremiah shucked his rifle from the long sheath he wore on his back. The weapon stretched before him as he sighted along the barrel in Eden's direction. Adam knew that as soon as any man stepped into sight, Jeremiah would take a shot, and they all needed to be ready.

Adam pointed Micah and Gideon toward the two outlaws lounging by the corral and then trained his own rifle toward the man in the tree.

With their slight height advantage and concealed position, their odds were good since there were four of them and four visible outlaws. But the guard in that tree was a long way off. Would he be able to make such a shot? Accurate enough to hit the guard from this distance?

More importantly, would Jeremiah be able to make his shot without hitting Eden?

And where were the boys? Had he arrived too late to save them? Or were they being guarded by other men somewhere out of sight? If so, how many men?

He clenched his teeth. Too many questions and he certainly didn't like Eden being down there where all the bullets would be flying! "Hold your fire, until we all have a clear shot," he whispered to his companions. They had to find a way to rescue her without putting her at risk!

Beside him the men shifted, but seemed willing to wait for his instructions. The problem was, he had no idea what those instructions ought to be! How were they going to pull this off without any of them or Eden getting hurt?

Eden moved further into view, calling out the names of the boys. The sound of her voice filled Adam with such a sweet relief! And the fact that she was calling for the boys...

That was good! She wouldn't be calling for them if she knew they'd been killed! He chose to see it as a good sign until he knew otherwise.

Whoever Eden was retreating from remained behind a patch of wild chokecherry bushes, too thick to even see where he was.

Eden took another step, and a man's hand came into view from behind the brush. But Eden struck out, and the hand disappeared from view.

Good. At least she had a weapon for the moment. Much as he didn't want to take his eyes off her, he had to keep his gaze on his target, for once the shooting started, they would all need to be fast and accurate. And yet, whoever Eden was holding at bay remained hidden by the brush.

Lord, please.

Eden backed another step into view, and then the next step took her into a patch of shade from the branches of a large oak that seemed to be leaning toward the water from the tree line. Massive branches stretched far out over the prairie and drew Adam's attention.

His heart began to hammer with hope.

He laid a hand on Jeremiah's arm to draw his attention, then swung a nod toward the tree. One thick branch stretched directly above where Eden and the outlaw had now paused.

Since they still couldn't see the man behind the brush, there was too much risk in making an attack. There could be any number of men scattered throughout this brush, for that matter. But if he could get to that branch above her...

Could he do that silently enough to avoid drawing the man's attention?

He had to try!

He touched Jeremiah's shoulder once again and spoke quietly. "I have to get her."

Jeremiah nodded and returned his concerned gaze to where Eden continued to speak to the hidden man.

Where he'd been frustrated with the brush moments earlier, Adam was now thankful for it as he snaked stealthily through it toward the base of that oak.

Chapter 22

Eden's hope surged another few degrees as Brad gave his head another shake. Was it the poison, finally working?

She retreated another step toward the river, but not too quickly. If she drew too near the fire, Brad's men would see that she'd escaped him and come to his aid. She might be able to fend Brad off for a bit, but she knew she'd never stand a chance against more than one man!

Lord, please give me strength. Don't let me be too late to save those boys.

Eden banished the last of her despair to its proper place. She wouldn't give in to it again. Still . . . the boys weren't answering her.

Deep sorrow filled her. They had deserved so much more than she'd been able to give them! What should she have done differently? She should have figured out a way to warn Wyatt not to let Brad know what an artist he was! She never should have allowed herself to be hauled away from the boys. She should have put up a fight right then and there, and maybe she would have been able to—

A thought hit her.

She hadn't heard any gunshots!

Would Brad's man have killed the boys in some other way? The revulsion in Killingbeck's voice when he'd been tasked with dispatching the boys made her think he would want to get the task over with quickly. His pistol would facilitate that. She felt certain that was the weapon he'd use. Surely on these flats, she would have heard those shots!

She chanced a glance behind her.

The fire still burned with deceivingly friendly pops and crackles. But the boys were not near the tree where they'd been a moment ago.

That despair again. Flooding her. All-consuming.

God, please...

Something hit her wrist hard, and her fingers went numb. Her grip on her paltry weapon faltered. The stone fell from her limp fingers.

Brad surged forward and clamped one hand around her throat! She wrenched at it in an attempt to loosen it, but he merely laughed and watched her as though he were enjoying the spectacle of her fight for breath.

Eden stilled. She was no match for his ferocity.

So much for hoping he was getting sick from the poison. He certainly hadn't lost any of his strength!

She closed her eyes.

She'd taken her eyes from the snake for one moment too long, and it had struck while she wasn't looking.

Adam wanted to kick himself as he sprinted back along the path they'd cut through the brush. *Why* hadn't he thought to bring his rope with him? It might have made things easier, but it was too late now.

At least the way was much faster going than it had been in coming.

Still, by the time he reached the base of the large oak, he was fighting for air.

Somewhere out there in the grass, he knew that his friends still lay on their bellies, keeping an eye on the situation below. After giving himself three short inhales to catch his breath, he chanced a glance around the tree trunk. His heart fell.

For Eden was once again firmly in the clutches of the outlaw. He could see the man's back. See the fear in Eden's eyes as the man gripped her throat.

Adam took a step, scanning for the best way to reach her. There was too much thick brush. The man would hear him coming for sure. It didn't matter. He would just have to risk it. He took another step and readied to leap the couple of feet into the brush below, but the outlaw released her!

Eden gasped for air.

Arms twirling, Adam barely prevented himself from falling forward off the embankment. He regained his balance just in time.

Adam's hands fisted. Only the recognition that making noise and alerting this outlaw to his presence would put Eden in even more danger kept him in his place.

He pivoted and put his back to the tree before his rage could make him act without thinking first. Each breath hammered at his ribs. Each thought urged him to immediate action. He forced himself to remain where he was.

From below, Adam could hear the low rumble of a man's voice, but couldn't make out what he was saying above the current of the river. He longed to look once again to make sure Eden was okay, but more than that, he wanted to get to her. It was good that the man was talking to her, because as long as he continued to talk, he likely wasn't going to hurt her too much.

Adam swallowed. Even having her hurt a *little* made him tremble with a rage he didn't know he possessed.

He turned now to assess the best way up into the tree. His mouth was as dry as the dust beneath his boots.

Movement drew his glance to where Jeremiah now slunk his way through the tall grass and brush on their level of the embankment. Since Micah and Gideon remained out of sight, Adam could only hope that they still had their rifles pointed at the other outlaws. He wished Jeremiah had stayed put. He didn't like what might happen without the man's rifle guarding Eden for even a heartbeat. But, he also needed his help, and from this spot on the bank, Jer would have a better line of sight to the outlaw anyhow. Jeremiah must have recognized that.

Could Micah and Gideon take out the other three men if necessary? He would have to leave that task up to them and concentrate on his own.

Saving Eden.

Trying not to worry about where the boys were, he turned his gaze to the spreading branches of the large oak above him. It was so still today. Not a breath of breeze wafting on the air.

How was he going to climb this tree without rattling the leaves and drawing attention to its movement?

Please, God.

Above him, the leaves of the oak stirred in a breath of a breeze. Then a full-out wind began to blow—so strongly that the branches of the tree began to sway. The first fat raindrop slipped through the leaves to smack him in the eye.

Adam grinned and bit back a whoop.

He leapt for the lowest branch on his side of the oak.

Thank You.

At least there was some hope now, where only moments ago he'd fought to find any!

Wyatt held Ash's hand and tried to be brave as the man named Killingbeck prodded them downriver toward a wall of upturned tree roots. A tree had fallen, taking a great section of the earth with it. The root ball was taller than his head.

He swallowed. Was this to be their burying place?

He tried to pray like Pa and Ma had taught him to, but couldn't seem to voice anything other than *God, please* . . .

Ash's hand trembled in his grip.

The closer they got to the fallen tree, the thicker the brush grew all around them, and Wyatt tripped over a bush and almost went down. A moment later, Asher slipped too, and only Wyatt's grip on his hand kept him from sprawling.

"Thank you, Wyatt." Ash's small voice made Wyatt want to turn and lash out at the man behind them. But he knew he wasn't strong enough for that task.

The man cursed and mumbled something under his breath. Wyatt caught the name *Baxter*, but not much else of the muttered ranting. Then the man said, "Get up there against those roots."

This was it then. Wyatt started to turn to face the man.

But the man smacked the back of his head and snapped, "No! Face the wall. Don't look at me!"

Wyatt's heart pounded in his chest. He felt sweat break out on his face. And something swirled in his head. But he had to be strong for Asher!

Just then, rain began to fall as though some heavenly lake had sprung a leak. Wyatt was soaked instantly.

He drew in a breath and gave his head a quick shake, thankful for the cool water that had cleared his wooziness. He took his brother's hand and pulled him to his side. A bolt of lightning flashed! Thunder crashed loudly overhead.

Wyatt tugged his collar tighter about his neck, irrationally wishing for a coat. Soon, neither he nor Ash would have need of warmth. He held his breath then, wincing his eyes into a tight scrunch as he waited. Would he feel pain? Would Asher? Or would—

"What the—" Behind them, Killingbeck cursed again. That was followed by the sound of his boots scrabbling through the brush and then all went silent.

Wyatt remained frozen. Unsure if he could move without getting them both shot.

Beside him, Ash's quiet voice filled the stillness. "Wyatt, look!"

Deliverance waited in the darkness at the top of the cellar steps, still uncertain if she could trust what Betsy had said. One thing she knew, she didn't like sneaking into a stranger's wagon to try to make her escape—man of color or not.

She would allow Betsy to help her to the wagon, but then she must make her escape from it first thing!

The doorknob rattled and Del jolted so high that she almost lost her balance on the stairs. She clutched for the rail.

The door swung in, and it was just Betsy peering in at her. She wore a blue cape now, and rolled her hand in a follow-me gesture. "Quickly. I sent the guard on an errand and told him I needed bring some parcels up to the wagons, but we must be quick."

Betsy hefted her skirts above the floor and hurried through the empty store.

Del stuck as close to her as she possibly could. Whether she could trust the woman or not, she was Del's only hope.

After they moved through Betsy's quarters at the back of the store, Betsy pushed open the rear door and glanced both ways. She stepped out, waving for Deliverance to follow. And then took the rucksack from her as she nudged her toward the necessary.

Del tried to hurry, but found Betsy pacing impatiently when she emerged.

"Good. Here, put this on." Betsy draped her blue cape around Del's shoulders and then took up the rucksack and strode out. "Stay close now." Betsy hurried down the gravel road at the back of the buildings. She furtively checked each alley between the buildings before they stepped into the open, but all remained quiet.

Del had never been allowed outside during daylight hours. To their left was a stretch of prairie that flowed into the horizon beyond. To their right lay a row of copycat buildings that seemed to have been built from the same pattern. No sounds disturbed the stillness of the day other than the occasional twitter of a bird and the crunch of the gravel beneath their feet.

Was it always this quiet? Betsy had said Boone had taken his men—but *all* of them but the one guard?

Del's heart beat from the region of her throat. Unaccountably, she wanted to sprint back to the safety and familiarity of the cellar. Foolish! She forced herself to put one foot in front of the other and stick close to Betsy.

At the end of the row of buildings, Betsy paused and planted one shoulder into the corner to study the area beyond.

From her position behind Betsy, Del couldn't see anything.

Her mouth was dry. Her palms damp. She scrubbed them on her skirt and huddled into the warmth of Betsy's cape. *Please, Lord, don't bring me this far only to have me caught.* Her hand moved to curve around her womb. *For the sake of this child, please, Lord. Have mercy.*

Betsy turned suddenly. She set the rucksack by her feet as she spoke. "Listen now. And listen carefully. Come here, by my side." She drew Del closer and tugged the hood of the cape into place, cinching it at Del's throat. "Up the hill there, you see the wagon train?"

Del nodded.

Betsy assessed her and then tugged the hood a little further forward and tucked some of Del's wayward curls back inside it. "Do you see the one that's painted blue? There's only the one."

Del searched and found the wagon. Thankfully it was parked on the near side of the party's circle. She nodded.

Betsy gave a firm nod. "That's the one. But from here you have to go on your own."

Del frowned. If she was to go on her own, why had the woman just put her cape on her? She reached for the ties at her throat.

But Betsy snatched her hand and held it in a firm clasp. "No. Keep it. You'll need something warm to wear on your trip west." The woman laid her other hand across their clasped ones and squeezed. "I wish

I could have done more for you. Get in that wagon and don't come out for anything or anyone, unless it's night. The men of that party rode out about an hour ago. It seems that Brad made off with one of their women. The rest of the womenfolk are hiding in their own wagons. Go on. Speedy like." Betsy gave her a hurried hug and a push.

"God speed!" Betsy whispered. And then with a wave, she disappeared around the corner of the building.

Deliverance glanced over her shoulder. To go back would mean she'd have to pass all the buildings of the fort. Someone was likely to see her. It was a miracle no one had spotted them up to this point!

She swallowed. Looked at that blue wagon.

The owner was off with the other members of his party? That was good. But what if he returned? What then?

She took up the rucksack and strode forward. She would simply have to be gone before he did so.

That was a problem for the future.

For now, she had to make it across this wide-open space from the fort to her hoped-for hiding place without getting shot in the back.

Del took a breath and another step.

But every muscle was tight. With every step, she expected an outcry to rise from behind her. Surely the guard would see her at any moment and come for her! A wave of lightheadedness made her pause to give herself a little shake. Spots filled her vision. She was working herself into a panic!

Lord, I need You now. Please help me escape without trouble.

Purposely, she took a slow breath. Forced herself to push it out slowly too.

A thought registered, then. How many of the men in the fort even knew that their precious Colonel Boone kept a slave chained in his cellar during the day—and often much of the night?

She suddenly doubted it was very many of them. Otherwise, why would he be so careful about chaining her away out of sight before anyone arrived in the store each morning? And, the day he'd first brought her here, they had paused to rest for several hours. It had been mid-afternoon, and she had been able to see the smoke from the fort's fireplaces in the distance, but Boone hadn't continued until after it grew dark. They'd arrived at his back door only a little later.

She suddenly realized why Betsy had made a point to say she'd told the guard she needed to bring some parcels to the wagons. Disguised as Del was with Betsy's cloak covering her from head to toe, anyone who saw her would, hopefully, think she was Betsy walking up to deliver the goods!

But... would the guard recognize her walk as different from Betsy's? Would he see that she wasn't quite as tall, so the cape nearly touched the ground? Her legs trembled as she forced herself to keep walking.

Lord, I will lift up my eyes to the hills.

That thought brought a smirk. No hills around here. Good thing the hills weren't her protection.

From whence comes my help? My help comes from the Lord, who made heaven and earth. Lord, You are my keeper. You are the shade at my right hand. The sun will not strike me by day, nor the moon by night. You will preserve me from all evil. You will preserve my soul.

Praying scriptures always seemed to calm her. And with each remembered promise from the one hundred and twenty-first Psalm, her breath eased a little, her trembling lessened.

One step at a time, she continued across the open, praying as she went.

When she reached the blue wagon, she hurried around to the back of it and glanced around the area. The encampment remained quiet with no one wandering about. Quickly, before she could lose her resolve, she tugged the cinched canvas loose and peered inside.

Relief swept through her. The interior was empty of occupants, just as Betsy had thought it would be.

After one more glance toward the fort and seeing no one watching her, Del tossed the rucksack inside and clambered in after it.

The dim seclusion behind the oil cloth immediately eased her tension. She'd made it inside without raising any alarm.

Lord, please bless that woman good for what she has done for me. Keep her safe from Boone's wrath. Keep these people of the wagon train safe also. Don't let him find me here and take his anger out on them, please Lord.

And that was when the truth hit her.

If Boone discovered her here among these people, he would destroy anything that got in his way of bringing her back—because she carried his child.

She sank onto the pallet at the back of the space and closed her eyes.

Betsy was right that she couldn't run during the day, but if she could just stay out of sight long enough to keep from being discovered until this party of folks were a few days down the road . . .

She scanned the interior of the wagon. There were a couple of large crates, but they would be filled with this man's supplies, and not even the largest one looked like she could fit all the way inside, even if she did manage to empty it in a way that he wouldn't notice.

With her fingers fidgeting in agitation, she rose and paced the short aisle between the goods. Could she crawl behind some of these crates? But every tiny crack she peeked through revealed more crates stacked behind. The wagon was jammed almost to the arched stays overhead with supplies.

With a sigh, Del turned and paced back the other direction.

The floorboards creaked hollowly beneath her feet.

She looked down.

And stilled.

Chapter 23

Striker Moss did his best to keep his breaths from beating too loudly against his teeth as he followed Cody, placing each step with precision and making sure not to step on any brush that might crackle or any stone that might dislodge and roll to give away their position.

He drew in a long inhale. Keeping up with Cody was like trying to keep up with a gazelle. The man could run without tiring, but they had run along the riverbank ahead of the others—Cranston had said he was too old to keep up, and Hawthorne had most gallantly offered to stay back to keep Cranston company. Striker grinned as he pictured the man's red face and heaving chest. They had descended onto the plain along the riverbank a ways back, and Cody had perused the area for footprints and then declared that no one had passed this way, so they had turned west again and started upriver toward where the other men would hopefully have found the outlaws, Mrs. Houston, and the boys.

Striker gripped his rifle in one hand and kept a keen eye on their surroundings. They needed to move fast, but he was ever mindful that anyone standing in the edge of the trees would be able to pick them off out here in the open like they were. Though they kept themselves as low as possible, both of them were too tall to be hidden by the grass if they wanted to move forward with any speed.

All the while he prayed. *Lord, don't let us be too late to save those boys. Keep that woman alive and safe. Guide us in safety.*

He had his eyes glued carefully to the tree line to their left when the torrential downpour hit them. He grinned. Driving rain like this was good for them because it would drive the outlaws into shelter and cut down on the visibility. Cody broke into a run again. Striker rolled his eyes self-deprecatingly and willed his legs to find the strength to keep up. Thankfully, they'd run for no more than thirty seconds when Cody froze and thrust up one fist.

Striker stopped, but here a tree had fallen and a large root ball rose to block his view of what lay ahead. What had the man seen?

Cody moved so fast that Striker barely had time to register that he had flinched before his bow was stretched taut and an arrow flew through the rainfall.

A man fell into view, clutching at the arrow through his throat. He only thrashed for a moment before going still.

Cody leapt forward now, no longer bothering to be cautious or quiet, and Striker stayed fast on his heels.

They stepped past the wall of roots, and Cody bent to kick the Colt away from the dead man. Relieved that at least this man would no longer be a threat, Striker took another step. A soft gasp drew his attention.

Huddled together where they'd been hidden by dirt and roots, the Slade boys stared at him, wide-eyed.

He whispered, "Boys! Thank God!" He fell to one knee in the mud and held out an arm toward them, still keeping his attention on their surroundings. Cody had another arrow nocked and was methodically sweeping his gaze down the canyon for any other men nearby.

The boys crashed against Striker. The younger one buried his face against his shoulder and Striker could feel his shuddering breaths against his neck.

"I've got you. You're safe now." He held one finger to his lips to let the boys know they should be quiet.

"Thanks, mister," Wyatt whispered. "Thanks ever so much!" The older boy was more sedate, though no less enthusiastic about their arrival. Then suddenly his head shot up. "They've got Mrs. Houston!" He thrust a gesture upriver. "Down there. That Baxter man said he was going to take her into the woods. But for some reason, he told all his men to stay at the camp."

Striker exchanged a look with Cody. Would the other men from the wagon train have found the outlaws yet? He and Cody might be that woman's sole hope! But they couldn't take these boys with them.

His gaze landed on the tall roots of the tree. It was a meager shelter from the driving rain, but it was all they had right now.

Striker stood and drew the boys over. "Sit yourselves down right here."

He despaired over lost time as he waited for the boys to settle. Cody was already moving on silent feet in the direction the boy had pointed.

Striker wanted to call for his friend to wait for him, but couldn't risk revealing their presence to others, and Cody never was one to wait for help.

As quickly as he could, Striker shucked his hatchet and set to piling the chokecherry bushes all around the boys. Water streamed off the brim of his hat and dripped down his neck.

He kept his voice to a whisper as he said, "This won't hide you for long, but it might keep them from seeing you right away. Sit real still and whatever you do, don't run if you see someone else coming, okay? I'll come back for you, I promise." With that, he piled on the last bush that would hide their heads.

Standing back, he was satisfied that the bushes would do the job. Because he knew they were there, he could still see that a couple of boys were behind the pile. But if he didn't know that, he would dismiss the pile without a second look as just a rather large chokecherry bush. It would have to do. He hated to leave them, but from any distance, the brush would disguise them.

There was nothing for it but to leave the boys here. He had to catch up to Cody so they could save Mrs. Houston.

He turned and sprinted in Cody's wake, praying they wouldn't be too late to save the minister's wife.

When Brad released Eden's throat, she gasped for air, choking and gagging, as he grabbed her arm and dragged her closer to the large tree's trunk.

She winced and touched the base of her throat. It burned and shot shards of spasms through her shoulders. Her chest begged for more oxygen than she could supply. Her heart pumped so hard that she could feel it knocking against her breastbone.

That despair, overwhelming and familiar, knocked for entrance, and black spots floated before her eyes.

She had failed the boys!

"Please. You could just let us go. Turn yourself in and do your time." The words were futile, and she knew it even before he barked a laugh.

Without a word, he continued forward with her wrist in that vice grip of his.

He stumbled, fell forward, and propped himself up with one hand. He gave his head a shake.

Eden yanked for her freedom, but his grip hadn't loosened.

He turned on her suddenly. "What did you put in that soup?" The moisture that had glistened on his brow earlier was now large drops, and he'd lost much of his color.

She searched his face hopefully. Were the mushrooms actually working?

"I said." He stepped toward her, yanking her close to wrap his meaty hand around her throat again. "What did you put in that soup?" He spat each word through gritted teeth. His eyes were fissured with red lines, and a bead of sweat trickled down his temple.

Eden swallowed. She didn't know what to say.

She could deny that she'd done anything, but that might get her killed because he wouldn't believe her. And it would be a lie.

But if she admitted that she *had* put something in the soup, he would definitely not be happy, and she didn't want to find out how he might react. But he had seen her put that wood sorrel in the pot, so she said, "The only thing I put in the soup that I didn't plan on was that wood sorrel, and you saw me eat some of that. It's completely harmless."

It wasn't exactly a lie. She had planned on adding the mushrooms.

Would he buy the story, though?

The wind, which had been still until this moment, picked up and began to chatter in the leaves of the trees. Eden shivered, willing herself not to hear them cackling her demise.

A slanting rain fell almost like a curtain, soaking them instantly.

Mumbling something to himself under his breath, he turned and dragged her under the leafier part of the tree.

Relieved, she went with him willingly for the moment, hoping that the poison would take him down before he injured her.

And then she would have to act fast to save the boys.

They were almost to the embankment where they would have to climb up a couple of feet to head further into the trees when Brad yanked his gun from its holster, spun on her, and pressed it to her temple. He scrunched his eyes open and shut a couple of times, and released her wrist to swipe rain from his face and tug at his collar as though he felt like it might be choking him. His pistol wavered. "You better start talking, woman!"

"I don't think she's gonna do that."

Adam's voice!

He leapt from the branch above and crashed into Brad's shoulder.

"Adam!" Eden pressed one hand to her mouth and leaped back. Oh! Had she ever been so happy to see someone in all of her life? He'd come for her!

She turned to run for the boys, but Brad reached out and grabbed her foot, sending her sprawling!

A loud thud, and Adam grunted in pain.

Eden flipped over just in time to see Adam strike Brad's temple with the butt of his pistol.

Brad grunted and stumbled sideways. He almost lost his balance, but caught himself with one hand against the ground. And then he was swinging his pistol in Adam's direction.

"Adam! He's got a gun!"

"Eden, get out of here!" Adam stepped inside Brad's arm and kicked the heel of his boot down on the man's arch.

Brad screamed in pain.

Then Adam hooked one leg behind him and shoved him over backward.

Brad landed hard, but lurched to one knee.

Fat drops of rain fell through the leaves of the oak now.

Eden ought to try again to reach the boys, but she couldn't just leave Adam here to fight alone! Yet, what could she do to help? She felt grounded to the spot.

"That way!" He pointed toward the embankment, and she now saw that Jeremiah was up by the tree trunk. If she could get to him, maybe he could help her get the boys! Eden sprang to her feet, and as she ran toward the embankment, Adam swung another kick at the hand in which Brad held his gun.

Brad tucked the weapon close to his chest.

Adam's kick missed.

Brad lunged at her as she passed, but Adam swung hard. This time it was his fist that connected with Brad's jaw.

Brad stumbled back, shaking his head, and gingerly working his jaw back and forth.

Adam placed himself between her and the outlaw, crouched at the ready, with his revolver before him pointed at the man. "Don't move, Baxter. I will shoot."

Brad moaned and shook his head like a dog with something in his ears.

"Come here, Mrs. Houston. Right here, ma'am." Jeremiah stretched a hand down toward her, though his gaze remained fixed on Brad. He wiggled his fingers as though to encourage her to hurry.

Eden ran toward him. She leapt for his hand, but missed and slid down the muddy embankment. Trying to ignore the pain in her knee, she limped a couple of steps back to get a running start and try again.

Behind her, she heard Adam's footsteps rustle in the grass. "Stay where you are. Don't even flinch other than to drop your gun."

Brad backed away several steps.

Adam moved with him, still keeping himself between the man and Eden. "Don't move. Drop your gun!"

Brad retreated a few more steps, leaving the shelter of the oak's branches and stepping into the rain that had eased some now.

Adam moved forward another couple of steps.

Eden's gaze darted to the maple by the river. "Adam, wait! There's a—"

"Malkovich! Shoot him!" Brad's gravelly bellow cut across the flat river plains. He dropped to one knee to give the guard the best possible trajectory, straight to Adam.

"No!"

A shot rang out.

Her call of warning had been too late.

Adam flinched. Grabbed at his head. Then fell headlong into the brush.

No! Eden's heart stuttered. Why hadn't she thought about the guard posted in that tree earlier? "Adam!"

Two more shots quickly followed the first.

Eden didn't even have time to wonder if she was being shot at. All she could think was that she had to get to Adam! She scrambled toward him. He'd fallen between two bushes, with one side of his face buried in the mud. Blood coated his cheek and dripped with the raindrops into the hollows of his nose and eye.

Eden lost the strength in her legs and fell to her knees. Dampness soaked through her skirts. "Adam." The word was barely more than a whisper.

Jeremiah yelled something, but she didn't register the words.

She must think, move, react. But she could only seem to stare at Adam's prostrate body.

And the blood. So much blood.

She felt herself sway.

"Mrs. Houston, you got to move now, so's I can take my shot." Jeremiah's voice rang sharp with command.

She glanced up to see that he'd taken partial shelter behind the trunk of the oak, but had his rifle leveled toward Brad. A glance at Brad, who was snaking toward her on his belly, showed that she must be blocking Jeremiah's angle. Would he even be able to see the man through all this thick brush?

Move! She must move. She worked to get one foot under her, but felt as though every movement was hampered by leaden weights chained to every limb.

Jeremiah dove to one side, trying to get a shot around her.

But Brad surged forward and grabbed her, holding her before him like a shield.

Once again, his pistol pressed with cold finality to her temple.

Eden's eyes fell closed in defeat.

Jeremiah stared down the barrel of his rifle, tasting the bitterness of failure. Was Adam dead? He'd certainly gone down hard. That guard in that tree must have been quite a shot. That had to be a hundred yards or better, and he'd been aiming through the rain!

There had been two more shots. Shots taken *by* Micah and Gideon? Or shots taken *at* them? Hopefully the former. And hopefully they'd both hit their marks. Even if that were the case, that left one man still unaccounted for.

And yet now, silence rang through the flats.

If Micah and Gid had been the shooters, shouldn't at least one of them have taken another shot?

He didn't like the silence. Didn't like this not knowing.

All those thoughts flitted through his mind as he kept a steady aim toward Brad and Mrs. Houston.

She'd gone to pieces there for a moment when Adam fell, and could he really blame her? Watching the man she loved get killed before her very eyes would throw anyone for a loop. But if she had moved just a moment earlier, the situation they now found themselves in could have been prevented.

Maybe he was the one who should have moved sooner, but with the brush growing waist high as it did here, and the way Brad had been belly-crawling toward her, the angle he'd been at, kneeling there on the embankment, would have been the best option for a clean shot.

Everything had happened so fast.

Now he must be calm and think through what to do.

He suddenly wished Striker were here. Ever since they were boys, Striker seemed to have a way with thinking through all the scenarios and coming up with the best possible solution. Even when Striker had talked his daddy into giving Jeremiah to him as a fifteenth birthday gift, they had laid out the plan ahead of time. And the situation had happened just as Striker had assured him it would. Striker, with his heart that was bigger than the whole of both Carolinas, had never been fond of his daddy's slave-run plantation. But he'd known that asking for Jeremiah's freedom outright would have been a request that was declined by his father. So instead, he'd told Jeremiah that he would ask for him as a gift. Jeremiah's heart had pumped with fear then, just as it pumped with fear now. He hadn't known yet just how much he could trust old Strike. His father had said no at first, just as Striker had told Jeremiah he would. But then Striker had lamented to a friend within his father's hearing about how he wouldn't be able to plant cotton on the piece of land that he had purchased because he had no slave to work it.

Wanting to encourage his son's entrepreneurial spirit, his father had relented and signed Jeremiah over to him.

They had taken their first trip west, not more than six months later, and Striker had given Jeremiah his freedom the day after they left.

Brad's feet shifted, bringing Jeremiah back to the present. The gunsight of his rifle centered on the one eye he could see just beyond Mrs. Houston's neck. There was no way he'd miss from this distance. But he didn't have Cody's confidence. He couldn't risk injuring Mrs. Houston.

The outlaw grinned and ground the pistol against Eden's temple, peering from behind her with a leer. "What's it gonna be, darky? You gonna lay down your weapon? Or am I gonna shoot this here pretty lady?"

"You shoot her and it will be the last thing you ever do." Again, he assessed the risk of taking the shot.

Brad hesitated at his words.

Had the man truly not considered what might happen if he felled his sole bargaining chip?

Jeremiah drew in a calming breath. "Don't want to shoot you. Just let the lady go and we'll take you in, peaceable like."

The man didn't look like he was feeling so good. Maybe it was the pressure of the situation getting to him? He seemed to be trembling, and was starting to sway so much that Jeremiah could see his whole head appear from behind Mrs. Houston before it disappeared again a second later. Still not far enough from Mrs. Houston's head to risk the shot, however.

Something drew Baxter's gaze, but with the thick leafy branches of the oak hanging in his way, Jeremiah could not see what Baxter had seen. Whatever it was caused the man to curse and drag Mrs. Houston closer to a chokecherry bush.

"Don't you move, mister. Don't you move another hair."

Jeremiah was glad to see that the man obeyed his command. Another couple of steps and he would be behind the bush, and Jeremiah would never be able to risk a shot. His chances were slim enough as it was. He couldn't worry about whatever the outlaw had seen. He had one job, and that was to try to get Mrs. Houston out of danger now. No other shots had come. He knew that if those two shots hadn't killed the man in the tree, the angle from him to Jeremiah's place up on the embankment would likely be blocked by the leaves of the oak. But to rescue Mrs. Houston, he would have to jump down from this embankment, and if he jumped down, he could be visible and vulnerable, just as Adam had been.

To keep Mrs. Houston alive, he had to stay alive.

After assessing the situation for a moment, he decided that he should remain on the embankment. The best thing he could do right now was to keep this man here until Striker, Cody, and the others arrived. Or maybe Micah and Gid? He hadn't seen them since he'd noted from the corner of his eye that they'd dropped into the flats a few minutes back, just after Adam fell.

Praying was also something he could do while holding this outlaw at bay.

Lord, I know You see this fix we are in down here. Adam dying. Maybe dead already. Certainly knocked out and needing help. Mrs. Houston in the very arms of danger.

"What will it be, stranger?" Did the outlaw recognize how badly his voice was trembling?

From behind the man and Mrs. Houston, Jeremiah caught movement.

Chapter 24

Gideon Riley had been on his belly in the wet grass with his rifle trained on the guard in the tree when one of the outlaws below had shouted, "Malkovich! Shoot him!" He'd known right then and there that the time for staying out of sight had passed. He surged to his knees to get a better angle, steadied his breath, and leveled his rifle on the man's chest through the rain.

In the grass on the ground near the corral, one of the other outlaws surged to his feet, but Gideon knew Micah would take care of him. The other man was either sound asleep or simply unconcerned for all that was taking place around him, for he didn't move.

As Gid was steadying his aim, the man in the tree moved to get a better angle, putting a branch between his chest and Gideon. Gideon raised his rifle until his sight was centered on the man's ear, just below his hat brim. But before he could get realigned, the outlaw squeezed off a shot!

Gideon felt despair rush through him even as he pulled his own trigger. The man slumped and fell, crashing to the ground in a heap beneath the tree, but Gideon couldn't find any relief in that. He had been too late.

"Don't you move! We've got you covered!" Micah called the words down to the camp.

But the second outlaw leaped to his feet and spun in their direction, raising his gun!

Micah shot him.

Together they jumped off the embankment and down onto the flats by the river. Their position was given away now, anyhow, and the element of surprise no longer needed.

Crouching low, they moved as quickly as they could toward the two fallen men. Would there be others? So far, they hadn't seen anyone else.

The man Gideon had shot was dead. Even so, Gideon kicked his rifle away from his body and shucked the pistol from the man's holster.

He looked over at Micah, who had his fingers on the pulse of the man he had shot. Micah shook his head and then proceeded to remove that man's weapons and move to the other outlaw who still lay on the ground.

When Micah bent over that man and touched his neck, the man groaned and clutched at his belly. He writhed a little, moaning something about pain in his stomach. Micah quickly snatched his weapons and stepped back. "Something is wrong with this one. Must be sick."

"He faking it?"

The outlaw rolled to his side and proceeded to upchuck into the grass.

Micah took another step back and looked over at him. He shook his head. "Don't think so."

Gideon had to concur. In the state that man was in, he wouldn't be going anywhere likely, but at least tying him up would slow him down a little if he tried.

He tugged a piece of rawhide from his pocket and moved to the man's feet. It scarcely took him a moment to tie his ankles together.

He stood and looked at Micah. "Now what?"

Micah pointed toward the large oak on the embankment across the way. They moved silently in that direction.

Gideon could only hope that his delay had not cost any of their party their lives.

A group of cavalrymen on horses surged from the tree line. One of them shot into the air, and another gestured for them to put their hands up.

Gid exchanged a look with Micah as they both lifted their hands into the air. With one of these outlaws being that colonel's brother, were these cavalrymen on their side, or on the outlaws'?

Eden closed her eyes and tried not to feel the press of the pistol at her temple. Brad trembled consistently now, and his breaths puffed against her cheek.

Upriver, a shot rang out! It echoed across the plains, making its origin hard to pinpoint.

Brad cursed and searched the riverbank, up and down. But he didn't dare turn his back on Jeremiah.

Thankfully, his attention was momentarily diverted from shooting her! But that shot . . . Was it in the direction of the boys?

No! Dear Jesus, please.

Hoofbeats thundered against soft soil.

She frowned. Hoofbeats? Killingbeck wouldn't be on a horse this soon. And there were too many horses for it to be a single man.

Also, there had only been one shot just now. But those other shots earlier . . . Could they have been Killingbeck taking out the boys?

Her emotions swirled.

Uncertainty.

Sorrow.

Horror.

Terror.

Brad cursed again. He was in a tight spot with some unknown riders approaching from behind, and Jeremiah holding him at gunpoint from the embankment that they faced.

Eden strained to see over her shoulder. Who was coming? Surely horses meant help! Quickly on the heels of that thought came another that sent a cold wash of terror through her. Did Brad have other men? Were these more of his band of outlaws riding to his rescue?

Please, God...

Something drew Jeremiah's gaze to a spot behind them.

With one swift move, Brad pivoted, yanking her with him, which put a chokecherry bush between them and Jeremiah. Adam lay sprawled just to one side near their feet.

Eden closed her eyes, refusing to look at him for one moment longer. She trembled, even as she heard Jeremiah's boots thump into the brush on the other side of the bush. She halfway expected Brad to end her right then and there, but then realized that if he wanted to make his escape, he still needed her as a hostage. She opened her eyes to see who was coming this way.

Surprise coursed through her when she saw a man in military uniform riding at the head of a group of soldiers.

She ought to feel relief. Instead, all she could feel was a mounting dread as the barrel of Brad's pistol dug into her temple. Rescue may be here, but it had likely arrived too late.

"You stay back, darkey. You understand?" Brad shuffled them further into the branches of the bush. "I hear you take one more step and this little lady here is done for."

Lord, if it's my time to go, please take care of those children.

At least she wouldn't have to go on living without Adam.

The cavalrymen rode close and spread out along the perimeter of the oak's branches, forming a half circle around them. With the embankment behind, they were effectively trapped.

The leader, who now sat in the middle of his line of men, leaned to one side and spat before he propped his forearms on his saddle horn like he was settling in to stay for a while. "Brad, you blazing fool. Let her go, right now, and maybe I can save your life!"

Eden felt a tremor work through Brad. The chokecherry bush rustled behind her as Brad stepped further into the concealment of its branches. "You know I can't do that, Boone. She's my insurance out of here."

"*I'm* your insurance out of here."

Something about the way the man said that sent a cold wash of premonition down Eden's neck.

"W-wish, I c-could believe that." Brad trembled so badly now that Eden feared the gun might go off accidentally. She felt more of his weight press against her throat like he was using her to help hold himself upright. He dragged her back another inch as though he wished the bush could swallow him and port him to another location. "Don't make me hurt her."

Footsteps crunched behind them.

"Stay back!" Brad yelled. "You keep that darky back, Boone, or I swear this woman is done for."

Boone looked weary. He swung a finger from one of his men toward where Eden presumed Jeremiah had been moving behind the bush.

The soldier swung his rifle in that direction. "Stay where you are, boy."

Revulsion filled Eden's chest. Jeremiah was just trying to help her. Couldn't these men see that?

The shuffling footsteps stilled.

"He's not moving, Brad." The colonel spat at the ground again. "Now let the woman go."

She felt Brad shake his head.

Beneath their feet, thick leaves left over from last fall and now wet with the rain made the ground slick. Eden felt Brad slip. The gun momentarily pointed away from her head as he automatically swung his arm out to catch his balance.

A feral yell split the air. Something crashed into them from the side!

Eden gasped as she was knocked to a sprawl in the brush. Her hands grated painfully against the ground. What had hit them?

She turned over to look back.

"Adam!"

He was alive!

Brad must have lost his grip on his weapon because his hands were empty as he and Adam wrestled in the grass. Adam knelt over the man and threw a fist. The loud crack of it connecting with Brad's cheek reverberated in the canyon.

Adam paused to shake his head and take a breath.

Brad heaved his hips upward and pitched Adam over his head. The outlaw barreled after him, taking up a large chunk of rock in one hand.

Eden covered her mouth.

Adam thrust out one leg and kicked the rock from Brad's hand. He scrambled to get to his feet.

Brad clutched his wrist and panted. Then lunged at Adam, taking him to the ground where he straddled him and began swinging.

The colonel continued to lean on his pommel, as though he were simply enjoying an evening at a theater. There was even a hint of a smile on his lips.

"Do something!" Her outrage filled her voice as she gestured for him to help Adam.

The man didn't even glance her way.

Still pinning Adam to the ground, Brad scrabbled his hand through the leaves in search of another rock. Adam panted and seemed dazed. Blood oozed from a gash in the side of his head.

When Brad's fist came up with another rock, Eden dove forward. Those men might be content to do nothing. But she wouldn't sit by and watch Adam bludgeoned!

When her shoulder crashed into Brad, it was like meeting a stone wall. He chuckled and flicked his arm, sending her flying. Eden's hip landed first and shot her through with sharp agony. She'd fallen on something. Another rock?

She rolled off it with a groan and reached to feel what it was. The gun!

She snatched it up and leveled it at Brad. "Stop or I will shoot you!" Her fingers felt clumsy as she searched for the trigger. The gun shook in her hands. She took a breath and tried to steady it. She may not know much about weapons, but she was only a few feet from the man. Surely she could hit him. But she couldn't see beyond the bush! What if she missed and hit Jeremiah?

Brad froze with his rock-filled hand in midair. He glanced over at her.

Behind her, the colonel snickered. "Best do as she says, Bradley boy."

Brad hesitated, but Adam didn't. With one quick arch of his back, he rolled and came out on top! He pinned Brad's wrist to the ground and rammed his forehead into the man's face with a loud crack!

Brad cried out as blood spurted from his broken nose.

Adam reared back again.

"Adam, stop!" Eden tossed the gun and scurried forward on her hands and knees.

"Stay back." Adam's sharp command didn't come soon enough.

Brad slammed his elbow into Adam's sternum and sent him flying again. Once again, she found herself in the grip of the outlaw.

At least this time he didn't have a gun in his hand. He locked one hand around her throat instead. "Let me go, Boone. Just let me walk on out of here. I'll ride west and you'll never see me again. I swear."

Eden heard the rustle of several rapid footsteps and then, from almost beside her, a man's voice spoke. "Let her go or this arrow's going straight through your ear."

Brad's grip on her relaxed, and Eden stumbled forward and into Adam's arms.

He drew her close, and she trembled with gratefulness to be leaning on his strength once again. He really was alive! She pressed her face into the hollow of his neck and inhaled the blessed familiar scent of him. She felt him broaden his stance to accept her weight and realized he was in no shape to be holding her up. She eased back. His focus remained fixed on the situation behind her.

When she turned to see her rescuer, she found Cody Hawkeye.

The colonel straightened in his saddle. "Easy there, scout. Let's let justice prevail here."

Cody didn't even spare him a glance. "On your knees." He pressed his arrow further into Brad's ear. "Don't even think about reaching for that gun."

"I'm not moving. Not moving." Brad carefully kept his hands in sight.

Eden noticed Striker Moss then. He stood a few short steps to one side, with his rifle stretched over the low branch of one of the river birches.

How had those two moved so silently through the grass? She hadn't even heard them coming until Cody was right next to them.

Brad suddenly slumped forward and threw up in the leaves before him. He clutched his belly and thrust a trembling finger toward her. "She poisoned me!"

Cody grimaced as he carefully avoided the pile of sick and kicked Brad's pistol farther away from him. After a quick frisk of the man and seeing that he had no more weapons on him, he stepped back and nodded from Adam toward the man.

"Stay here, please." Adam set her to one side, stepped over to Brad, and, taking him by the shirtfront, hauled him to his feet.

He marched the man toward the half circle of soldiers and only loosed him when the colonel gestured at one who swung down and set to tying Brad's wrists with a strand of rawhide.

Stepping back, Adam wiped the heel of his hand at the corner of his mouth and spat blood. Then he looked at the colonel and thumbed a gesture to Brad. "This is the outlaw who attacked that wagon train and killed those folk. Kidnapped my wife and two boys from that train that we helped—one of whom drew that sketch I showed you." He touched the side of his head and showed the colonel his bloodied fingers. "Tried to kill me."

The colonel sighed and swung down from his mount. "I'm very sorry about all this." There was a note of dejection in his voice. "This sorry lout of a cuss may be my brother, but he'll face a trial just as soon as we can get one set up. I'll need you to testify. None of you are to go any further than your current encampment until the trial is concluded."

"Boone, you can't mean it!" Brad practically wailed.

A group of three soldiers rode up. One of them spoke. "Found three other men, Colonel. Two were shot. One is so sick we can't get him to wake up."

"It's the poison! I'm telling you she poisoned us!" Brad wailed.

Micah stepped forward. "We shot those two men, but not until after they shot Adam there."

Colonel Baxter didn't acknowledge Micah or his brother's lamentation. He only turned his horse and started away, presumably heading back to the fort. He snapped his fingers from a soldier to Brad. "Load him onto his horse and bring all the bodies back to the fort."

His men rushed to do as he instructed. All except the soldier who held his gun on Jeremiah—he remained where he stood.

Eden frowned. Why was he doing that? The danger had passed.

Yet there was a gleam of something feral in the soldier's eyes. Water dripped from the man's hat, giving him the appearance of a statue.

Jeremiah didn't move a muscle either.

Striker lowered his weapon and strode toward her. "You okay, ma'am?"

Eden nodded, noting as she did so that Striker had stepped into the line of fire between the soldier and Jeremiah.

"I'm right glad to hear that." Striker spoke to her, but his gaze was leveled on the soldier. The man smirked, then turned, mounted up, and rode away through the sleeting rain.

Eden heard Jeremiah release a breath. He lowered his hands and rolled his shoulders as though to relieve some tension. Gave Striker a nod of thanks.

Eden pressed her hands together. She wanted nothing more than to get Adam back to their pallet where he could lie down and she could tend his wounds. But... "We have to find the boys. I'm afraid—"

"We found them." Striker started back in the direction from which he and Cody had just come. "They're safe. I'll fetch them. Be right back."

"Oh!" Eden wanted to collapse with the relief of it. "Thank you. Thank you so much!" She felt torn between seeing to Adam and going with Striker.

Adam waved for her to follow Striker. "Get the boys. I'm fine."

"You're sure?" She searched him from head to toe.

He smiled. "I'll still be alive when you get back."

Eden started to turn but then froze. "Afton! Did you find her? I had to leave her alone in the wagon."

Adam nodded. "She's fine. Mercy is watching her."

Relief took the last of her tension. She tossed up prayers of thanks as she hefted her skirts and darted into the rain on the scout's heels. Toward the boys. Her boys. Boys whom she wasn't ever going to let go to another family!

She willed herself not to cry, but couldn't seem to stop the silent tears that fell to meld with the rain streaming down her cheeks.

She'd held herself together just fine until this moment.

Ahead of her, Striker called above the rain, "Boys? It's safe now. Come on out."

A pile of brush moved and Wyatt surged through the leaves, hauling Ash with him.

"Oh, boys, come here!" Eden pushed past Striker and drew the boys into a tight embrace. She was suddenly sobbing with relief. "Thank You, Jesus. Oh, thank You, Jesus!" She pressed kisses against both boys' curly wet mops, then turned to Striker. "Thank you. Ever so much."

Striker smiled and touched the brim of his hat. "Weren't nothing, ma'am. We should all rejoin the others. We need to get Adam back to camp. I think he'll need stitches."

"Yes. Come on, boys. The outlaws have all been rounded up. We're safe now."

When they reached the others once more, she found that Adam was seated on the log where they'd first collected the mushrooms. He rose as they approached, and all the other men suddenly found other things to do.

"I'll find Cranston and Hawthorne," Cody said.

Striker nodded. "Jeremiah and I will get the horses."

Micah and Gideon strode in the scouts' wake with parting touches to their hats.

Eden didn't spare them more than a glance because she couldn't seem to take her eyes off her husband. The rain had plastered his hair into wet curls against his head, which covered the gash carved by Malkovich's bullet. The blood had also mostly been rinsed from his face.

She was glad the boys didn't have to see how bad he had looked only moments ago.

She walked into the circle of his arms.

"Eden." He pressed a kiss to her hair. "Thank God." He turned then. "Boys, you all right?"

Wyatt and Ash nodded.

"Yes, sir." Wyatt said.

"I'm tired!" Ash proclaimed.

Adam and Eden exchanged a laugh.

Eden reluctantly withdrew from Adam's arms and took the boy's hand. "As soon as we get back to the camp, we'll get you tucked in for the night, okay?"

Wyatt folded his arms and frowned as he stared off toward the river. "I couldn't pray. I tried. But no words would come."

Adam sank back onto the log, and Eden recognized the pain pinching his features even as he gestured the boy closer.

Eden worried. They needed to get him back to the wagon quickly. But for now, she was content to simply have all of them together again.

She could worry about doctoring him and getting everyone dry once they returned to the wagons.

When Wyatt sank onto the log beside him, Adam swept one arm around the boy's shoulders. "Do you know that I had the same thing happen to me? A few times over the last few days, actually. The first time was when I thought you were about to be trampled by that herd."

Wyatt shot his gaze to Adam's. "Really?"

Adam nodded. "I was scared. I'm sorry that I yelled at you that night."

Searching his face, Wyatt asked, "You were scared I would be hurt?"

Adam nodded. "And again today, I was so worried about Eden and you boys that no thoughts seemed to want to form in my mind. All I could cry out was 'God, please.' But you know what? That's okay, because God looks at our hearts. He knows we are but dust. And the book of Romans tells us that the Spirit helps us in our weakness. When we don't know what to say, He makes intercession for us. God can fully understand our cries of 'God, please!'"

Wyatt sniffed and swiped a hand at his nose. "That's good, because we sure did need Him." He lifted his gaze to Adam then. "Thanks for coming after us."

Adam gripped the boy's shoulder. "I'll always come after you, son."

Again, Wyatt scrutinized Adam's face, uncertainty in his expression.

Eden drew in a breath. Had Adam just said what she thought he'd said?

"What about me?" Asher chirped.

Adam grinned and pinged a glance off her before lowering it to the boy by her side. "You too, Ash. You too."

Wyatt shifted. "We don't want to be a burden, even though we know we've been one already. We ain't family and you don't have to—"

Adam raised a hand. "I have something to say."

Eden held her breath.

"I've been a coward." Adam snatched a blade of grass and shredded it methodically in his fingers. The pieces fell into a puddle forming at his feet. "Sometimes it's hard for a man to face his feelings, boys. But a real man, well, eventually he can learn to face them."

There was humor in the gaze he settled on Eden.

She covered her own smile with one hand.

"Sometimes it's easier to hide from things that we are afraid might hurt us. But God tells us that in this world we will have tribulations, but we are to take heart because He has overcome the world. I don't know what the future holds. What I do know is that I want us all to face it together, if, well, if you boys are okay with that. And we'll let you make the decision for Afton too."

He reached to ruffle a hand through Wyatt's hair, grimaced, and clutched at his ribcage.

Wyatt frowned and folded his arms, kicking one toe at a clump of grass.

Eden stepped forward. She hoped Adam could read the caution in her gaze. They couldn't push these boys too far. They'd lost so much, only days ago. "Tell you what? Why don't you boys think on it, and we can talk more once we are back at camp and in the shelter of the wagon this evening, okay?"

Wyatt nodded, looking thoughtfully serious. He stood and reached a hand through the rain to Asher. "Come on, Ash. We're gonna have to walk back to camp because we don't have any horses. We might as well get started."

Jeremiah drew up beside them, riding a horse and leading another. Striker rode his Morgan beside him. He swung down and hefted Asher up behind Jeremiah, then looked at Wyatt. "I'm gonna swing up into the saddle and reach down and sling you up behind me, all right? It's best we make a beeline for the camp because it looks like another doozy of a storm is headed this way." When Wyatt nodded, the man transferred his gaze to Adam. "You going to be okay to ride that far? You'll have to share your horse with your wife."

Adam's smile returned in full force as he glanced over at her. "I'm feeling better already."

Eden felt heat surge into her cheeks. She reached to tuck a drenched strand of hair back into her bun. Of all the times for him to flirt with her? She probably looked like a drowning prairie dog.

Striker took in her face and chortled. "I guess that's our cue to get out of here, boys." He handed Adam the reins to his mount, and when he had hauled Wyatt up onto his horse behind him, he set off at a canter in Jeremiah's wake.

Chapter 25

Jeremiah was bone weary and soaked to the skin by the time he returned to the encampment. He had stood watch last night and ridden through this day on only three hours of sleep, and now, as he stripped his saddle and turned his horse into the temporary rope corral in the center of the circled wagons, he tipped a look at the sheets of rain falling from the sky. "I sure am glad that it's your turn to stand guard tonight." He reached out and clapped Striker on one shoulder.

"Yeah, yeah," Striker grumbled good-naturedly. "See the boys to the Houstons' place, would you, before you climb into the Slade wagon to get all dry and cozy, like the mollycoddled man that you are."

Jeremiah chuckled. "Sure thing." If there was one thing he appreciated about Striker, it was that the man saw him as just another man. Another friend that he teased like any other. That he stood up for like any other. "Say, Strike?"

"Yeah?" The man turned to squint at him through the rain as he hunched his shoulders and tugged his collar beneath his hat brim.

"Thanks for what you did back there." For several moments, he'd wondered if that soldier was going to shoot him just for the fun of it.

"Saving those boys? Of course! That's what we heroes do." Striker spread his hands as though to say he couldn't help but be amazing. "The way you were just standing around there, though, it's a good thing that

I showed up when I did. I don't think you could've got the job done without me, Jer. And maybe Cody. He helped a little." The small gap between his upheld fingers emphasized his teasing.

Jeremiah couldn't fall in with his friend's light treatment of the matter. He shook his head at his yarn-spinning friend. "I mean it, Strike. I thought I was looking at my end there for a moment."

Striker turned serious, sighed, and stared off toward the west. His shoulders seemed to take on the weight of Jeremiah's burden as he hung his head toward the ground. He bent and snatched a blade of grass and tucked the stem into one corner of his mouth. "I hope we'll be able to make things better in the west, Jer. Truly, I do."

Jeremiah believed him. He hoped Striker could hear the seriousness in his tone when he offered, "I'm glad you're my friend, Strike. Sure am glad."

As though coming back from a far-off land, Striker grinned and pummeled Jeremiah's shoulder with one fist. "Aw, Jer. Don't go getting all soft on me. Now if you'll excuse me, I think I'd better go prepare Miss Acheson for the arrival of the parson because he's gonna need her ministrations." His friend turned and dashed through the rain toward the Acheson wagon.

Jeremiah loosed a bark of laughter. "Go on with you, then! I hope Miss Acheson doesn't give you the time of day, and that it rains all night!"

Striker's laughter floated through the rain as he waved one hand over his shoulder.

Jeremiah glanced down to see the two soaking wet boys staring up at him from where they both huddled into their shoulders.

"Come on, boys. Let's fetch you some dry clothes from your folks' chest and then get you settled for the night." He picked up Asher and dashed with him through the rain to the Slades' wagon. Once they were inside, he settled Asher on his feet and glanced around. "Now then. Which trunk is yours? You'd best get dry and then plan on sleeping on that pallet there for the night. This storm seems like it's going to be one doozy of a blow. You boys certainly don't want to be trying to sleep in that hammock on a night like this one."

Wyatt stepped over to a trunk on one side of the aisle. "If it's all the same to you, mister. We've got family business to discuss and need to fetch Afton." He opened the trunk and pulled out two pairs of britches and two clean shirts. These he rolled into a tight bundle that he tucked close to his chest. He bounced a glance off the empty pallet at the front of the space and then turned his back on it. "We'll just run through the rain and fetch Afton from the Morrans and then get changed in the Houstons' wagon. We can sleep on the floor over there in the middle of the aisle tonight. You might as well make use of that dry bed as anyone. My folks would want you to make yourself at home."

With that, he nudged Asher back out into the rain, and Jeremiah stood peering through the oil cloth opening to watch as they ran to the Morrans' wagon. Wyatt said something to Mrs. Morran, who shook her head and shooed them toward the Houstons' wagon. Jeremiah guessed that Afton was already asleep and Mrs. Morran didn't want the boys disturbing her. Jeremiah remained where he stood until the boys had disappeared inside.

Only once they were safe did he take up his pack and drop it on the bed at the back of the space. He didn't usually sleep in here, but on a night like this, it sure seemed to be the best alternative. Tonight, a bedroll beneath would be soaked clean through before it hardly touched the ground. And the wagon box surely wouldn't keep much of that slanting rain off. He would sleep a sight better in here, and that was certain.

He hooked his hat on an S hook looped into one of the stays overhead and then shucked out of his sheepskin coat. That, he draped over a stack of crates where it would have the best chance of drying. Even so, it would likely still be damp by morning. He unhooked his holster and hung it from the S hook before rehanging his hat, then toed off his boots and tugged a dry pair of buckskins and socks from his rucksack. He stripped out of the soaked ones he'd been wearing. These he also draped over crates in the space.

It sure felt good to don dry duds and sink down onto the edge of that pallet.

With his elbows planted on his knees, he bent forward to rest his weary head into his hands. "Lord, You surely been good to me."

It was in that moment that he took note of the rucksack on the floor. Slowly, he straightened. The bag was brown leather, supple and new. Certainly not anything he'd seen in here before. Not a bag the Slades were likely to have, poor folk that they were.

Jeremiah's gaze fell to the trap door that led to the compartment Mr. Slade had built beneath the floorboards. A soft gasp emerged from the darkness below.

Slowly, he stood and withdrew his Paterson from his holster, never taking his eyes off the floor.

He stepped off the door, and then in one swift move, he bent and snatched the compartment open.

"Don't shoot me. For the love of God, please don't shoot me!" A woman's voice, barely above a breath of a whisper, emerged from the darkness of the space.

Jeremiah's mouth fell open.

For there, lying in the floor of the wagon, with trembling hands held up before her, was quite possibly the most beautiful woman he'd ever seen!

"I can explain," she said tremulously.

Jeremiah checked both ends of the cinched canvas. Looked down at the woman with her honey-hued skin and hazel eyes. Took in the rucksack, once more. His thoughts turned to the fort and the fact that all the soldiers had been out hunting Bradley Baxter today.

His heart hammered in his chest. "I think you better do that, yes."

Eden couldn't move as the men and boys rode away. All she could do was stare at her husband with so much relief and thankfulness and amazement coursing through her. This man that she had been so certain had traveled on to eternity without her just a few minutes ago.

He inched a step closer to her and smiled softly. "Do you know how good it is to see you standing there safe and whole? I thought I was going to lose you."

A huff of laughter spurted from Eden's lips. She stepped close to him and parted his hair on the side to see what his curls were hiding. She gasped when she caught sight of the shallow trench of missing hair just above his ear. "Adam! You thought you were going to lose me? For a moment there, you were stretched out at my feet like you were prepared for your coffin."

He winced away from her touch. "Let's not talk about coffins. I think both of us came closer than either of us is comfortable thinking about."

"I agree. Please sit down." She nudged him onto the log and then bent and took hold of the sides of the tear in her skirt from when she had fallen on the stone earlier. She tore away the bottom six inches of her hem and hurried to the river to clean the material as much as possible. After wringing it out, she returned to stand in front of him and stepped close. She wrapped the strip of cloth around his head and tucked in the end to hold it in place. "This is bad, Adam. Come on. We need to get you back to camp."

The fact that he didn't resist as she led him to the horse and helped him mount set her heart to hammering even harder than it already had been. He must be in a great deal of pain, indeed, not to brush away her concern. There was no way he would have the strength to haul her up onto the saddle before him. Besides, she'd ridden out here with a pommel gouging into her thigh, and she had no desire to repeat that discomfort on the way back.

She took up the reins and started toward the forest at a jog, leading the horse behind.

Cody Hawkeye emerged from the trees and met her. "Here, Micah and Gideon are riding double, so you can ride Gid's horse back to camp."

Relieved, Eden didn't even protest the offer. "Thank you so much." She mounted and settled into the saddle, not even caring that her ankles were showing.

He handed her the reins. "They are ahead of us. You got your seat?" Eden nodded and was never more thankful to turn leadership over to someone in all her born days. She wasn't even sure she would have known how to find her way back through all those trees to the camp near the fort.

Cody set out at a ground-eating lope, leading Adam's horse. Eden trailed behind.

Adam looked like he barely had the strength to hold onto the saddle. Several times she saw him clutch for the saddle horn.

It seemed forever before they emerged from the trees, and in the distance, she could see the light of several campfires near the wagons. "Hold on, Adam. We're almost home."

Adam's head lolled, bouncing like a rag doll atop his shoulders.

She leaned over and gripped his arm, but if he went over, there was no way she'd have the strength to hold him up! Worry pinched her brow. He didn't look good at all.

Was she going to have his life miraculously returned to her only to lose him again?

Men surged toward them now, and Striker reached up to steady Adam as they moved the last few yards to stop near Tamsyn's place. She was there, waiting beneath the canvas at the back of her Conestoga.

The woman jumped down and started snapping orders almost before they got Adam to the ground. "In here, please, where I'll have all my supplies." She pointed and then followed Striker and Cody inside.

There was no room for Eden, so she was left to pace the damp grass.

But she heard Tamsyn say, "Cody, fetch me another lamp, please. Mr. Moss, you hold this one. Now then, Parson Houston, how are you faring?"

Adam mumbled a reply that Eden couldn't quite make out.

Cody leaped down and darted the few steps to knock on the Morrans' tailgate.

Eden paced the circumference of Tamsyn's fire.

From behind the canvas, she heard Striker say, "He gets to be Cody, but I'm Mr. Moss?" There was a tenor of mock hurt in the question.

"Move the light closer, please," was all Tamsyn curtly replied. "Parson, you'll feel some pain as I clean your wound. Try to hold as still as possible."

"What about the, ah, Hawthorne woman?" Striker asked.

Eden frowned and glanced toward the Hawthorne place. It was too soon for the baby, wasn't it?

"These things take time," Tamsyn said.

It must be the baby!

Water trickled, and Mr. Moss fell silent so she supposed she'd have to content herself with guesses. Cody returned only a moment later and clambered in to join Tamsyn, Striker, and Adam with another lantern.

"Set it there and then get out, please. I need room to move. No. Not you, Mr. Moss. I need you to hold that lantern close."

Cody emerged through the canvas with a smile on his face and a shake of his head. He tilted Eden a look through the drizzle. "I'd say he's in good hands. All the best healers I've ever known were grumpier than grizzlies straight out of hibernation."

"I heard that!" Tamsyn called.

Despite her concern, Eden couldn't help a smile.

Cody gave her a companionable nod of encouragement. "Your husband's got sand, ma'am. Anyone with a head as hard as his will be fine."

"I heard that." Adam teased.

"Hush, please, and lie still." Tamsyn snapped. "Unless you want me to sew your ear right to your head."

Eden blew out a breath of relief. And suddenly she didn't have any strength left in her legs. She sagged onto one of the seats by Tamsyn's fire.

Rain continued to fall, but the drops had settled to naught but a mist now, and she couldn't get any wetter than she already was, so she was just going to sit here and enjoy the fact that none of them had been injured beyond repair and that the Lord had brought them all home rejoicing.

A happy sob caught her unaware. She recalled the verse Mrs. Hawthorne had reminded her of on the day they'd come upon the Slades' wagon train. *He that goeth forth and weepeth, bearing precious seed, shall doubtless come again with rejoicing.* "Oh, Lord, thank You." That was all she could think to say in that moment, and she hoped that, like with cries for help, the Lord's Spirit could understand prayers of thanks that were so heartfelt they couldn't be spoken.

Rejoicing indeed!

She felt impatient now. Impatient for Tamsyn to finish with Adam so they could return to their own space, where they could spend time with the children.

In the aisle between the Houstons' crates, Wyatt handed Asher his dry clothes. "Get changed. We need to talk." Maybe they should have just stayed in their own wagon, but that place was still too full of painful nightmares to be tolerated.

"We should stay with them." Asher spoke the words matter-of-factly as he yanked his wet shirt off.

Wyatt sighed. They were good people and would take care of them, but it felt a bit like betraying Ma and Pa to move on with this other family so quickly. Yet . . . what were their other options?

They could strike out on their own like he'd been pondering previously, but after just one half day of driving the team, he'd felt like his hands might fall off. Doing grown-up work was hard. He wasn't sure he was strong enough for that yet.

Asher flung his wet clothes into a heap on the floor and turned to face him. "You ever gonna get dressed?"

Wyatt moved to pull off his shirt. "You can't leave those clothes in a heap like that. They'll never dry. Hang 'em over the tailgate."

Asher frowned at the rain slashing down from outside. "They ain't gonna dry in this storm no how."

Wyatt glared at his stubborn sibling. He tossed a gesture to the outside. "At least wring them out as best you can, and then we'll drape 'em over those crates. If we're staying with these folk, we don't want them to regret keeping us on the first night."

Asher grinned. "So we gonna stay?"

Wyatt sighed and slipped into his dry pants. "Don't see as how we have any other choice."

Asher thrust his arms and his wet shirt out into the rain, working fruitlessly with his small hands to try to wring water out of the garment that was soaked just as quickly as he could wring it.

"Give me that." Wyatt stepped up beside him and wadded the shirt into a twist then quickly drew it inside and gave it a shake like Ma used to do. Water flung everywhere, and Asher swiped drops from his face.

"You just got me almost as wet as the rainstorm!"

Wyatt had to acknowledge that was true. "Sorry about that. Here. Hang this on that crate."

By the time he got their clothes wrung out and hung up to dry, he felt bone weary and ready to be done with this day. He was glad that Afton was sleeping at the Morrans' tonight because she likely would have wanted a story, and he was already more than half asleep. But before he and Ash could make their bed in the aisle, a sound at the back of the wagon drew their attention.

Parson Houston thrust his head through the back canvas. Mrs. Houston was fast on his heels.

Wyatt swallowed as he took in the large white bandage swathing the parson's head. "You gonna be okay?"

The man smiled, but there were hints of pain in the reflection of his eyes. "Yeah. Just a scratch. A few stitches."

"Sit, Adam. Sit." Mrs. Houston hovered over her husband just like Ma used to do with Pa.

"If we don't stay with you, what happens to us?" Wyatt blurted the question before he could chicken out.

Mr. Houston hesitated, then turned to sit on the edge of the pallet. Mrs. Houston went to work cinching the back canvas closed.

The minister rubbed a weary hand over the back of his neck. "Well now, the colonel says there's a Children's Aid Society back in New York City that might be able to find you kids a home." His gaze bounced off his wife's. "But there's no guarantee that you'd stay together, or what kind of home you'd go to." He cleared his throat. "The colonel mentioned some families wanting good workers."

Asher shook his head and tugged the quilt the boys had been using in the hammock from where it lay folded on a crate. "I'm too tired for this. Wyatt knows we're staying. He's just worried you don't want us."

Mrs. Houston sucked in a quick breath.

"Asher, hush." Wyatt had been worried about that, but out at the river the parson had said . . . He angled a glance at the man. "Did you mean what you said? That you want to take care of us?"

The man met his gaze without flinching and nodded. "I really meant what I said, Wyatt. And I'm sorry that my fears, fears of growing attached to you and then experiencing pain because of it, have caused you more pain in a time when I should have been a comfort to you."

Asher shrugged, laid out the blanket, and flopped onto it, then pulled one side over himself. "Night." He closed his eyes and was sound asleep before Wyatt could even nudge him to allow Mrs. Houston to pass.

The couple met each other's gazes with a chuckle.

Wyatt stepped out of her way and motioned that she could pass. Once she was seated on the pallet by the parson and looking at him, he sighed, scuffed one toe at a corner of the quilt he would share with Asher. "Okay, if you'll have us, we'll stay."

Mrs. Houston covered her mouth, and tears glimmered in her eyes.

For a heart-stopping moment, Wyatt wondered if he'd misjudged, but the woman was nodding. So why the tears? He frowned.

"Yes!" she said. "Yes, we'll have you!"

He felt relief sweep through him. "Okay. I'm pretty tired, so . . . night."

"Good night." They both spoke at the same time.

For the first time in days, Wyatt felt like things were going to be okay again as he nudged Asher closer to his side of the aisle and lay down beside him, tugging his side of the quilt over himself. He was just drifting off when he felt Mrs. Houston settle another quilt over top of them.

He was glad God understood prayers, even if he didn't know how to voice them.

Eden sank back onto the bed beside Adam. She faced him.

He grinned and reached out to tug one of her soaked hair strands. "Guess we'd better get dry." Though he said the words, neither of them moved. They simply looked at one another, looked at the boys, and then looked at one another again.

He chuckled and started tugging off his boots. "I'm so glad that we got to you in time."

She smiled, plucked the pins from her hair, and set to drying it with a scrap of toweling. "And I am so glad that he did not win once you got there."

Adam blew a breath of dismissal as he winced his way through tugging off his soaked shirt. "He wasn't even close to beating me."

Eden knew he was joking, but couldn't find humor in the situation at that moment. She handed him the towel and then reached to touch the area where she knew the gash lay beneath his bandage. "This would beg to differ."

Adam cast a glance at the boys. They both breathed the deep breaths of sleep. He took her hand and pressed a kiss against the back of it. His other hand splayed warmly against the curve of her back. "It wasn't my time."

She nodded, then leaned to blow out the lantern so she could change out of her dress. But once again, Adam held her in place. "I was scared, Eden. Terrified, even. Back when I left." He held his finger and thumb a spare space apart. "You came this close to—" He groaned and turned his gaze to the canvas to blink hard a couple of times. He sucked his teeth, trying to compose himself. Finally, he returned his gaze to hers. "I feared what losing you would do to my faith, if I'm honest. I already had so much anger in my heart toward God, and I just . . . Didn't want to chance what might happen if I stayed and you never came back to me. Or I stayed, and . . . then we patched things up and I lost you in another birthing."

Eden felt as though all the oxygen had been sucked from the wagon. Her heart seemed to be taking up too much room in her chest.

He still loved her.

"I've been a fool, Eden. Worrying about God's job and trying to do it for Him, instead of allowing Him to do it for Himself. But back there, when I didn't know whether you were alive or not, God challenged me."

Eden tilted her head. "He did?"

Adam nodded. "'Choose for yourself this day whom you will serve.' That's what He said to me. And I chose Him." He pointed a finger upward. "I think I had you on a pedestal, Eden. I love you so much, and that pain of loss scares me more than a little. I've never felt any emotion that powerful before, and I knew it could break me if I let it." He stroked the backs of his fingers along her jawline. "I've kept you at arm's length because I was terrified of all of it. Loving you. Losing you. Losing my relationship with the Lord if I lost you. I've been a mess. But

I'm letting go of all of that now. God can do His job, and I'm going to try to stay in my place and do mine, which is simply to love those God puts in my path. That's you. That's those kids." His voice broke. "It's God's job to carry the unknown future, not mine."

Eden concentrated on the beat of his heart beneath her fingers. On the blue of his eyes looking down at her, filled with so much love. So much *life*. "I thought I had broken us, Adam. I didn't even know if you still loved me." A sob caught her by surprise. She covered her mouth. "You still love me!" Awe filled her.

Adam winced. Swept the back of one of his fingers down her cheek. "It pains me to think you doubted my love for you. If anything, my love may have been disproportionately weighted to you. Can you ever forgive me?"

This time it was a laugh that bubbled free. "Are you saying you're going to try to love me less?"

He grinned and swayed her from side to side. Stroked a damp strand off her forehead. "I'm saying I'm going to try to keep you in your proper place, which is the person I love just a little less than I love my Savior."

Eden's heart hadn't been this full in a very long time. She smiled. "I can live with that."

He leaned over her, looking deep into her eyes. "You never answered my question. Can you forgive me?"

She grinned and reached to sweep her thumbs over his waterlogged eyebrows. "Only if you let me get out of this soaking wet dress."

Adam glanced toward the sleeping boys and growled low in his chest. "Do you think we could move them to the hammock without them noticing?"

Eden smacked him with a chuckle. "You concentrate on getting out of those soaked pants, and I'll concentrate on donning a dry gown, and then we'll concentrate on *sleeping*. But we'll be together."

Adam released a long-suffering sigh. "Fine. I can do that. But first . . ."

He dipped his head and captured her lips with his own. Eden forgot about needing to don a dry gown. She forgot about Adam needing dry pants. And she forgot about the chill in the air as Adam's warm lips covered hers with a firm promise for the future.

They had come through barren years, but God was the author of life, and He would see them through what was to come.

Epilogue

Eden woke the next morning, feeling contentment deep in her heart. Adam said that his head ached a little, but he would be all right, and a check of his stitches showed that Tamsyn had done an excellent job, leaving him with minimal scarring—though he declared that he needed a haircut to show off his manly scar while he still could.

The storm had passed in the night, and though the air outside was cool, the canvas kept enough of the breeze at bay that the sun warmed the interior into a humid oven. Eden was thankful that their damp clothes would be able to dry today while they attended the trial.

Wyatt and Asher scrapped and argued so much as they donned their dry socks and boots that Eden shooed them off to fetch their sister for breakfast.

She glanced at Adam with a laugh. "Is that bickering what we are in for all the way to Oregon?"

Adam took her hand and tugged her onto his lap. "I don't mind, if it means we get to shoo them out of the wagon first thing each morning."

Eden chuckled and forked her fingers into his hair. She could hardly believe how wonderful it felt to share the pleasure of an intimate kiss with the man she loved. He lingered over the task, tantalizing her lips gently with his own, and all the while, a twinkle in his eyes.

But as the kiss grew more heated, Eden knew they were dancing on the edge of something more. If the boys popped back inside... She lingered for a mere moment more, relishing the feel of his curls between her fingers, of his stubble, scratchy and rough against her chin, before she stood and scooted out of his reach. When he lunged playfully for her, she smacked his hand and retreated another step. She rubbed the pads of her fingers over her lips and straightened her hair as she whisper-laughed, "Stop that. I have to go make breakfast."

Adam grumbled his protest good-naturedly but he did reach for his boots instead.

Eden took another moment to make sure her clothes were straightened before she stepped out onto the crates Adam had set up as steps.

Mrs. Hawthorne was tottering by on her morning constitutional with one of her grandsons skipping by her side. The woman's gaze sparkled as she swept Eden with a glance. But she didn't pause. Simply offered a wink as she continued past.

Feeling heat blazing in her cheeks, Eden hurried to start the fire. She took up her pot and headed in the wake of several other women toward the fort, relishing the glorious clean slate of the sky overhead. The air was crisp and the blue of the sky so sharp and clear that it made her feel happiness just to see it. Her heart was light as she filled the pot with water from the fort's well, and returned to hang it over the flames.

By the time she returned, Adam had invited Jeremiah to join them, but the man didn't seem at ease this morning. He paced the edges of their camp like a hemmed-in cougar.

Eden scooped oats into the pot, offering him a quizzical frown. "Everything okay, Jeremiah?"

"What?" He froze and spun to look at her. "Yes'm. Fine. Just fine." He plunked himself down on one of the crates that Adam had pulled near, but one knee bounced up and down, and he cast a strange searching glance toward the fort. "You heard anything about Mrs. Hawthorne?"

Eden shook her head. "Not a peep."

Jeremiah surged to his feet and continued to pace.

Was he truly that worried about the woman having a baby?

Eden exchanged a quick look with Adam, but he only wagged his head and lifted one shoulder.

The boys returned with Afton in tow. Mercy had done her hair up in a red ribbon, and the child's cheeks were pink, bunched into a smile as she skipped along by her brothers. She was the picture of health, which filled Eden with relief. Maybe whatever had plagued her had simply been a passing illness.

Wyatt carried a small bucket and held it out to Eden. "Mrs. Morran told me to tell you that they got a milk cow and we should expect a small bucket of milk like this from them every morning."

"Oh, that's very generous of them." She looked into the bucket, frothy with cream. It was still so warm that it steamed in the cool morning air. "You kids sit down there by Mr. Jackson." She gave the man a pointed look and was thankful when he took her meaning and sank down again. Eden gave him a nod, then continued speaking to the boys. "Parson Houston will say a blessing over these oats and fresh milk! What a wonder! Maybe I'll be able to set some cream by and we can make butter of an evening."

As soon as Adam prayed, thanking the Lord not only for the food but also for His abundant protection over all of them the day before, Eden doled out bowls of oats and mugs of milk.

Afton swung her feet, and her heels kept clunking on the crate she sat on, but Eden couldn't bring herself to chastise her. The child ate with gusto and downed the entire cup of milk before wiping a chubby hand across the white mustache left on her lips. Eden grinned and used the hem of her apron to clean the little one's face fully.

As she gathered the plates and cups, she noted that while the children may have eaten with hearty appetites, Jeremiah barely picked at his food. And when, a moment later, he looked up to see the colonel of the fort headed their way with a group of soldiers trailing him,

Jeremiah leapt to his feet and hung his thumbs on his gunbelt, looking like he was ready to take on the world.

Maybe it was the incident with the soldier from the evening before that had him jumpy this morning?

Eden dumped the plates and mugs into the bucket that she would use to wash them momentarily. For now, she wanted to see what the colonel would have to say.

The man paused just outside their circle of wagons and waited for them all to gather around. His eyes were red and glassy, and a weary severity seemed to sag his features. As he waited, he searched everyone who approached. When his scrutiny reached Jeremiah, it snagged and lingered.

Jeremiah offered the man a smile and a tug of his hat brim. "Morning, Colonel."

The man's eyes narrowed, but he did give a nod and continued his perusal of the rest of the gathering. His lips pursed into a tight bunch and twitched a couple of times.

Something was wrong. Maybe simply the fact that the man was tasked with standing as the judge in his brother's trial?

Adam paused at her side and took her hand in his, and Eden clung to the warmth of him, willing down the trembling that had suddenly risen from inside.

The colonel took hold of the crown of his hat, removed it, and scrubbed his wrist over his brow before returning his hat to its place. "You all will be happy to know that I chose to step aside and allow my lieutenant colonel to judge this trial. The lieutenant colonel has already made a judgment. Considering the circumstances in which we found my brother—him holding Mrs. Houston there at gunpoint—"

Eden shuffled closer to Adam needing to feel the safe strength of him

"—and considering that he tried to have Parson Houston there murdered, the lieutenant colonel has decided that my brother will . . . hang. The judgment will be carried out in one hour and you all are welcome to attend. Chairs are being placed on the parade ground there." He pointed to where several soldiers bustled about.

Eden couldn't withhold a gasp as she noted men rapidly assembling gallows not too far beyond that.

She returned her focus to the colonel.

No wonder that poor man was a mess. His brother was about to hang. *As he should.*

Eden had no desire to watch the sentence carried out. She certainly didn't want the boys to see it. She hoped their whole party would be long gone by then.

"You'll also be happy to learn, I'm sure, that we expect the ... proceedings to be quick. You folk will be on your way before midmorning."

Men and women alike rumbled their relief and began to turn back to their departure preparations.

"However!" The colonel shot one hand into the air. "I regret that my soldiers and I will need to examine each wagon before you get on your way."

The rumble in the crowd grew louder, this time turning to curious protests.

"Please, folks, please." The colonel held up a hand and waited for silence. "A slave has gone missing from the fort is all. She's quite dangerous, and we want to make sure that she hasn't slipped in to hide among your supplies unbeknownst to you."

Eden felt a wave of horrified shock. She met Adam's narrowed gaze. Her lips thinned, and she lost all measure of the charity that she'd felt for the colonel moments earlier. Here she'd been thinking he was concerned for his brother, but what he really was concerned about was a runaway slave?

Dangerous indeed. The poor woman was probably running for her life. Eden hoped she had gotten away and that was the truth of it.

The colonel snapped his fingers, and his soldiers began spreading throughout the encampment. Families followed them, but the soldiers didn't even ask permission before climbing into wagons!

The audacity!

However, there was no use in protesting. None of them had anything to hide and a soldier had already climbed into her and Adam's wagon and begun poking through their crates. Lifting one. Looking behind another. He even lifted the tick on the pallet at the front and knocked the butt of his rifle against the boards below but since they had nothing but filled crates beneath the bed it didn't ring hollow.

"What's in these crates?" he demanded.

Adam's lips pressed into a thin line. "Those are filled with Bibles. I'm happy to open one to show you."

The soldier nodded that he should.

Adam sighed and climbed up to do so. Not until he'd opened every one of the large crates did the soldier relent and drop the tick back into place. "Sorry for the inconvenience, folks. Thank you for your cooperation."

Eden huffed and folded her arms. Like they'd had any choice. She set about righting the interior of their space and rehanging the damp clothes that the soldier's search had knocked to the ground.

By the time she climbed down and stood by the firepit once more, soldiers all around the circle were leaving other wagons.

Mercy Morran approached with irritation in her expression. She spoke quietly to Eden. "Wherever that poor woman is, I hope she makes her escape."

Eden nodded. "I was thinking the same. Did they leave as much of a mess in your place as they did in mine?"

Mercy flapped a hand. "They wanted to look inside every crate bigger than a child. She must be a tiny little thing, if they think she can fit in something that small. They even made Micah open the compartments where he stores our tools and such below."

At the Slade wagon just ahead, several soldiers converged. Jeremiah stood to one side, arms folded as he waited for them to conclude their business. The soldiers seemed to be focused disproportionately on that wagon. They even pulled open the compartment where the children had hidden on that first day, but as expected, it was empty.

Striker Moss approached and shook the colonel's hand with a smile. "Morning, Colonel. We about done here? We'd like to have a meeting of our folk as soon as possible."

Two soldiers emerged from the Slade wagon, shaking their heads.

Across the way, Tamsyn Acheson stood in the opening of the Hawthorne's oil cloth with her hands on her hips. Inside, Eden could see two soldiers still poking through the supplies. All the Hawthorne children, huddled around the back of the wagon like a brood of chicks eyeing a couple of hawks.

"This woman is having a child, gentlemen. If you're quite done?" Tamsyn's voice rang loudly through the encampment.

Mrs. Hawthorne moaned loudly.

A soldier emerged from the shadowed interior, looking rather horrified and with his cheeks as rosy as the flower painted on the side of the canvas. He, too, shook his head at his commanding officer.

The colonel hung his head, propped his hands against his hips, and stared at the ground. Then he pivoted toward the fort, swinging a gesture for his men to wrap things up. "We're done here, folks. Thank you for your cooperation!" He took a step toward the fort but then paused and turned to look at Adam. "If you have those children's things packed, I can take them with me now."

Eden drew in a sharp breath and stepped forward, but Adam was already shaking his head. "The children say they have no family, and my wife and I are willing to care for them. They've agreed they want to stay with us."

Colonel Baxter hesitated, opened his mouth as though considering a protest, but then seemed to decide to let the matter drop. "All right." He twirled his arm again and headed back toward the fort.

A breath of relief puffed from Eden's lips. And then she was grinning from ear to ear. Adam took in her expression and smiled too. He gave her a nod. She wanted to rush across and throw her arms around him, but with everyone looking on, that would be quite the spectacle for a minister and his wife, so she remained where she stood, simply relishing this feeling of complete happiness. It had been a long time since she'd felt this joyous.

The soldiers followed the colonel out of the encampment without so much as a backward glance.

As if by mutual agreement, all the train's folk clustered in the middle of the wagons save Mrs. Hawthorne. Cranston climbed onto a crate and held up a hand for silence. "Who wants to stay to watch the hanging?"

Not a single hand went into the air.

Caesar looked at Tamsyn. "Can that woman travel?"

Tamsyn clasped her hands so tightly that her knuckles turned white. And for some reason her gaze glanced off of Jeremiah before returning to Caesar. "I believe it will be some hours yet. She can labor in a moving conveyance just as well as she can in a still one. We may have to stop early, however. Delivery will be another matter."

Caesar nodded. "Right, then. Everyone, hitch up, and we'll head on out. I, for one, will be happy to see the last of this place."

Everyone disbursed to gather their oxen.

Eden blew out a breath and hurried the children toward the wagon. Afton tugged on her hand. "I'ma be sick."

"Oh no!" Eden hurried her to one side and held her hair. Once the child had lost her breakfast and Eden had cleaned her up, she drew the girl into an embrace. "I'm so sorry you got sick again."

Tamsyn approached, prodding their oxen with her brother.

"Tamsyn?" Eden called. "Can you check on Afton when you have a moment?"

Tamsyn gave quick instructions to her brother. "Get the team hitched, Edi. I'll be right there." Then she hurried over. "Was she sick again?"

Eden nodded. "Yes. She seemed fine before we ate."

Tamsyn frowned. "You're right. I saw her sitting by the Morrans' fire this morning. She did. What did you have for breakfast?"

"Oats, like normal, but Micah got that cow, and so we also had... milk! Could that be causing her upset stomach?"

Wyatt stepped close. "We used to always have milk with breakfast, back when she was often sick in the mornings."

Tamsyn splayed her hands. "That would make sense why she seems fine most of the time but feels sick at others, if it's a food bothering her. I say, hold off on giving her any milk or butter for a few days and let's see how she does."

Eden felt relieved to have at least the beginnings of a diagnosis for the child. She hefted her into her arms and snuggled her close. "No more milk for you, okay?"

"Otay." Afton clasped her chubby arms around Eden's neck and squeezed her tight, and Eden had never felt so much love fill her as she did in that moment. She hustled the children up onto the wagon bench, settling Wyatt closest to where Adam would sit, and Asher and Afton in between.

Asher smiled up at her, his blue eyes sparkling. He held up a stick of candy. "Can I share this with Afton and Wyatt?"

Eden frowned. "Where did you get that?"

Asher shrugged. "Mr. Jackson gave it to me this morning. I like him. He's nice."

Eden smiled. "Yes. He is."

She glanced to where Jeremiah was pulling the Slade's wagon into line right ahead of them. She heard him whistling a tuneless ditty and wondered at his change in temperament from breakfast this morning. He'd seemed tense and uptight then. But now he seemed relaxed and happy.

Maybe as she'd suspected, his tension had simply stemmed from the soldiers who had treated him less than respectfully?

Eden brushed the questions aside a few minutes later as Adam settled onto the bench beside them. He called to the team and set them moving west behind Jeremiah once more.

They weren't more than a mile outside of town when Striker rode up beside Jeremiah, and Jeremiah pulled to a stop. The men quickly changed positions, and Jeremiah rode ahead on Striker's horse.

"What could that be all about?" Eden asked.

Adam shook his head. "Just scouting business, I presume."

Eden didn't suppose it was any of their concern. She listened to the happy chatter of the children as they shared the stick of candy and tipped her face to the sun. Adam reached across the bench to squeeze her shoulder, and as she looked at him above the heads of the three children the Lord had blessed them with, she knew such contentment that she heaved a blissful sigh.

They had started on this journey, all of them broken by pain, but the Lord had caused each of them to come again rejoicing, bringing their sheaves with them.

Sheaves of happiness, love, hope, and peace. And an even greater joy lay in knowing that He would be with them in the future, too, no matter what they faced.

Please Review!

If you enjoyed this story, would you take a few minutes to leave your thoughts in a review on your favorite retailer's website? It would mean so much to me, and helps spread the word about the series.

You can quickly link through from my website here: https://www.pacificlightsbookstore.com/collections/the-oregon-promise-series/

Coming soon...

Upon the Broken Range

Oregon Promise - Book 4

You may read an excerpt on the next page...

Chapter 1

Jeremiah stared at the beautiful woman who had somehow appeared in the sunken compartment in the floorboards of the Slade wagon. Outside, thunder crashed and a flash of lightning lit the sky so brightly that for one brief moment, he could see the fading bruise on her face that the lights from the lanterns hadn't revealed.

He released the floorboard door to rest against a crate and stretched a hand down to her. "Setting to blow a fierce one tonight. Don't think you'll get much sleep down there."

Her hand was delicate in his—no bigger than that of a teenage child. And when he hauled her to her feet and helped her balance in the aisle of the wagon on the other side of the trap door, he realized that she wasn't much taller than a child either. How old was she, this delicate, tiny, trembling package of uncertainty?

Her large eyes studied him above curled arms and fisted hands that she tucked beneath her chin.

She looked like a wary boxer about to throw the first punch. Jeremiah folded his arms so she'd hopefully understand he meant her no harm. "How'd you get in here?"

She made no response other than her eyes growing a bit rounder and her lower lip trembling slightly.

Right. He was frightening her. He eased his arms to his sides and lowered the trap door into place. He angled his body and stepped to one side as best he could in the cramped aisle of the wagon, then swung a gesture to the tick stretched across a bed of crates at the back of the space. "Please, take a seat."

She continued to look at him for a long moment before finally easing past him to sit on the pallet.

Good. "Let me get you something warm to drink." Would she still be here when he returned?

He paused at the tailgate to peer out. He dreaded going back into the weather he'd just escaped. His dry clothes would almost immediately be as wet as the set that still lay in a heap on the floor and he had no others to change into, but there was naught for it.

He reached to swipe the canvas aside.

"Please," she said, the word barely audible above the storm pounding the canvas.

He paused and turned to look at her.

"Please don't go out into that caterwaul on my account. I ate not long ago and need nothing."

Relief eased through him.

There was a slight touch of the South in her words. The sound of it took him straight back to the shanty where he'd grown up behind the plantation home owned by Striker's parents.

He tilted her a nod and bent to retrieve his wet clothes. He wrung them out at the back opening of the canvas and took the opportunity to check the area, but thankfully, no one seemed like they were headed his way. One good thing about this storm was that most folks would be tucked away in their wagons, trying to stay dry. A break in the clouds to the southeast showed that the storm should ease within the hour.

He could still see a lantern light in Miss Acheson's wagon. Likely, she was working on the parson. Other than that, most wagons around the circle lay dark and silent.

Another crack of thunder rolled, followed more distantly by a lesser flash of lightning this time.

He turned back into the wagon, gave his pants a flick, and draped them atop a stack of crates. He did the same with his shirt.

Then he settled into his heels, folded his arms, and looked down at the bit of a woman who was now at the farthest edge of the tick with her arms wrapped around her knees. She huddled into her blue cape like it was a shield that could protect her. The whole package of her didn't take up more room than a sack of flour. His mammy would have said she looked no more substantial than a "cob o' corn the chickens done picked clean."

She was of mixed blood, like him—that much was clear. But he knew all too well that it made no difference to many a man who held power. One drop of black blood was enough to mark a person as lesser in their eyes—enough to justify chains, cruelty, and stolen lives.

Chains which she had only recently escaped, judging by her raw wrists. He eyed her abrasions and felt his fists tighten, ready for war.

Purposely, he drew in a long inhale and forced himself to relax. He leaned his shoulder against a stack of crates. There had been many times in his life that he'd been ready to go to war, but if there was one thing he'd learned, it was that some battles would drag a man down into the mire of inhumanity, and he never wanted to be that kind of man.

He would need to wrap her wrists, and maybe her ankles too. But he'd give her a minute. Judging by her dry hair and clothes, she'd come this way before the rain.

"What's your name?"

She rolled her lips in and pressed them into a tight line. "Maybe it's best you don't learn my name. I won't be here long. I promise."

He frowned. They could deal with that later. "You want my help, you're gonna have to trust me. You ended up in my wagon. I presume that's because you knew I was a man of color like yourself?"

She shook her head. "I didn't know. Leastwise not until Betsy told me. The mercantile owner—she's the one who helped me escape and told me to come here."

Ah. That would explain why the woman had stepped out onto the store's porch. She'd wanted to see which wagon was his. But her sending this girl to him could get them both killed. He bit back a sigh before he could make the girl feel like she was putting him out.

"My name's Jeremiah Jackson." He waited. The silence stretched long.

Finally, she said, "My master calls me Delilah."

Something curled in Jeremiah's stomach. A reference to the woman who had been Sampson's weakness? Such a man would want his prize back.

"Don't want the name your master gave you."

Her brow slumped, and she worked her teeth over her lower lip. The silence stretched as she searched his face.

His hands clenched tight again. Some fool who would one day stand before God had her afraid to even speak her own name.

He softened his voice. "You can trust me. What's your real name? The one your mammy gave you."

She frowned and swept a glance around the inside of the wagon as though trying to decide. Finally, she settled her gaze on his. "My mama named me Deliverance. You can call me Del. Never had no second name."

Deliverance. He smiled at the woman, pleased that she'd decided to trust him. "Deliverance is a good name. Right glad to meet you."

Now to figure out who she was running from.

Even as the thought registered, weariness washed through him. He pressed his fingers and thumb against his eyes. Wished he wasn't so tired. Last night had been his watch, and he'd only gotten about three hours of sleep. With the long day of rescuing Mrs. Houston, exhaustion about had him dead on his feet.

He eased to his haunches in the aisle. Maybe if he weren't towering over her, this conversation would go easier.

"Who you running from?" For some reason, that question set him on edge. Evil was about to be named, and evil did not like to be dragged into the light.

She swallowed. Licked her lips. "My master. Colonel Boone Baxter."

Jeremiah jolted his head back as the name hit him square in the chest. The man with the most power for hundreds of miles. That was the man she was running from. The man whose brother had just kidnapped the parson's wife and those two kids. The man who now held the kidnapper in his jail down in the fort.

Thank God they were pulling out first thing, and yet a man like that one wouldn't tolerate the loss of a woman such as this. The loss of his Delilah.

If she were caught—

Jeremiah didn't want to think about what would happen to either of them if she were found and he were discovered helping her.

And now it would be up to him to make sure that didn't happen.

Lord, You gonna have to show me how to help this woman. I know it's not Your will for either of us to end up at the end of a scourge and then a rope simply because we have different colored skin.

Deliverance wrapped her arms more tightly about her knees as she studied the man squatting in the aisle before her. She'd shocked him, that was certain.

Also certain was the fact that Master Boone was going to tear this wagon train apart as soon as he discovered she was missing! Would he even go down to the basement where she ought to be tonight? Sometimes when he was tired or overworked, he didn't take her to his room. On those occasions, he left her in the basement overnight and only let her out early in the morning to use the necessary before returning her to the basement for another day.

Her arms ached just thinking about it.

She'd planned to simply rest in that hidden compartment until dark and then make her escape, but then the storm had come, and she'd known there would be no shelter for miles in any direction. With a child on the way, no matter how unwelcome—guilt pierced her at that thought—she'd needed to stay dry.

And then this man had found her.

Now, as she waited for the man to speak, she studied him. What had she expected to find in a free man of color as Betsy had described him? Certainly not this young, strapping man with the broad shoulders that stretched his shirt to near capacity, and certainly not those gray eyes that studied her in the lantern light. She'd expected an elderly man perhaps, set free after years of service to a master. Or maybe one bent with years of servitude.

He hung his head and studied the boards between his feet. Ran one broad hand around the back of his neck.

"You really free?" The words blurted out before she could think better of them.

He lifted that gray gaze to her. "Yes'm. Grew up on a plantation in South Carolina, just outside of Charleston. My master's son took a liking to me, charming sort that I am." He offered her a scallywag's grin.

She tucked away a smile, lowering her mouth behind her knees.

"Striker talked his daddy into giving me to him, and then he gave me my manumission papers."

"Striker?" She felt her eyes go a little round. That name sounded rather lethal, like a bounty hunter or a marksman. A cold sweat broke out on the back of her neck.

Jeremiah grinned. "He earned that nickname working at the forge on his daddy's plantation. That fella could shoe a horse faster than anyone in five counties. Can you keep a secret?"

The twinkle in his eyes raised her curiosity. She nodded.

"Striker's real name is Sebastian Jebediah Moss." He grinned. "I like to remind him o' that every once in a while so's to bring his feet back to earth, if you catch my meaning."

Deliverance wanted to smile. She liked this kind man who made her feel at ease even though she'd inserted herself into his life without permission. But a smile wouldn't come. She was weary. Weary clean through.

Only when she heard him stand did she realize that her eyes had fallen closed. She opened them to find him standing close, reaching for her.

She gasped and cowered back.

He stilled and raised his palms. "Easy. I was just reaching for that extra quilt there." He pointed past her to a folded blanket on a shelf that extended beneath the driver's seat.

She couldn't seem to shake her tension, but she did hand it to him, if only to get him to retreat. "Sorry."

He clutched the quilt in one hand, but didn't step back. He hung his head instead for a moment. "You can trust me. Understand?" He lifted those gray eyes to her, brows raised.

It was his hopeful expression that eased her. "Okay."

"Good." He stepped back and, with a quick flip, unfurled the quilt in the narrow aisle of the wagon. "I'm gonna need a couple hours of shut-eye before we decide where to hide you."

Del frowned. "I can't hide here?"

"Not if you want to live." The man said the words wearily as he sank onto the blanket on the hard wood floor and pulled the covering over himself. He was breathing deeply before she had the presence of mind to realize she'd stolen his bed.

But with him asleep, maybe this was her time to skedaddle? She rose to her knees and parted the cinched canvas above the bed just enough to see out.

The rain was naught more than a drizzle at the moment. She glanced back at the man. *Not if you want to live.* He was right about that. Boone would search this wagon train, top to bottom, as soon as he discovered she was missing. And if he found her here in the company of this man . . . Fear pumped a breath past her lips. She didn't want to bring trouble.

Another quick peek at the sky outside. The clouds didn't seem so dark and ominous against the blackness of the heavens. Maybe she could make it to the trees by the river and find shelter before the storm grew heavier? That would be better for these folk, if not for her. She shivered at the thought of wandering through those woods in the dark. Were there wolves? Mountain lions? Snakes? Spiders? She shuddered. But all of that would be better than getting innocent folk killed.

She turned back to look at the man sprawled in the aisle. He took up most of it with his big frame. She would have to scoot past him to get out.

She stood and scooped up the rucksack that Betsy had packed for her, ignoring the pain that flared to life in her wrist when she hefted it. With the pack on one shoulder, she assessed the best path forward. Moving past his legs wouldn't be a problem; she had plenty of room to tiptoe past them. It was his shoulders that would be an issue. Each one nearly touched the crates on either side, and there was no room for her foot. She would have to jump over him, then.

She took a couple of steps back and hefted her skirt enough that it wouldn't encumber her feet.

The man surged upright, rubbing fingers and thumbs into his eyes.

She gasped and plunked backward onto the pallet in surprise.

He looked at her, weariness drooping his shoulders. "Listen now. You go out there and you finished for sure. I spent the evening with the colonel today, and he's got a good tracker."

She felt a swirl of lightheadedness. Of course he did. She'd heard Boone mention him more than once. She pressed one hand to the base of her throat.

He rested his arms against his knees and clasped one wrist with his other hand. "You believe in the Lord?"

Tears blurred her vision. Oh, how she did. She nodded.

"Good. Then I'm asking you to believe that the Lord brought you here to me. And I'm asking you to trust me, weary man that I am at the moment." He pointed to the bed. "Please sleep for just a little while. And let me do the same."

She moistened her lips. "I thought you already was asleep."

His lips tilted upward almost imperceptibly. "You thought right."

For a long moment, they looked at one another. His weariness was evident in the sag of his shoulders and the sleepy squint of his eyes. But there was an alertness, too.

He tilted his head. "You gonna let me sleep and get some for yourself?"

She frowned. "Don't want to bring trouble on you. It's dark now. Best time for me to slip away."

"You won't be able to run fast enough or far enough to outrun that tracker and Colonel Baxter's mounted men." His expression was sternly fierce as he continued. "Come morning, that man will be on your trail. The rain will help with that. But if you run out there . . ." He thrust a blunt finger toward the outside. ". . . they will find you." He pinned her with a stern look. "I'm thinking on a plan. But first, you got to let me rest a bit."

She frowned, but nodded. "Okay."

"Good." He flopped back down and tugged the quilt over himself once more.

Almost immediately, his breaths filled the space, deep and steady.

Deliverance eased the pack to the floor and settled herself against the soft tick on the pallet. Weariness washed over her. How long since she'd slept in a bed this soft?

That thought sent a shudder through her. She'd slept in Boone's bed plenty of times—if one could call the subconscious tense alertness sleeping. But alone? That had been a very long time ago.

She pulled the coverlet on the tick over herself like a shield and relished the warmth of it. Closed her eyes. Allowed her weariness to pull her under.

Boone arrived back at the fort, weary and heartbroken over Brad. He wanted to fetch Delilah. To relish the warmth of her in his arms as he slept. But there were too many men still wandering about tonight.

He couldn't have word getting about that he had a weakness for a woman. Especially not a woman like her. A man in his position had to maintain authority. And respect.

And he was too tired to wait for all the hubbub to settle.

Tugging off his gloves, he tromped the stairs to his rooms above the store.

Brad. Stupid fool. He was going to die, and Boone wouldn't be able to do a thing about it. He couldn't risk his career on his no-account brother.

He shuffled into his room and sank slowly onto the edge of the bed to tug off his boots.

Ah. That felt better. He massaged his aching feet and then slipped off his uniform, and took time to hang each piece carefully in the wardrobe.

After a quick rinse of his face and arms in the washbasin, he toweled dry and then sank against his pillows. Closed his eyes.

Tomorrow, he would shore up his strength. For tonight, he allowed himself to weep for the brother he would lose. Not the adult brother who had caused him so much angst and anger, but the boy he had been. The boy Boone had loved.

That thought registered and eased through him. It was true. He no longer loved Brad. He was simply a burden that Boone couldn't disassociate himself from because they shared a last name. Soon, he'd no longer have that burden.

He would cling to that truth. It would help him get through the next few days.

That and Delilah. He always found comfort while with her.

Chapter 2

Deliverance woke to hear the voices of two men speaking quietly at the back of the wagon. She sprang upright, clutching her blue cloak around herself. Was it Boone? Had he discovered her missing and come looking already?

It was still dark outside. Two silhouettes stood at the other end of the wagon, one inside and one outside, speaking in tones too quiet for her to hear. Was Jeremiah still asleep in the dark shadows between the crates? Or was he one of the men in the conversation? She wished she could see. But it was so dark that the moon must be hidden now by either clouds or trees. Only because another wagon's canvas was a lighter spot behind the speakers could she see the two shadows in conversation.

Terror had her breaths beating against her teeth as she waited, one of her hands clutched tightly into the material at her throat.

But then, the man inside clapped a hand onto the shoulder of the man outside, and that man turned and walked away.

She blew out a slow exhale and scrutinized the shadow turning toward her. He strolled the length of the aisle without tripping over a sleeping man, so he must be . . . "Jeremiah?"

"Yeah. Sorry if we frightened you." He sank to a squat.

She appreciated how he kept lowering himself so he didn't tower over her. But she couldn't see his face in the darkness. "What is it?"

A brief flash of white must be him smiling. "The good Lord sent you a baby."

She snatched a silent inhale. How did he know that? She wasn't far enough along to even be showing yet. Only two months of missed cycles. And she could hardly feel that this child had been sent from God. "Not all children are hoped for." The bitter words were out before she thought better of them.

The sound of his boots shifting against the ground made her feel ashamed of her sentiment.

"What time is it?" she asked, wanting to move on from the talk of babies.

"Just before dawn. That was my friend Striker. He'll be back in a moment. Got your pack?"

"It's here." She fumbled for it in the darkness.

"I'll take that. You'll get it back, don't worry none." Jeremiah stood, and she heard him swing the pack onto one shoulder.

At the back of the wagon, someone whisper-whistled. "Jer? We're ready."

"Follow me." Jeremiah turned and scrambled out into the darkness.

Swallowing down her trepidation, Del eased off the pallet and padded after him. *Lord? You still watching me?* At the tailgate, she found Jeremiah holding a burlap sack. He had handed her pack to the other man, based on the shadowy lump on one of his shoulders.

"Don't get down just yet. You need to put your feet in here."

Del's heart hammered. What was going on here?

Jeremiah must have sensed her uncertainty because he hurried to add, "It's so the tracker doesn't have as easy a time with your trail. This will keep you from leaving an inadvertent footprint in the dark. Hopefully, the Lord will send more rain after we get you across, but we can't take that chance. Here, sit yourself down."

He took her hand and helped her sit on the tailgate. Then held the sack until she worked both her feet inside. She was thankful for the darkness that gave her some privacy for the task.

Across? Across where? But she didn't voice the questions hammering through her.

"Good. Now, work your toes into both corners there at the end. We'll take the walk slow, so no need to worry about that."

"How far are we going? Can you just carry me?" She felt heat blast into her face at that blurted comment.

But he didn't seem to mind her question. He was already shaking his head. "A good tracker can assess the depth of a man's footprints. If one of us carries you, our prints will be deeper and raise questions. The sack will leave an odd mark in the grass, but we'll be able to rough that out after we get you to safety."

Safety? Where was that, exactly?

She could hardly believe she was here, working with such diligence to keep Boone from finding her. Did she really want to leave him and bring such harshness on these folk? He obviously hadn't checked the basement. She could go back right now, and he'd never know she'd ever been gone.

When Jeremiah took her hand again and helped her jump down from the tailgate, she clutched the sack covering her feet with one hand and looked toward the fort. He released her and stepped back.

Starlight stroked enough highlights on wood and rooftops that she could even discern Boone's window on the top floor of the mercantile. The moon was not behind the clouds, then. She looked for it and found the half-moon in the distance, hovering above the western horizon, most of the light obscured by dark clouds. Yet here above them, the skies were clear and the fort lay quiet.

Boone must not have gone down to fetch her earlier, or all manner of chaos would be brewing. Yet, if she went back, how would she get in? Surely Betsy would have locked the back door of the store? Besides, there would be any number of guards roaming about now that all the soldiers were back at the fort.

"You thinking of going back, you're a fool." Jeremiah's voice was quiet but firm. His feet shifted through the grass.

She turned to search him out in the darkness.

He shook his head. "Don't mean to speak so harshly. But it angers me to think what you must be running from."

"Jer, we gotta go." The other man whispered.

Jeremiah spread a firm hand against her back, turning her away from the fort as he swung his hat to the shadow man. "This here is my friend Striker Moss."

Del shuffled a couple of steps away from Jeremiah's touch. Her fears were foolish. The man wouldn't be able to tell she was expecting by touching her back. However, she still wasn't certain what baby he spoke of, even though she felt sure he couldn't have meant hers. But she didn't want any of these folks to know about this child growing inside her. She still hoped she might resume her cycle any day.

Guilt slammed through her at the thought.

She glanced toward the stars above. *Lord, forgive me for such a callous thought.*

"Pleased to meet you, ma'am." Jeremiah's friend's words drew her attention from the heavens as he touched the brim of his hat and lifted it.

She almost laughed. Only this morning she'd been chained to a wall, and now men were doffing their caps to her? Was she still chained and only dreaming? "Pleased to meet you, Mr. Moss, sir."

"This way." Jeremiah strode out in the wake of the man with her pack a shadowy lump on his shoulder.

All around, the camp lay silent. Not even the birds were twittering the announcement of dawn yet.

Del was thankful to see that the men were true to their word and took the way slowly. They strode right across the middle of the circled wagons to one across the way with the dim glow of a lantern lighting the inside.

Behind that wagon, a woman paced the ground. She was too slender to be the one expecting, though taller than Del by a good several inches. Otherwise, it was too dark to make out other features.

Mr. Moss stepped close to her, and they spoke in low voices.

Del was too tired to strain to hear their conversation, so she glanced back toward the fort. All remained silent and dark.

Why this disappointment pumping in her chest? Was she surprised that Boone had, to his way of thinking, left the mother of his child chained up like a dog in the dark? He obviously hadn't even gone down to see if she needed the necessary.

A shadow loomed between her and the fort, bringing her focus back to the here and now. Jeremiah's gray gaze seemed even more piercing in the dim light of the stars. "You going back? Or going forward?" He swept his hat through his fingers repeatedly.

Back to familiar chains and abuse? Or forward into an unknown future that might bring pain and misery on those trying to help her? *Lord, this seems an impossible feat, this escaping from such a monster. But I got to try. For the sake of this child.*

A child she didn't want, her guilt reminded her.

But the child was not at fault. And the Lord, who was the author of all life, must have a plan for this one because He had allowed life to form out of so much misery.

She drew in a fortifying breath. "Forward."

Jeremiah nodded. "Good. I knew I liked your gumption." He swung his hat toward the wagon. "This here is the Hawthorne wagon. Mrs. Hawthorne is laboring to bring her eighth child into this world, and Tamsyn seems to think it will be a good long while yet. God's timing is always perfect."

He stepped between her and the fort as though to indicate her decision had been made and she ought to move.

Del turned toward the wagon, confusion still pinching her brow. How did a woman giving birth offer help to her?

When she reached the tailgate, Jeremiah's hands swept about her waist and hoisted her up onto the wood. He reached a hand up. "I'll take that gunnysack."

As Del clutched the overhead stay and worked to keep her balance and remove her legs from the bag, Mr. Moss helped the other woman climb up into the wagon as well.

Once Del was free of the bag and had handed it to Mr. Jackson, the woman held her hand toward her. "My name is Tamsyn. Pleased to meet you. Deliverance, correct?" She didn't wait for Del to confirm before waving her into the interior of the wagon. "Come on, let's get you hidden inside. Quick now because Mrs. Hawthorne is standing until you get inside."

Del took one more look at the men. They were already almost all the way across the field. She saw Mr. Jackson toss the gunnysack into the campfire near his wagon, take up a bucket, and begin scrubbing the tailgate of his wagon where she had sat a moment ago.

That sight set her heart to thrashing even harder than it had all day.

Was he worried the fort might have dogs? Did Boone have access to dogs? She wasn't sure. She'd never heard any baying sounds, but locked up in the basement during the day as she'd always been, would she have heard them?

Dear Lord!

Yesterday, she'd feared what might happen to anyone who helped her, but now that she had faces to go with those people, she knew that she would never be able to live with herself if anything happened to these good folk simply because they'd tried to help her escape evil.

"This way." The other woman urged her inside by placing a hand on her back.

Taking a fortifying breath, Del stepped into the dim light cast by the lone lamp in the wagon.

An unknown future lay ahead, but she knew the One who had known that future from the beginning of time. She would have to rest in that.

ABOUT THE AUTHOR

Born and raised in Malawi, Africa. Lynnette Bonner spent the first years of her life reveling in warm equatorial sunshine and the late evening duets of cicadas and hyenas. The year she turned eight she was off to Rift Valley Academy, a boarding school in Kenya where she spent many joy-filled years, and graduated in 1990.

That fall, she traded to a new duet—one of traffic and rain—when she moved to Kirkland, Washington to attend Northwest University. It was there that she met her husband and a few years later they moved to the small town of Pierce, Idaho.

During the time they lived in Idaho, while studying the history of their little town, Lynnette was inspired to begin the Shepherd's Heart Series with Rocky Mountain Oasis.

Marty and Lynnette have four children, and currently live in Washington where Marty pastors a church.

Made in United States
North Haven, CT
02 August 2025